# THE FLIPSIDE

By

Kimbeth Wehrli Judge

ISBN: 1502573822
ISBN 13: 9781502573827
Library of Congress Control Number: 2014917603
CreateSpace Independent Publishing Platform
North Charleston, South Carolina

# DEDICATIONS

Always to my husband,
Bernie Judge

Also to my brother,
Michael Wehrli
And to my collected memories of
my mother, Lorraine,
and my father, Robert,
who forever encouraged my imagination and my
writing.
(Belated thank you, Mom & Dad, for forcing me to
take Latin)

*Ad astra per aspera*
(To the stars through difficulties)

# CONTENTS

*The truth will set you free. But first, it will piss you off.*
~ Gloria Steinem ~

*Express your feelings all the time unless you're trying to hide something.*
~ Miss Piggy ~

# THE FIRST SUNDAY

On a balmy fall day in Chicago, three people descended from high up in their condominium at about the same time. Helen and Steven Clark took the elevator, while Max Shaw plummeted through the air, crashing at least twice into his neighbors' windows on the way down.

All three landed on the ground at the same approximate time, two of them alive and well.

And so it was that upon exiting out into the blinding sunshine, first Steven and then Helen came upon the surreal sight of a freshly smashed and dismembered dead man. In a millisecond, Steven grabbed his wife and told her not to look. Helen, of course, did.

"Jesus Christ," she said loudly. She saw a bleeding head twisted at its torso. The body lay on the sidewalk at the bottom of one of the marching mulberry bushes planted smartly down the length of their building. One of Max's legs was lodged in the lower branches of the same bush; the other, still attached to Max but bent underneath his torso, was missing its shoe. Max's right arm was jutting out at a peculiar angle, but his left one was nowhere in sight. The oddest thing, some would remark later, was that a margarita glass sat upright nearby. His margarita glass had survived.

Helen froze in place, eyes dilated by flashes of red and white lights coming from three emergency vehicles savaging the air with their screaming sirens and finally winding down their flash/scream struggle with a jolt of stopping right THERE.

People were gathering and gawking, responding with hand-on-chest-oh-my-Gods.

To Helen's right was the horrified doorman croaking orders to his staff through his crackling speakerphone. When Helen quietly asked who that man on the sidewalk was, he replied that he thought it was Mr. Shaw.

"What? It couldn't be. God, don't repeat that to anyone," she whispered.

"O...K." Now he had even less composure as he dug into a situation utterly beyond his scope.

They walked away quickly.

"God, that was horrible." Helen's voice cracked as she and her husband automatically joined hands. Steven managed a throat clearing.

Forgetting about Steven's old injury, Helen dropped his hand and began power walking. He huffed an aggressive "Hey," and she flinched and halted with a "Sorry," a sad reminder to them both of his limitations.

Each was processing the previous scene in his or her mind's eye, examining a unique perspective of the images newly burned into memory, more of a dramatic struggle for the artist who replayed the scene in vivid colors than the pragmatist's images of blacks and grays.

After a spell, Helen began muttering. "Mr. Shaw! Mr. Shaw?...I thought Greg had better sense than to be guessing..."

"James," said Steven. "James."

"What?"

"James is on duty right now."

"What the hell, Steven. I'm in the middle of collecting my thoughts and you correct me on the doorman's name? Is his name the important one here? Who cares if I got his name right?"

Peevish silence.

"Are you OK, Helen?" asked Steven.

"Oh brother, not this. Come on, Steven. I'm as OK as you are. How're you doing? How's this day workin' out for you?"

"You know what I mean," he shot back. "Are you sure you still want to see a movie?"

"I need to. You should know that about me, Steven. You should know that I need to," said Helen.

He said nothing.

"...Great," she said sarcastically, "no response. I guess we're filling the air with silence. Let's just keep it that way."

"Fine...Am I allowed to say fine, or is that breaking the silence?"

He instantly regretted this juvenile remark; she let it go, and silence was achieved, enabling both of them to privately collect themselves as they crossed the Chicago River.

Steven was all but certain that the body had been Max Shaw's, whose unit, for one thing, was about forty-five stories directly up from the body on the cement. He'd already briefly entertained the scenario of Max dreamily sitting on his windowsill sipping his margarita and then simply losing his balance. But no. The windows had no sills. There was also the matter of the screen, which would have had to be removed. Now why would Max struggle to remove the window and the screen to perch on a strip of metal?

The whys would be answered slowly over the next few days, some easier to believe than others, but no explanation would be as strange yet as simple as the secret truth.

As they approached the theater's entrance, Helen was able to drop her abrasive tough-girl armor, at least temporarily. "Look," she said bravely, "by the time we return, everything...will be sorted out...and...calmed down. Let's just see the movie and forget about this for a couple of hours." She withdrew her arm from Steven's and briskly twirled through the revolving door.

As soon as her husband came through, Helen pulled him to the side and stretched up to kiss his cheek.

"I've never seen that person," she said, "and therefore it's really none of my business...our business...my business."

"Our business," said Steven as he firmly returned her kiss.

They escaped into Hollywood's take on reality, which was—no matter what—a welcome respite from their own at the moment.

Two hours later, Helen and Steven smacked into the disorientating afternoon sunshine and headed for home.

The minute she turned her cell phone back on, it jingled their daughter's alert tune and showed that she'd left three messages.

It rang again now, and there she was on the other end, excited about having farewell drinks together before she and her three flatmates on holiday from Cambridge left on the nine o'clock flight back to London.

For the past week, the girls had been all over town with Camille's friends, enjoying Chicago's late summer reprieve. Last night they'd stayed out until three, slept until ten, and with plenty of coffee, they'd showered and finished their packing. They'd left by cab to join their friends for brunch just a few minutes before Helen and Steven. Just a few minutes...

"Where are you?" asked Camille. "I've been calling and leaving messages that we wanted to meet up with you guys earlier. The cab dropped us at the Museum Campus and we've been walking north along the lakefront. We're almost home, so I guess we'll see you when you get there...now that you finally answered."

Camille sort of huffed on the rare occasions when her parents weren't around exactly when she wanted them. She was an only child, and she'd been such a nice one that she'd gotten all the attention she'd ever wanted, so of course she expected it.

At thirty-one, Camille belonged to the unique group of fortunates born into the luxury of financial freedom with the perk of unlimited educational opportunity.

Professional students who were financially dependent but hardly children, these young people had mostly avoided life's harsh realities. While trying to figure out what to be when they grew up, they'd grown up and still hadn't decided.

Just yesterday, her father had told the young women that "by now you geniuses are qualified to become isolationists and run some kind of a small utopian village." Helen had laughed and wondered aloud how many remembered the cautionary tale of *Animal Farm.* (All had, provoking lively conversation.)

But today, Camille's doting mother was using her self-control on the bloody accident, so she spoke without humor.

"Oh, uh-huh," said Helen. "Well you and I agreed to have farewell drinks together at four o'clock and it's not even three-thirty. Anyhow, sure. Great. Can't wait to see you ladies. I've got some snacks semiready and some white wine chilling..."

She stopped walking and took a breath. "You know, Camille, there are a few other things to use as amusements in this city besides Dad and me, for God's sake. Also, are you really packed, or is there going to be one of those last-minute mad dashes that..."

"There's no need to get annoyed here," interrupted Camille, "and, yes, I am completely packed. In fact, if you'll think back to four hours ago, Daddy helped us bring all our luggage to that room off the lobby this morning before we left for our farewell with the gang. Our luggage is awaiting our limousine," she finished smugly. "So, Mom, in this part of the world, we're fine. What about yours?"

"Mm…mine?" Helen tripped, then righted herself.

Steven took Helen's phone and spoke to Camille. "Listen, kiddo, about the lobby, you should know that…an accident occurred a couple of hours ago and…so, you should,…you should walk quickly past any crowd and straight through the lobby and the security door and right into the elevator and then into our unit."

Was it really only four hours ago that that person had been alive? thought Helen.

"Daddy, what happened?"

"I'm not sure but somehow…someone…"

Helen grabbed the phone back. "Someone died. And so just walk through the park and then straight into the lobby and…and don't talk to James…" and the airwaves went dead. "Crap," said Helen and clicked off her phone with more force than necessary. "Well that tears it," she said, looking up. "…Christ, are those the Harrises?"

"Oh yeah, heading toward us," said Steven. "Straight this way…. Annnnd here we go."

"Hello," he said, with false cordiality.

Helen kept her concentration on the phone problem, choosing to ignore their neighbors as long as possible. She mumbled, "Is that it then? Do cell phones just always roam when they're actually needed?"

"Max was such a happy man," Jean Harris was saying.

Al Harris was glumly shaking his head from side to side.

"Max? Did you say Max?" asked Helen.

Jean and Al both slowly shook their heads yes.

Again, Steven tried to somehow protect his wife, but from what, the truth? He slid his arm around her back. Helen pretended to switch her purse from one shoulder to the other, thus successfully shrugging her husband's arm away without embarrassing him. She was becoming annoyed with his behavior. When had she ever needed to be coddled like that? And why did he stop to talk? Was there some kind of a suicide-discussion etiquette that had been left out of her mother's somber drills?

"Just because his last name may have been Shaw doesn't mean it was Max," stated Helen belligerently. "We saw the person, you know…right after it happened, and, and that was not Max, that wasn't Max Shaw."

Now the Harrises were looking puzzled and did the sideways glance at Steven several times.

Steven feigned surprise as he checked his watch, took his wife's arm firmly, and began leading her on as he talked over her.

Helen was turning her head and finishing her point, "People should NOT be sharing false information…Christ, it's blogging without a computer…" while Steven was withdrawing with "We are beyond late, Jean and Al. Sorry to be so abrupt. See you later."

"Stop whisking me," Helen whispered loudly as she tried to free her arm. "You're treating me like some kind of an embarrassment."

He slowed their pace. "Naw, really? Let's take a moment, Helen. Let's wonder why…"

The cell phone rang again and this time Steven grabbed it from Helen's purse. "Yeah, hi, sweetie…No…He seems to have fallen out…Let's just talk about this when we get home. GottaGo. Bye." Click.

At this point, another shocked neighbor walked toward them, shaking his head sadly. "What a shame. What a shock, Max, of all people."

"What a shame What a shock What the fuck," murmured Helen to Steven. She squared off with him and said, "Where in the hell are people getting this information...this identification?"

He blanched at Helen's surprising hostility. "The, the building manager drove over and her boss showed up, and they talked with the medics before Max's, uh, the body was taken away. They identified him."

Helen slit her eyes and crossed her arms over her chest. "Only next-of-kin can do that, pal."

Steven spoke up quickly. "Where's Max's wife, Janet?"

"Oh, wait till you hear this." A true Irish gossip, he spoke with enthusiastic sadness. "Patty Marshall and Janet were on their way home from grocery shopping for their usual Sunday barbecue. So they're walking toward our building, maybe two blocks away, and they see the commotion and see the flashing lights, so Janet apparently calls Max to ask him what's going on. Patty's husband, Jim, is in the crowd of onlookers surrounding Max. He recognizes Janet's personalized cell phone jingle and realizes it's coming from Max's pants pocket. Instinctively, he looks down the street and there they are, the two wives, walking straight toward the bloody scene. Jim walks quickly toward them and stops them about a block away."

The narrator was highly flushed and all but beaming as he dramatically described how the action had unfolded, the way Jim stopped the women, and told them. How they had listened, screamed, and sprinted down the street, talked with the paramedics, and collapsed—how Janet had to be pulled away from the ambulance, and how the police took her to Northwestern Hospital.

He took in a deep breath, which afforded him the opportunity to switch from memory vision to the now of observing Helen's reaction. He softened his voice and spoke sympathetically, "So, Janet Shaw actually did identify her husband, Helen."

Steven was watching his wife very closely. Watching her reaction to the horrible truth she'd been resisting. As if in slow motion, Helen somehow became smaller, more delicate; a sad, vacant kind of surrender showed in her eyes and spread across her mouth.

"Here, honey, let me carry your purse for you," said Steven. "Would you like your sunglasses?" he asked as he got them out and said. "O...K...Well, uh, that was some kind of an update. We'd better go digest all this, don't you think, Helen?"

"Hmm?"

"Let's go, honey."

Helen allowed Steven's arm to stay on her back as they escaped the messenger. She was forced to refocus her attention on to the task of repetitive swallowing as the vomit of popcorn and Pepsi rose up in her throat.

They reached their building, which now blurred with activity and seemed to Helen to be strangely colored-over as if it had been tied-dyed and surrealistically illuminated, repainted in high-gloss colors of wet flesh and brilliant Chinese red, the dull gray cement color receding into the distance. There were maintenance men scrubbing the blood off the sidewalk. Window washers were setting up their gear to wash away the vertical trail of smeared blood. There was that squashed mulberry bush again with even brighter blood-red berries. It would have to be replaced, thought Helen, but the House Committee will surely see to that immediately. Her mind idled there for a moment to calm itself...there with those pleasantly composed committee faces...so efficient...

"What's that?" Her body trembled as she was snapped back to reality at the sight of a bright white tennis shoe dangling from a high mulberry branch.

Steven stabilized his wife by enveloping her into his left side with his arm and chest and hip. She leaned into him as they tangoed their escape toward the serenity of their unit, swiftly stepping through a blurry newsreel crowd of sad, stunned neighbors, some of whom were addressing Helen, but all she heard was a whirring sound.

And there they were—alone, thank God—back in the same elevator they'd taken earlier in the day. Helen remarked upon this in a small monotone voice. "We, we seem to have shared a moment in time that could have gone so many other ways…"

Steven interrupted her. "Helen, if you're thinking we're linked with Max's tragedy in some peculiar way…"

"You know what, Steven? Small talk would be great. The smaller the better."

Steven aggressively unlocked the front door and yelled, "Hello."

Helen yelled, "It's show time."

Four young ladies came bursting into the foyer, warmly greeting them. A sympathetic inquisition began at once: "My God, what happened?" but was drowned out by Camille's confrontational need-to-know in the form of a loud, "What's with the GottaGo/Bye/Click?"

Camille's aggression caused Helen to burst into tears.

Aghast, Camille took her mother into her arms, uttering a horrified, "Oh."

Helen buried her face in her daughter's curly thicket of long blond-brown hair and cried.

Camille gently rocked her a few times, chanting, "Oh, Mom," so softly, so sweetly.

Steven's description was brief, "The commotion that you girls saw when you came back was the aftermath of a suicide that happened earlier today, period."

The girls reacted with a flurry of dramatic oh-my-Gods, oh-nos, and how-awfuls.

Helen inhaled her tears and whispered to Camille, "Come here a minute, will you."

"We'll see you two at 'the Diner,'" Steven said, and led Phyllis and Eileen and Julia down the long gallery hall.

Helen took Camille into the first room off the foyer, where Camille hugged her mother and stroked her hair.

Camille said, "Do you want to tell me about it?"

Helen said, "No."

Camille said, "Mom, we should go. We could just go to the airport early. This is too hard for you."

Helen hugged her daughter tighter.

They could hear Steven talking pleasantly with the girls, probably getting some wine for everyone.

"NO. I...I'll be OK. Let's, let's just let this go for now. Live in the now. Right? We've got a couple of hours to spend before you're back at school finishing out the year. I can postpone my reaction...If I could, but I can't, I'd lie down on the tarmac to delay your flight..."

"...Although..." Mother and daughter automatically delivered the line together, giggling.

If nothing else, Helen Clark was a master at disguising and delaying her emotional pain. Now, she attempted a smile, and when that didn't work, she easily faked one. She blew her nose, wiped her eyes and combed her hair with her fingernails. "Let's just...let this go for now."

"I can do this," she said brightly, as she assumed perfect posture and took in an athletic breath.

Camille understood her mother's bravado, so she aided the effort by tenderly threading her arm through her mother's, slowly walking her down what was called the Camille Gallery toward the party life of the kitchen.

"I love this one," she said, pointing to a portrait Helen had done of her playing dress-up at age three. "And here's Daddy's favorite of me on my tricycle." She began pointing to every portrait on the wall. "And he likes this one, and this one..." achieving the sought-after smile.

"Oh," blurted her mother, "I'm almost done with your over-the-hill thirtieth birthday portrait."

"WOW, Mom...I'm...I didn't know you'd been painting lately."

"Well whatever gave you the idea I wasn't?"

"Because you hadn't asked me to actually pose."

"But you know I work off memory and photos as well."

"Yeah but then you get face time in."

"Little hard when you're not here, kiddo."

Camille adopted the voice of her little-girl self and began jumping up and down. "Can I see, can I see, can I see?"

Helen smiled widely at the memories of all the fun times her daughter had done that. But her eyes clouded over as she realized she hadn't put away the frenzied charcoal sketches of another person that she'd created from memory in the middle of last night. Don't deal with that now, she told herself. Don't even dare think about that until you're alone.

"Can I see?" repeated her daughter.

Helen gave her a coy "Possibly," her standard word announcing cautious optimism. It promised an answer based upon open-mindedness, and it bought time to mull over the conceivable outcomes of a yes or a no.

She turned to Camille and began tickling her. "I actually do need you to pose a little, so maybe you could quit school." Camille tickled her back as the two women spilled into the kitchen giggling.

The black-and-white diner-tiled kitchen had an orange neon sign high up on the back wall that glowed "EAT." Below the sign were silver appliances, shelves filled with sturdy white dishes, and a counter with soda fountain equipment at one end.

Another long counter faced the open kitchen and had eight swiveling silver stools with black leather seats.

Beyond the stools was the dining room with its oak floor and huge mahogany table and armchairs. Behind them was a floor-to-ceiling bookcase housing bunches of cookbooks and fancy tins of family recipes, as well as various colored crockery.

The bottom section of the bookcase held the board games of Camille's youth, with framed photos scattered among them of her and her friends playing these games in the big old River Forest home where she'd been raised.

Now everyone was sitting on the stools facing Steven, who was holding court from behind the counter, answering Eileen's question.

"Good question," he was saying. "The GottaGo/Bye/Click was a Camille ploy that sort of backfired. Her original purpose was to buy time for parental reconsiderations. Apparently her theory was that, out of touch, we might understand the logic of her latest urgent request and grant it.

"In those days, if she called either of us for some sort of permission, always involving freedom, and Camille sensed we were about to deliver the NO answer, she'd say, 'Whups, there's my bus,' or whatever. Then she'd utter a speedy wrap-up…'We'll talk later. Love you. Gotta go. Bye.' She'd hang up leaving a dangling parent on the receiving end.

"So," mugged Steven, "immediately after several months, we realized that our little teen-ager was attempting to manipulate some guidelines in her favor. We shared a brain, using mostly Helen's, and turned the tables, employing Camille's trick ourselves.

"All these years later, it's still useful as a stalling device, and obviously still annoying to the person on the receiving end." He laughed at Camille.

She made a face and said, "The parental units have allowed the entire game to get out of hand. Now it's become a contest—who can activate faster."

All three Clarks quickly formed imaginary phones, each holding the splayed fingers of one hand to their ear and mouth. They yelled, "Gotta go, bye," closing their fists as they said, "click."

A laughing Camille sat on a stool as her mother hugged each of the three young women, remarking on their new looks. "Well, yesterday's pampering at Tony's Salon paid off nicely I see, and the Oak Park boutiques seem to have gotten your business as well. Very nice."

The women formed pouty lips, dramatically fluffing their hair, and displaying their fingernails.

"Party under way," Helen announced as she rounded the counter into the kitchen and began assembling the prepared snacks.

Steven had poured everyone a wine. Helen turned to him, glaring so no one else could see, and said, "Where's mine, honey?" She had never in her life needed a drink so badly.

He was in the middle of sipping his and immediately gave it to his wife. He smiled gallantly to cover up his oversight. "Why, it's right here, darling. I was just making sure it was good enough for you."

The phrase seemed to just slip out.

It was on his list of the top-ten-favorite-ways-to-rile-Helen, because it held several grains of truth, and so it worked. But why in God's name would he want to provoke her right now? She was the center of his happy universe. She was his life. Where did this sudden hostility come from?

Now it hung in the air. Good enough for you. Good enough for you. Good enough for you.

Camille came to her mother's defense. "Common, Daddy, play nice. Mom can't help her perfectionism."

"Thank you, Camille," Helen said darkly. "And, Steven, maybe you could focus your hostility on to yourself..."

"What hostility? I was kidding," he interrupted lamely. "Kidding...where's your sense of..."

Helen interrupted him back. "Yep. I'm sure in the mood to be made fun of."

The couple suddenly became aware of the discomfort they were causing and stopped.

"I'll be right back," said Helen as she sought the sanctity of her bathroom.

She could hear Steven diligently lightening things up. "So. Did you ladies hear the one about the guy whose bus stop happens to be near the fenced-in grounds of an insane asylum?"

She heard the girls' appreciative laughter, the knowing laugh of a bad moment having passed, with relief on its way in the form of humor. But then she realized that Steven was telling one of Max's favorite jokes, which sent a powerful shudder through her.

Helen pep-talked into her mirror while applying some eyeliner. "Could you possibly be any more hormonal?" she asked herself aloud. "You're laughing, you're crying. You're happy, you're sad. You're sweet, you're sour. Stop it. Suck it up. A couple of hours, baby. Thick skin." She blushed her cheeks, kicked off her sandals, and marched back down the Camille Gallery with a healthy look of determination.

The group sat at the dining room table as Helen glamorously swept through the French doors with an empty wine glass, puffing on one of her Nat Sherman Fantasias. She called them her party cigarettes. They were extra-long and thin, with gold filters and a choice of five colors. Helen found the phrase that was printed along one side of the glamorous box amusing, because it somehow managed to imply that the cigarettes were good for you. "Made from the best tobacco."

Helen Clark had difficulty sitting or standing still for too long at a time and so she viewed her smoking as a secondary activity when she was drinking, which wasn't that often... although, actually, her consumption of alcohol and tobacco had slowly increased these last several months. It was about to skyrocket during the following week. In fact, by week's end, she would be chain-smoking.

"Well don't you look all fresh and fun," said Steven, as everyone smiled and agreed. "Hey, this swiss cheese you sliced is wonderful," he said as he put a slice on a cracker for her. "Is it from that new Italian deli across the river? And the spinach dip you made for the sliced zucchini. And your famous guacamole dip and chips..."

Helen patiently smiled as she poured herself and others more wine and interrupted her husband. "...He's trying to get me to eat instead of smoke, ladies. Steven is under the impression that he's protecting me from myself," she said coyly as she strolled behind his chair and kissed him gently on top of his head.

In fact, that's exactly what he was attempting.

"I know you all smoke occasionally, so if any of you would like to try one of these, why you're welcome." She took another from the pack, lit it with her beautiful slender gold lighter, and put them in the middle of the table with all the appetizers. "See, I share my toys," she said.

Camille took a pink one. Eileen chose a bright blue, Julia, a yellow. When Phyllis's fingers went toward the red, Helen gracefully handed her a green.

"Green is more you." She smiled, and made a mental note to throw out the blood red ones.

Steven understood her reaction exactly, and protected her frailty by saying, "Hey, she's an artist, Phyllis. No arguing color with a master."

This loyal endearment broke down Helen's tough-girl barrier for a split second, but Camille helped her regain it, by reverting to the stop-smoking subject.

"Poor Daddy," said Camille. "A control freak with no one to control."

"You got that right," said Steven, deciding to assuage the unfortunate earlier "good enough for you" remark by taking this one on the chin. This socializing under traumatic conditions had turned into a real workout for him. All these females with their right-brain reactions...Camille was a whole-brainer, but that didn't matter because in these circumstances she would be siding with the F's. The pinks outnumbered the blues, five to one. Not that there was a contest going on, but more to the point, a compassionate understanding of male viewpoints and logic would have been nice.

He could tell by the way she was behaving that Helen would be up for hours going through this trauma, and he'd be the one to help her calm down for all those hours. The other wrench for him was that he was actually suffering quite a blow over Max's death himself. He and Max had become very close in the six months they'd known each other.

Julia was studying Helen's lighter and asked about the engraving. "So what's this, then?" A very fancy MINE was written along one side.

Helen blinked twice. "Oh that," she said. "That's a botched engraving for my friend Mimi. She now has the correct version, and since there was a replacement, I got to keep the original mistake at no charge. I got MINE." Helen would have bet money that this bit of nonsense would be accepted because of the group-inebriation factor. It was.

She thought she put out the story's embers by rising and suggesting they all resettle in the family room.

The girls brought in the hors d'oeuvres, but Steven stayed behind opening a bottle of wine, saying, "Mimi? Who's Mimi?" while Helen poured a fresh can of cashews into a crystal bowl and laughed her way out of the room as if he were kidding to have somehow forgotten Mimi of all people. Christ, just kill-me-now, she thought. What a disgusting liar I am.

But hell, what's one more deception at this point, she thought, as she placed the nuts on a table. Everyone was pleasantly conversing, so she took the moment to put some music on while collecting her thoughts. Old favorites began playing: the Doors' "Riders on the Storm" came on and then "Break on Through." Helen smiled at the ladies' sounds of approval over her choice of music, as she rested by the sound system, pretending to select more. Just kill-me-now.

Kill-me-now. It was a common thought for Helen, albeit one that hadn't been in her schemata until it had reared its paralyzing head several months ago. When it came, those times before and now this time around, an overpowering urgency to stop herself from wakening her buried cheerfulness combined with the equally powerful urgency to move closer to the irresistible light of doom.

Kill-me-now. It was the tornado territory of her soul reliving the torment of being punished for having fun. Her life experience had taught her to never ever go to that place of utter joy because it could flip to sheer horror. She had learned long ago and several times since that happiness flips to unhappiness faster than you can say wait.

Kill-me-now. This schizophrenic pattern had occurred before in Helen's fifty-four years of life. She knew it as her nastiest of companions, yet it also offered the comfort of familiarity. She didn't welcome it, tried to avoid it, but when it appeared on her doorstep, she was unable to deny herself the magnificent crescendo by barring the door. She was vaguely aware that her heightened pleasures seemed to take up all available airspace; her happiness seemed to cost others theirs. She had been brought to her knees over this hideous conflict four other times in her life, and now here was one more of those Hello/Good-byes. Another death.

Kill-me-now. This had been her first thought of the morning and the last one at night during their two and a half months. Her morning mood of calculated indifference would baby-step toward optimism by three o'clock in the afternoon when he called, and then accelerate into several hours of what she recognized with untold gratitude, not to mention utter astonishment, as genuine happiness.

But later in the same day, unless there were party plans, the mood would begin to deteriorate, and when it did, it didn't slide backward; it plunged into one of hideous torment—a desperation of unnamed sadness, with a final bed tuck of kill-me-now.

At two in the morning, she would fly to him for their hour of ecstasy, then peacefully sleep until the kill-me-now first thought of her morning guilt.

Now in the family room, Helen placed her two CDs of *Gotan Project* in the player and brought her attentions back to the group.

The girls watched Helen admiringly. She watched them watching her...as a role model, as a beautiful woman of substance who had it all. This façade always upset her. Her pose of a centered female was honed for her demanding mother, was kept afloat for her loyal husband, and shone its brightest for her precious daughter.

In private, Helen worried that she presented an unrealistic standard. She knew herself to be an intricate puzzle with missing parts and sometimes thought she should share her past with Camille simply to show her that life's possibilities are not endless, that authority interferes with those possibilities. Should she tell her that? But what if that wasn't always the case and revealing her personal tragedy somehow thwarted Camille's achievements by altering her optimism?

Enough. Helen stifled a yawn. Steven caught it and gave her a comical look, causing her to further stifle a laugh.

Right now she was pleased with the enthusiasm over her city, and that her daughter's classmates had enjoyed the show of it all. On the other hand, this repetitious conversation was feeding her exhaustion. She'd heard this kind of praise about herself and Chicago enough times to circle the world and certainly more than enough to last a lifetime.

What about Max's lifetime, she suddenly thought, and then immediately sipped some wine and lit another Fantasia.

Steven, on the other hand, never tired of talking. Teachers never do. He liked the subject of their condo, the way the exterior walls of floor to ceiling glass presented such magnificent views of the heart of Chicago, and how the interior walls were lined with either Helen's amazing artwork or their collection of books. Steven needed little coaxing to discuss each painting, each book, and then on to the colors Helen had chosen to use in the décor of their rambling space. He enjoyed informing people who really wanted to absorb all this pleasure.

Helen got a kick out of this sometimes, but not today. Please don't go on and on today, she thought—and then, just to assure a proper outcome, she turned the attention back on to the girls.

What was the dating scene like lately?

"Mutually agreed upon sexuality with no commitment," was basically the answer. The females were busy launching their careers just the same as the males these days.

Phyllis was an exception in that she had earned the money for her education, so it had taken her even longer to get where she wanted to go. In her final year of studies, she was four years older than the others, and at thirty-five, she had the only serious relationship. She and her fiancé had gotten engaged last Christmas with a plan to marry in two years' time. This would give her the chance to begin her career in medicine and be settled enough to begin their family. By then, they'd both be thirty-eight, and she could safely bear children until age forty, so if she had their two children back-to-back, there they'd all be. Happy, healthy, and financially comfortable.

Mapping out life was a difficult subject for both Helen and Steven, and now she wished she'd let her husband ramble on about their condo. They had learned the hard way that detailing a life plan was stupid and audacious, a dangerous presumptive move on God. Both parents began fidgeting, Steven clearing his throat, shifting in his chair, rubbing his right leg, and Helen calming her hot flash by holding the cool glass of wine to her cheek.

Now Phyllis was merrily describing the love of her life, blithely unaware that their many lean years of thoughtful and cheerful diligence might very well end up being remembered as their highest point, and would not necessarily be rewarded with their happily-ever-after plan.

"Andrew has been intrigued by computers his whole life," Phyllis said to Helen and Steven, "because his dad was a professional technician, and after Andrew earned his master's degree in science and technology, father and son opened their own business, bringing in a few good men his dad had worked with as well as several of Andrew's classmates. Trust is everything. That and hard work. But I don't have to tell you Yankees that," she finished.

"Always good to reiterate, though," said Helen. "And this decade of humans is totally dependent on tech support, so, really, I can't think of a better gig. You and Andrew will probably be gazillionaires," she said enthusiastically.

In fact, Helen regarded money as a curse, and spoke this way as an encouragement to Phyllis, because she knew how hard she and Andrew had worked for the promise of it all. She wanted them to find the happiness they'd worked so hard for, but she'd lived plenty long enough to know that money wasn't the ultimate answer. Phyllis seemed to think it was.

Helen said to Phyllis, "Honey, you and Andy love each other and you're a conscientious team. You've already got what you need."

There were thoughtful murmurs of agreement from the others.

Helen's family money hadn't gotten her the life she wanted. Did money have anything to do with her God-given artistic talent? Did money stop flukes? Had money stopped the never-ending nightmare of Steven's accident? What was the dollar price of a child like Camille? And likewise, emotional train wrecks aren't stopped with money. Money never stopped humans from hurting each other, did it?

Duty bound to offer her hard-earned wisdom to Phyllis, Helen took a moment to phrase her advice in a nonlecturing way. She directed her commentary to Camille, who understood exactly what her mother was doing.

"I was just appreciating an article I read the other day," said Helen. "It pointed out that the intangibles of life aren't for sale. We can't buy love or joy or insight...and, boy, if that isn't a mouthful..."

Quiet reflection momentarily filled the room.

This kind of conversational philosophizing had fascinated Helen for most of her life because her own sense of ease had hit a brick wall at the age of twelve. She'd lived in a tense state of bated breath for so long now that it had shifted into the familiar, which had traveled further afield and landed in a zone misnamed "comfort." She was fine with it, or thought she was.

To Helen, life's meaning was one of the most fascinating of conversations. But this line of thought generally upset the comfort zones of others.

Not wishing to drag her friends down the long and winding road of reality, Camille reiterated the importance of these "sought-after priceless life qualities"—love, joy, insight, and then cleared her throat at her mother, signaling "the end."

Her father understood the freedom of apathy and airily offered up her mother's joke. "So," he said, "speaking of American ethics, did you hear Helen's latest political joke?"

Helen froze. Max. Max had told that joke at the last party. But they were so alike, it might as well have been her. She forced out a jovial, "Fine."

As she told the joke, Steven found himself admiring his wife's social grace one more time. Helen could have invented the phrase, back on track. Her joke telling was new, though... She must have honed that skill under Max Shaw's watch, come to think of it. Max had been great at that too, thought Steven. He ached with the sorrow of losing their new friend, remembering how he'd felt a connection the day they were introduced. "That's rare in adulthood," he'd said to Helen with unusual enthusiasm. He recalled that she'd liked Max too in her laissez-faire Helen kind of way, but not as much as he.

At last, the doorman double-rang the phone to announce that the girls' limousine had arrived. Good-byes and hugs all around.

Steven said, "Now, Eileen, don't forget what Mrs. Clark asked for."

Eileen laughed and reiterated her promise "to send back a London cab and one of our livery instructors to teach grooming and manners and smooth driving and..."

"AND geography," added Helen.

"A required one-year course on attitude might cover all that nicely," said Steven, summing up, as he winked at his wife.

When Camille hugged her mom good-bye, Helen felt an overwhelming desire to not let go of her. Then, grabbing her daughter by the hand with an "Oops, I almost forgot," she led her to the desk in the den, opened the hidden drawer, and took out a watch, which she put on Camille's slender wrist.

"See. It's got two faces, so you can know what time it is here as well as there. I've set it so that, as you can see, it's six o'clock here and midnight in London."

"How perfect, Mom. I'll call you tomorrow when it's ten o'clock here, in case you're sleeping late. Let's see, it's a seven-hour flight, departing at nine tonight, which means that by the time we get to Cambridge, it'll probably be six a.m. there, eight a.m. here..."

"No," corrected her mother. "Six a.m. there would be noon here."

It seemed that Camille had always messed with time in some way or another. Yet, actually, this quirk hadn't shown up until around age ten. At ten, she'd become, what her father called, purposely off-center. "Our little genius is time-challenged," her mother had announced. Her parents had been amused. Camille herself had known why she'd shifted from the dullness of normalcy and was fine with it. The shift away from time constraints had served as a convenience, allowing her daily curiosity to develop at its own pace.

This latest confusion over the time differences between Chicago, Illinois, and Cambridge, England, had gone on all school year.

Six months ago, time-conversation number two thousand and nine had occurred after Helen and Steven had settled their daughter into Cambridge for the year, and they were hugging good-bye one more time.

"Call anytime," her mother had said.

"Well, try during waking hours," her father had said.

"Time is so irrelevant," Camille had theorized. "Or perhaps it's crucial. I've vacillated on the subject for years now…Maybe I'll invent a time machine…Maybe I've already invented it and I'm visiting you from the future." Her eyes, her hauntingly beautiful turquoise-blue eyes, became moist when she spoke this way.

The parents had shot each other amused isn't-she-fascinating-and-adorable looks. Helen privately thought her daughter's postulations were possible.

"It won't matter what the plan is if you don't make the plane," Steven was now pointing out.

No one was listening because Camille was showing the girls her fancy new watch. "Look on the back." She giggled and turned it over to reveal an engraving of a fly.

"My mom's idea of course."

Julia let out a sigh of pleasure. "Time flies," she said.

"Exactly."

When the phone double-rang again, everyone realized Limo-man was probably getting restless. Their laughter subsided, replaced by sweet good-byes.

Helen and Steven smothered Camille with kisses and let her go.

The party ended with Mother and Father, and Daughter speaking over each other as they said, "See you at Christmas," recklessly assuming their tomorrows.

The minute the door closed Helen let out a huge sigh of energy loss and collapsed onto the Oriental rug.

This threw Steven and, fairly typically, when he most wanted to offer words of comfort he came up with something confusing. "Oh, Helen, what is it, sweetie?"

"What is it? What IS it?"

"Well no. I know what it is. I just don't understand your reaction. You're so typically stoic in these types of situations..."

Helen interrupted. "These types of situations? I've never seen a fatal accident, Steven. I've never seen a person smashed onto a sidewalk. None of this makes sense. Was he washing the window screen?"

She got up and he followed her into their living room. She stood in front of one of their operable windows, demonstrating her thoughts. "When our screens are washed, the maintenance men just crank open the window, then reach in and unhook the screen and...you know this isn't as easy as it looks..." She struggled to angle the screen past the cranked-open window and into the room.

She picked up their wine glasses from a nearby table, gave her husband his, and held on to hers as she leaned over the window to look out.

"Careful," said Steven, as he hovered over her protectively.

"No. I don't want to be careful. I'm feigning curiosity. I'm wondering what the weather's like. I'm leaning over to test the weather conditions. I'm..."

"It's cold," he said. "Let's put that back and close the window."

She shot him a look of reproach. "It's not cold. Here. First see how far out you can actually lean. Keep your glass in your hand."

He held his glass and leaned out. The angled window itself stopped him from further movement. "I don't need to, Helen. This is nuts."

She briefly watched him reassembling the window, and then headed for a wine refill.

"Would you like a wine or something, Helen?"

"You mean like the glass I'm pouring?"

"I'll have one too."

"Would that be why I've taken your glass?"

Her testiness upset them both.

Steven entered the kitchen and grabbed his wife around her waist from behind. She stopped pouring. Set the bottle on the counter. Turned around to hug him. Buried her face in his chest. And burst into tears. He just kept stroking her hair and kissing the top of her head, and softly saying, "OK, honey. OK. Let's just do whatever it is you need to do to accept what happened."

This calmed her down. His voice calmed her. He had a deep, almost gravelly-type voice, and when he lowered the tone to nearly a whisper, she was hypnotized. "It's OK," he kept whispering as he kissed her head, her cheeks, her ears, her neck—and finally she stopped sobbing and went limp. She gave into the comfort he offered her and was quiet.

They stayed like that a wonderful while.

The ringing phone jarred their respite. They let it ring and go to voice mail but then it rang again, the family signal to pick up, so Helen grabbed the cordless as she cleared her throat. "Hello," she said, using her mechanical everything-is-fine voice.

"Hi," said her best friend, Cate, calling from New York. There was a puff sound. She was smoking, which meant she felt like chatting. "Is this a bad time?"

The minute Helen heard Cate's voice she burst into tears. "Oh. My God. I'm so sorry. I. Just. Can't seem..."

"I knew something happened to you today. I could just feel it. What's wrong? What happened?" Cate was a true New Yorker. She liked change. She really didn't mind if it was good or bad. She thrived on change itself. To Cate, change and complication were healthy challenges.

"Hold on. It's Cate," she told Steven dismissively. He mouthed, I figured, collected his wine, and gladly sought the escape of television, trading his day of relentless reality for that of the Bears.

Helen lined up the five red Fantasias, and lit one. Between bursts of tears, she was able to tell Cate what happened. But only to a point. She couldn't background Cate about what this Max person really meant to her, so the base was sadly superficial.

Without opening the private life of herself and Max Shaw, there was no hope of resolve. No other living person knew the truth except Max's sister, and even she only knew the beginning, so what followed was the agony of listening to her best friend's heartfelt attempt to problem solve in quicksand.

After a good hour of both of them talking slowly and calmly, Cate was under the impression that she'd rationally reached some understanding of Helen's reaction and suggested that Helen might want to think about making an appointment with her sister's psychiatrist who was located five blocks from Helen.

"I've been raised to tough it out, Cate. I'd ruin my self-image if I sought professional help, and that would lead to more depression."

"All righty, then, be obstinate at your own expense..." Big puff and exhale..."Here's the thing, this doctor I'm suggesting is my sister's link to any possibility of normalcy. She actually trusts him and keeps her appointments, which is a major deal, considering her schizophrenic condition. He's the only man who has ever reached..."

"...me, was the son of a Preacher man..."

"What?"

Helen felt lightheaded and giddy as she sang the lyrics: "The only man who could ever reach me was the son of a preacher man. Yes he was, yes he was..."

"Pour the wine out and get some sleep, Helen."

"Uh huh," said Helen pouring herself another glass of wine. "...I. I'm so tired...Maybe in a few days..."

"Why don't I call Dr. Savage and let him know that you're calling him on my recommendation. I can tell him you witnessed a suicide. Then when you call for an appointment, you won't feel like so much of a stranger...How about that, Helen?"

"I don't think so..."

"Just to see, Helen. You're definitely relating to this suicide personally and you need to figure out why that is. I mean, just consider all the adjustments you've made in your life. And yet you're reacting to this trauma as if it's in the same league with Steven's car crash, or Camille's birth."

"...Helen?"

"...Helen?"

Out of love and respect, Helen collected herself and tried to give her devoted friend an explanation rooted in pure truth. "I can't do life, Cate. I'm just not tough enough to do life. I guess Max Shaw maybe figured out that he couldn't either, and so now, I guess he's reached peace."

Dead silence.

"Look what he's left behind, Helen. Don't you dare talk like that. A coward puts himself at ease by harming others. He's left an incalculable emotional mess. He's permanently damaged all those who cared for him; everyone who ever related to him is worse off because they did. But he's OK? I don't think so, Helen. There's no hiding in this life or the next. Where's the logic?"

"You know what, Cate? You're probably right about that. And having said that, I'm feeling worse than ever that I told you, because you can't help me. Even you, the best of the best, cannot help me. Only I can get through this. And now, now all I've done is pull you down into this chasm of hell..."

Cate interrupted. "How about no man is an island?"

"How about clichés aren't gonna do it?"

Silence.

"I'm sorry, Cate. I love you, and I just…don't want to hurt anyone else. I need to hang up…and I need you to know that just the knowledge that you're…in my life…is a gift from God."

"I'm not hanging up until you agree to see Dr. Savage."

Emotionally trapped, Helen physically and mentally recognized the shift in her nature. Cate's relationship with Helen went way back, but not as far as the one to whom Helen now surrendered. Her old sidekick, Self-Hatred, said, "Hello, Mess, give us a kiss."

"No," said Helen.

"What?"

"I will, Cate," said Helen as she walked quickly down the hall to her bathroom. "I have to go, Cate. I'm about to throw up. I'm sorry. I love you. I'll call him tomorrow."

After she'd hung up, and thrown up, Helen laid on her bed, wondering for the hundredth time if she just should have told Cate everything. It seemed somehow cruel to let Cate think her reaction mystifying, when really it wasn't at all. She lit the last of the red Fantasias while Self-Hatred took a stroll around her soul.

How could I have exposed myself like this? Before Max, I'd managed to simplify my life to one of beautifully choreographed style. My life was controlled. My life was smoothly simple—not a hint of complication.

Cate's mother suddenly popped into Helen's thoughts.

*Years ago, when Cate was promoted and moved from Chicago to New York, she'd been concerned about her mother's well-being, so Helen had volunteered to drive the hour or more to the rest home once a week to look in on her.*

*Helen had taken her watchdog position seriously.*

*Now she recalled what she'd learned.*

She reacted fairly typically on the first visit, becoming slightly nauseous over the unmistakable odor of elderly habitats; a mixture of medicine breath, urine, and extra-strength cleaning solution.

There was also the visual physicality to overcome. The old bodies were all slouched into wheel chairs. This troubled Helen. It was anyone's guess as to their conditions, but Helen remembered wondering if this confinement was more beneficial to the staff than their charges, because it must certainly be far easier to handle the mentally and physically slow when they were all in wheel-able chairs.

The second visit was only slightly easier. She knew what to expect, but the fact that Cate's mother seemed irritated, frankly rankled her, because of all the thoughtful attention and expense involved in the upkeep of the old woman.

But then on the drive home, she realized it probably was irritating for her to be asked what she wanted. Old people probably all wanted to be self-sufficient, and preferred not to think about their deteriorating energy. So the best solution was probably the one already in place; don't ask them what they want...just provide what they need.

Helen came a different day on her third visit, with the idea of catching everyone off guard, seeing how the place was run during a typical nonvisitation day, trying to figure out the key to the calm.

Cate's mother wasn't in her room, so Helen went about arranging her fresh flowers and comingling Hershey chocolate kisses into her pretty candy dish to share. She hung a new leisure outfit in the closet and then went down the hall to the beauty parlor to find her friend's mother. Pleasant beauticians and happily pampered old ladies greeted her.

But she wasn't there.

Next she peeked into the social room. She saw wheel chairs filled with nodding off ninety-year-old lumps contentedly watching *I Love Lucy* reruns.

Cate's mom wasn't there either.

She looked here and there, noticing the order, the cleanliness, the quiet patience of the staff members.

Helen finally located Cate's freshly coiffed and manicured mother in the craft room, covered in a pretty yellow smock, creating greeting cards. There she sat, yammering on and happily working away at a table with some fellow inmates. There was a perky aid, helping the women with their creations, making suggestions, and supplying them with materials. Helen was mesmerized by the scene's childlike appeal.

She stood there watching them, longing to be a part of their simplistic existence.

Apparently, the key to the calm, was in accepting the slowdown while maintaining a schedule of various degrees of simple stimulation.

Helen wrestled her covers and turned onto her other side, imagining the simple daily pleasure of being taken care of in that way. She placed herself in the scene. She could be running the class, or she could be taking the class. Either way, the imagery was nice. She was in a simple little class of pleasantly creative women...

When whatever game Steven was watching ended, he came into her room, leaned over and kissed her tenderly on the cheek, relieved that she'd given up the day. She feigned sleep as she felt the kiss, the tenderness, and his relief.

Tears streamed down her face and onto her pillow as she began to accept the unbearable truth. I'll never feel Max again. Never hug him again. Never kiss him again. Never wrap my legs around him again. She couldn't imagine how she'd get through the rest of her life without his smile, without his kisses, without his eager sex.

That caused her to remember what Max had said after the first time they had been intimate. He had looked at her so earnestly and said, "There's no turning back, you know. You know that, don't you? Our lives will take on different dimensions."

The clarity of this perception would take a few lifetimes to appreciate. In the distant future, Max and Helen's great granddaughter, Daisy, would eventually be able to calculate the complexity of youthful sexuality and bring it back full circle to simplicity. But she wasn't even a thought yet.

Helen resettled her head and arms around her pillows several times. Oh, Max, she thought. Why did we go so far? They had passed three points of no return in their long history together.

For him, it had been easy to request a change, because he didn't want to be free. His was a life befitting the Janis Joplin lyrics, "Freedom's just another word for nothin' left to lose." If granted, his request would have grounded him, would have been his dream realized. He didn't seem to grasp the meaning of victimization, of claiming happiness at the expense of others.

Helen did though. For her, there was the complicated matter of being the mother, of being the apex of happiness for her husband and daughter.

Helen had figured something out that Max had not. His shallow life hadn't shown him the signs that her complicated one had: Beware. Danger. Keep out. Changing dynamics. Flip Side ahead—Don't go there—Stop.

She tossed her soft linen sheets, shifting her leaden exhaustion once more, tired, but simply unable to settle down.

It had never occurred to Steven that what his wife really needed was to be held and cuddled through the night.

Max would have known that and done that, though he'd only had the proximity during their three-night "honeymoon." The dazzling memory stimulated her body's raw nerves, sending shivers of unwanted ecstasy.

Had it really only been two weeks ago?

"Open it." Max had beamed.

MINE, said her new cigarette lighter, her "honeymoon" remembrance.

"Helen, you've really always been mine," he'd said as she'd opened her gift.

*No one can make you feel inferior without your consent.*
~ Eleanor Roosevelt ~

*Sometimes I wonder if men and women really suit each other.*
*Perhaps they should live next door and just visit now and then.*
~ Katherine Hepburn ~

# MONDAY

The next day was a Monday with everyone going about their business as usual because they had to, and besides, it was a way of normalizing. Helen's Mondays were typically her laundry days, coupled with catching up on correspondence and confirming planned events for the week ahead. But this one took the path of the unforgiving day before and was therefore second in a series of days from hell.

She'd slept fitfully, finally REMing at 6:00 a.m. At 6:30 a.m., the phone wakened her. When she went to pick it up, she noticed the time and was furious that anyone would have the indecency to call at such an ungodly hour.

"Hello," she answered crabbily.

"Hi, Mom. Did I wake you?"

"Camille," said Helen. "Think back to yesterday, and the double-faced watch I gave you with London time and Chicago time. Are you wearing the watch, Camille?"

Helen's sarcasm was met by silence at the London end.

Helen waited.

Finally Camille said, "Mom I am SO sorry. I'm putting it on as we speak and I won't take it off ever again, and…Is it waterproof, or should I not wash my left arm anymore?"

An image of Max's missing arm shot to the front of Helen's brain.

"Hold on," she said weakly. (Deep breaths.) "Oh-so-funny-you," she said in a monotone.

"Yeah. Can I ring back later and pretend this call never happened?"

"That's my girl," said Helen. "Let's begin again. I got no sleep, you've got jet lag, and what a way to startle a day, huh?"

"Exactly. I'm safe, Ma. And I'm sorry."

"I love you, kid. And your safety keeps me (from blowing my brains out) happy." Helen could hear Julia and Eileen and Phyllis chatting in the background. "Say hi to the gals," she added.

Mother and daughter blew kisses through the airwaves and hung up.

She made some coffee, padding around her home as it perked. And for the millionth time, Helen realized that the only thing that kept her grounded was her daughter. When Camille was in the house, Helen forced herself to behave normally. And now Camille was across the ocean until Christmas, during which time Helen could do a lot of damage to herself, though how it could get worse was impossible to imagine.

She found herself in Camille's lovely bedroom and climbed under the tousled comforter, falling instantly asleep and waking peacefully a few hours later in this wonderfully cocooned place.

*Treasured Camille moments popped up, one delightful picture after another:*

Baby girl Camille, safely in her mother's arms suckling at her breast with her rosebud mouth and fat little cheeks, all pale and rosy, with huge and trusting turquoise blue eyes, looking at her mother (her everything), who's looking adoringly back at her.

Little girl Camille, seriously contemplating the question her father had asked her, "Camille, what do you want to be when you grow up?" And then her answer, "A parking place." Laughter, then, "Why?" "Because Mommy's always wanting to find one."

Serious third grader Camille, same question, phrased: "Camille, what will you be when you grow up?" Two minutes of contemplation, then a wise and self-assured, "Older."

Momentarily aggressive fifth grader Camille, rushing in the door to announce that she'd done what Daddy suggested and popped Timmy in the mouth for mercilessly taunting her half the school year.

Tragically upset eighth grader Camille, wondering why her principal asked her to choose another American hero to honor and to then rewrite her valedictorian speech (followed by an intense parent/teacher meeting and no rewrite).

Earnestly righteous Camille, delivering that same wondrous Martin Luther King speech. (You could hear a pin drop.)

High schooler Camille, deftly handling the ins and outs of popularity, choosing genuine classmates, some athletes, some geeks, some geniuses, some just plain nice, and all hanging out at her River Forest home.

The sophomore Camille, forced to give up basketball (only five-five) but eventually starring as a team captain and star pitcher on the baseball team. (The life-sized portrait of suited up MVP number 22 hung in the condo hall gallery.)

A stunned Camille on the front porch of her home at seven in the morning, looking out at her surprise "Sweet Sixteen" birthday party. (Among many others, the football team showed up, all crazy for this girl who was smart, funny, darling, and nice besides.)

A restless seventeen-year-old Camille and two best friends, all in bib overalls painting the garage and themselves (hired by her sly grandmother who wanted them home and safe that crazy summer).

A pensive Camille, parents hovering, exploring the vast possibilities of university choices, causing the three to joyfully explore some campuses together.

Camille had literally never acted negatively to her parents, ever. The only heartache during all those years had been to ease her into the harsh realities of adult life. Steven had been willing to occasionally cause her overreaction to life's tragedies via newspapers and PBS news reports, but Helen had been gentler, more lighthearted, couching Camille's personal reality run-ins as "first-world problems," reminding her that if she thought THAT was bad...Still, it was true that Camille had been spared most of life's harshest realities.

Now what?

Up for the day, Helen sighed, poured herself some half-coffee/half-milk, and found the phone number Cate had given her for that psychiatrist, that Dr. (something) Savage.

He said he was expecting her call, and why didn't she just come over today. He'd had a cancellation, so he could see her at 4:15 p.m.

This threw her, because she really hadn't thought about how she would be able to expose her life to anyone, trained or not.

"Yes, all right, then. I'll see you at four-fifteen." She crawled back in bed to think this through.

Moments later, the phone rang again. A neighbor wanted to know if the Clarks would give her a ride Wednesday to the church service for Max. Helen's voice cracked. "It...it's Wednesday? I...I'll call you back."

She buried the phone between her mattresses.

Helen felt the weight of grief seeping through her. She propped up her pillows and sat there in bed, leadenly staring at the coffee mug, listlessly sipping its cold, near-empty contents. The seconds ticked toward minutes and steadily accumulated for over an hour as she stared at hazy nothings while a confused disorder of past-life tragedies relentlessly tumbled through her addled brain.

The need to pee got her up and moving again. Disgust over the stupidity of self-induced pain powered her mobility awhile as she put in a load of wash to catch up on the day and more importantly to keep from thinking about anything meaningful. Multitasking usually helped her gain energy, but not with today's multifaceted hangover. Today she had the conglomerate constraints of toxic wine and cigarette remnants and a heart-shattering tragedy to lug around.

After five cups of coffee, and the first load of wash drying while a second load gyrated in the washing machine, she stood under the shower and cried.

Finally, exhausted again, she managed to throw on slacks and a sweater and sit at the kitchen table with a banana and juice. She read about Max Shaw's death in the two daily papers. It said nothing of suicide—just that he had passed away, leaving behind family and friends who dearly loved him. This produced a burst of tears.

She cleaned up the party remnants, folded some laundry, put the phone back on the hook and listened to ten or so messages, all related to Max Shaw's suicide. She did not return the calls, but did begin contemplating her appointment with Dr. Savage.

Helen pulled her hair back into a ponytail, put on some lipstick and her sunglasses, and went down to the lobby to check out the situation, under the guise of collecting the mail. Neighbors were talking in hushed tones. Several came to her for hugs, which she put up with. Certain hypocrisies were already under way. Some of the people moping in the lobby barely knew Max. Helen allowed for the fact that they might simply need hugs because the situation was so traumatic, so she held a few pretend-pals altruistically. But the self-control it took to address the suicide so directly caused her to feel weak and breathless.

While this was going on, she was looking at the outside activities through the lobby's glass wall and could see neighborhood people talking and watching the maintenance men scrubbing the sidewalk again.

Now, see, this is something I never knew, thought Helen. Apparently blood stains cement…or maybe blood only penetrated pavement when it was mashed into it after gaining the momentum of four hundred feet…

Or? Or maybe Janet Shaw had jumped out the same open window before maintenance had time to put the screen back in place.

Helen suddenly realized that she needed to be upstairs. Yes. And search out everything that was the dazzling, gleaming, screaming red of fresh blood and the brownish red, the umber color of dried dead blood. She needed to throw certain clothes away…also any red or brown nail polish. Pink was OK. And clear. And…brown? Hmmm…blood looked brown when it dried, didn't it? But maybe not. The sidewalk had dried and hadn't turned brown. So brown shades of nail polish would be OK, then. Wait. The sidewalk blood was deceiving because it was mixed with water and cleaning chemicals. Was brown OK or not? Hadn't she just made a distinction about ruby and umber?

There Helen stood amid her neighbors in a zone no one else could enter, pondering cause and effect and reaction and related matters, logically illogical like the Mad Hatter in *Alice In Wonderland*, only he scurried as he thought his thoughts, whereas she had become rooted to the spot.

Perhaps this bloody tragedy was written in the stars long ago. Maybe, somewhere deep inside her, she had expected Doom for a long time, and maybe that's what all these tears were about. Because, really, Max Shaw was so much a part of Helen that she might as well have jumped with him.

No. There was Camille to consider. Camille, whose innocent part in all this seemed otherworldly, remained safely inside another dimension.

The weaver himself had unraveled a corner of their densely tangled web. How could he do this? He simply couldn't have. He couldn't have meant for this to happen.

...Actually, though, hadn't he always been their audacious playwright? He'd certainly thought up the first and second acts, with her as eager leading lady, but still...And the third? Apparently, they'd just finished the third and final act, leaving her to take the curtain call alone.

She became aware that someone had been speaking to her and that she'd been making the appropriate uh-huh responses. Another neighbor joined them, giving Helen her opportunity to politely exit.

Helen was now begging her legs to walk her to the elevator, to the safety of her home, but apparently one of her had an important mission. She was on automatic pilot as she worked her way to the front desk, seeking out the poor brave doorman who had handled the whole horrible ordeal yesterday. Was it only yesterday?

Back on duty, he was out from behind his desk, holding the door for someone. She waited nearby pretending to look over her mail so that no one would talk to her. When

James circled to return to his security desk, Helen touched him lightly on the arm.

"James, you did a great job yesterday of controlling what could have led to a panicked crowd. I hope you were able to get some sleep last night. How are YOU doing today? Are you OK?"

James's eyes welled with tears. "I. I'm getting there. I'll be OK. It takes time. It just takes time. It takes time."

Helen gave him a hug and said, "Thank you for your strength and intelligence," at which James had to break away and blow his nose. "OK, then, see you later," said Helen. Why did she always provoke such emotion in people, she wondered as she headed straight for the elevator, head down, studying her mail. Christ, what were those? Her fingernails were still painted bright red. She furrowed her brow. "I thought for sure I removed that," she said aloud.

Safe in her unit, she reluctantly answered her ringing phone, cradling it as she began roughly peeling the nail polish off. It was their friend, Peter, who was calling to suggest that Helen and Steven share a taxi on Wednesday with him and Christine.

She forced the polish off in clumps.

They needed to cab to the church service for Max and then to the luncheon where Max would be eulogized.

"Yes, good idea..." said Helen. "Meet in the lobby at ten thirty...You'll have a cab ordered," Helen repeated in a deadpan voice.

She clawed at her nails.

"Are you OK?" asked Peter.

Helen had to hold her nose to stop another burst of tears. "Well, not really. I mean, is anyone OK?"

Several fingernail beds began throbbing.

"No," choked Peter. "We...Well, you know. All of us were at the Randalls' dinner party with him just last week for

God's sake. He was fine. Remember? He joined in the conversation. He told that great ostrich joke."

Actually, thought Helen, I told that joke, I'm the one who told the ostrich joke that night, and come to think of it, it's one of those cautionary jokes...I wonder if I was already warning me, warning us...she half-listened to Peter as she remembered the party, and saw herself telling the joke:

*She's seated at the disheveled after-dinner/after-dessert table in the Randalls' elegant dining room, wearing her pale blue knit dress (Max's favorite), sitting among her friends enjoying a liqueur and cigarette. Max has just asked her to tell the ostrich joke. (He'd told it to her and Steven earlier in the evening and they'd gotten a bang out of it, but, besides the fact that their friends would enjoy it, Max wants so very much to have a reason to stare at her, to watch her tell it.) She demurs, "It's YOUR joke; YOU tell it." "No YOU tell it," he says. "Well, someone tell it," says Steven. "Yeah," says Janet. Rather than continuing this juvenile banter, Helen says, "Fine."*

"A man walks into a restaurant with a full-grown ostrich behind him. The waitress asks them for their orders. The man says, 'A hamburger, fries, and a Coke,' and turns to the ostrich. 'What's yours?' 'I'll have the same,' says the ostrich. A short time later the waitress returns with the order. 'That will be $9.40, please.' The man reaches into his pocket and pulls out the exact change for payment. "The next day, the man and the ostrich come again and the man says, 'A hamburger, fries, and a Coke.' The ostrich says, 'I'll have the same.' Again the man reaches into his pocket and pays with exact change.

"This becomes routine until the end of the week. 'The usual?' Asks the waitress. 'No, this is Friday night, so I will have a steak, baked potato, and a salad,' says the man. 'Same,' says the ostrich. Shortly the waitress brings the order and says, 'That will be $32.62.' Once again the man pulls the exact change out of his pocket and places it on the table. The waitress cannot hold back her curiosity any longer. 'Excuse me, sir. How do you manage to come up with the exact change in your pocket every time?'

"'Well,' says the man, 'several years ago I was cleaning the attic and found an old lamp. When I rubbed it, a genie appeared and offered me two wishes. My first wish was that if I ever had to pay for anything, I would just put my hand in my pocket and the right amount of money would always be there.' 'That's brilliant!' says the waitress. 'Most people would ask for a million dollars or something, but you'll always be as rich as you want for as long as you live!'

"'That's right, whether it's a gallon of milk or a Rolls Royce, the exact money is always there,' says the man. The waitress asks, 'What's with the ostrich?' The man sighs, pauses, and answers, 'My second wish was for a tall chick with a big ass and long legs who agrees with everything I say.'"

Nothing like a clever joke. Funny? Yeah, the group sure laughed—so, yes, funny. But clearly this was a "be careful what you wish for" joke, and in that way, Helen now wondered if she and Max had somehow, maybe intuitively, been warning each other to STOP.

Helen became conscious of holding the phone, of Peter still yammering on about Max's behavior at the Randalls' last party, saying "He...He was preoccupied. But fine. He was always preoccupied. Jesus if any of us knew how upset he was, we would all have talked it through with him."

Helen began feeling faint, couldn't get enough air, and had to end Peter's call way too abruptly. "Thanks, Pete, for calling. There's my cell phone."

It wasn't ringing, but what she said allowed her to escape further conversation without actually lying. Helen had mastered the art of double-talk way, way back during the endless summer of her first trauma.

From that point on, time seemed to reverse in on itself. She collapsed onto her bed and automatically focused on the ceiling. This was a favorite coping skill she'd developed that same summer of long ago. In her imagination, she lived on the ceiling. She lived in a large white room with windows and a door. It was free of furnishings, and had the safe but interesting boundaries of angled walls, so in this room, she was clearly free and safe. Sometimes when she lived on the ceiling, she would furnish it minimally with her favorite necessities. But today, for example, she wanted it to be completely empty, so it was.

Time passed in this comforting way for a while, until, logy and disoriented, she became bleakly aware of a periodic buzzing. Ah yes, the clothes dryer was signaling "done." Suddenly the chore overwhelmed her. She lay back on her bed collecting her thoughts, the bits of life she must absolutely deal with, like getting off the bed to turn off the dryer, and she fell asleep.

When she awoke, it was to the same insistent clothes dryer demanding her attention. She made her way to the machine and turned it off, while cutting her to-do list down to a bare minimum.

Back on the bed she did damage control: Keep her doctor appointments—the one today with Savage and the one tomorrow, which was her annual gynecological appointment, and could not be broken, because she was booked four months in advance, and anyway Helen wanted to tell her doctor that she'd been traumatized. Maybe she could prescribe some kind of sedation to get through Wednesday, or another thought she now recalled conjuring up in the middle of the restless night, maybe this guy she was seeing today would give her some Valium or something stronger.

Eventually Helen dressed for her shrink appointment while developing her strategy of nonanticipation. She'd never met the man, and even though her best friend had raved about him, Cate's sister's situation was far different than hers. She would wing it.

The five-block walk to his office in the fresh air would have done her good, but she was so late, she had to hop in a cab. In her mind's eye, this failure of time management framed her as a loser.

When she located the office of Dr. Savage, his previous patient was just leaving. The patient looked like one step up from a bag lady. Her troubled face with darting eyes, and her unkempt appearance indicated the type of patient Dr. Savage took on. This gave Helen a reality jolt and caused her to change the direction of her "interview." She now thought that she had no business complaining about her life. And that she should be able to get herself together by her own wits.

Soon enough, the doctor came out of his office to greet Helen. They shook hands cordially and proceeded to sit where they belonged, he behind his desk where he counseled truly sick people, and she in a chair to the side of his desk, adopting her "perfectly at ease" look. She crossed one leg over the other, disconcerted to realize she'd exposed one of her "perfect" ankles, her mother's word. She put her leg down and adjusted her shoulders so as not to seem to be showing off her figure. But then she began twirling her long black-brown hair.

His eyes flickered ever so slightly.

She stopped at once, took a deep breath, and placed her arms on the arms of the chair.

He continued to study Helen as she wondered what he was learning.

"So tell me what brings you to this place," he said.

"Well, I..." And Helen burst into tears. "This," she finally managed. "I...can't...stop...bursting into tears."

"I understand you witnessed a suicide yesterday. Is that right?" asked the doctor.

"Um. Yes," said Helen and burst into tears again. "Oh, God," she managed. "I don't know why this keeps happening." She held her nose between her thumb and index finger, which stopped her crying.

He asked her to describe the suicide and she did. She kept hesitating, remembering more details and adding them to her description. He sat there patiently through the hesitations never taking his eyes off her, until finally she let out a sigh and said that was about it.

"How well did you know this man?" asked Dr. Savage.

This was her chance, she thought, the moment of truth, of finally freeing herself from keeping all those memories to herself and wondering time after time if she'd made the right choices. She prepared to unload her lifetime of burdens, but at the last moment, she opted for the cover-up. "That's the weird part," she answered. "We saw him socially. That's it.

"We saw him a little over a week ago at a dinner party, for example, but see, that's disconcerting, because how come no one noticed he was that far down? How come his wife didn't notice, for God's sake?

"Every single one of us would have talked through the night with him if we'd had the slightest clue that he was that troubled." She put pressure on the area of her face between the bridge of her nose with her index fingers and held them there until her tears were derailed and she could speak normally.

"And see, that's not even entirely true, because, for example, my husband, Steven, thought that Max Shaw was an alcoholic, and, well, he probably was. But is that someone else's business? Are acquaintances supposed to step in and insult their friends if they drink too much?" She cleared her throat to regain composure.

The doctor said nothing. This annoyed Helen and she reacted.

"Look, Dr. Savage, I really don't think this is going to work out. I saw the patient who came out ahead of me, and, man, I need to go home and count my blessings. I have nothing to complain about comparatively speaking. And besides that, I'm really fairly stoic. I don't like whiners."

She was about to rise and leave when she remembered her goal, which was for the doctor to prescribe some heavy-duty drugs to get her through the week ahead.

He finally spoke. "Mrs. Clark, there are all sorts of reasons for you to need professional help right now. Witnessing a suicide is a traumatic event, and needs to be recognized, not covered up.

"Also," he continued, "I have a feeling you've experienced other traumas, and have, in fact, suppressed them. Because, Mrs. Clark, what I see is a person who's highly proficient at hiding her heartaches. You may have finally reached your limit."

Helen began tapping her fingernails on the chair arms. She saw herself appearing neurotic and stopped, but not before she noticed that she hadn't removed the nail polish on the third finger of her right hand, causing an immediate flashback to bloody Max Shaw. That one nail was still the color of blood. How the fuck could she have missed that one nail? Maybe because Max Shaw's ring was on that finger. She sat up straighter and shoved her hand into her pocket.

Savage watched as he said, "What I see is a person who's stuffed her sadness so many times that the basket is out of room. No more room to stuff anything. You've reached your limit."

Helen stared at him almost belligerently. This came close to being pretty insulting. What did he know about her attempts at understanding her sadness?

"Well, Dr. Savage," she began, "I've read many books describing and explaining trauma, and I am aware of the seven stages of grief." She proceeded to count them on her fingers as she recited: "Shock, denial, guilt, fear, anger, despair, and acceptance."

The doctor raised his eyebrows slightly and smiled. "You know, Mrs. Clark, you may be the most intelligent woman around and capable of helping all sorts of people through crises, but I doubt if you've consistently helped yourself. And I doubt if you've even shared some of your worst experiences," said Dr. Savage.

She remained silent as she measured his condescending manner, and considered a volatile response. But, again, she remembered her goal of powerful drugs.

"That may be true," she agreed. "It's possible that I need to hone those skills. But right now, all I need to do is to get through this week of hell, with the eulogy and luncheon, and just try to erase that awful image of Max Shaw's bloody head…" she pressed her hands to her temples and gritted her teeth, "…on the pavement."

Dr. Savage continued studying her. "You really are a master at controlling your grief. I see that you've adopted many tricks to stop your tears. This tells me that you've been through a hell of a lot more than you maybe even realize. Can you tell me some more about your past?"

Helen stared at him. "Well, Doctor, they're the typical complaints of psychiatric patients—the big kahuna being that, between the ages of twelve and twenty-three, I thought my mother was a cold, controlling bitch and treated her with distance and distain for ten years, until I finally understood her sacrifices for me. She's dead now, so it's over, anyway," she said flippantly.

Dr. Savage asked her how that realization had affected her, and she replied that she'd simply transferred her hatred of her mother over to her pile of self-hatred.

Dr. Savage said, "Tell me about that, Helen."

Her tone was defensive. "About what?"

"The pain associated with those traumatic memories," he said.

"Oh. Uh huh," Helen wore her hard, expressionless face now. This was useful when entering into any memories of the horrible events in her life; the ones she managed to suppress most of the time.

"OK, Dr. Savage, here's something you can wrap your trained mind around: I've taught myself to forget my most unbearable past memories, which is a good thing. But the flip side is that I truly have practically no memory at all, so I barely remember my glorious life experiences either..." She paused, then continued.

"I usually can't recall a movie I saw a day ago. I don't remember what I read, unless my husband or daughter reminds me. I've labeled this 'jump-starting' me, and we've made it into a family joke, but it's not all that funny. It's frustrating and embarrassing."

She asked for some water. The doctor got her some. She chugged the entire glass.

"Tell me," he said, "when was the last time you were happy?"

"Happy? Happy," she repeated. "Well, life is filled with moments of happiness. I...have my moments." She was hesitating as this question sunk in. "I've actually been fine most of my life."

She paused to consider the question seriously. "You know what though? I remember what stopped my happiness, better than I remember the actual happy times. For example I remember the year I married Steven, before his accident. I was happy then. But my father died suddenly. That trumped that happy card. Then we were OK for a bit, happy to use your word, and then, some months of happiness later, Steven was permanently maimed by an oncoming truck, thus successfully scattering my happy cards all over the floor—life's floor—if you will."

Savage watched her, studied her cynical expression, and waited for the rest.

Helen hated to be watched and filled the silence with, "My life's been one fun surprise party."

He didn't laugh at her dark humor. This unnerved her.

She said, "Anyhow, Doctor, the flip side of happiness is too bleak. Dull gray seems a safer place."

He waited.

"There was also a period of eighteen years of happiness," she gestured quotation marks as she said the silly word, "as we raised our daughter, Camille." Helen continued, speaking more slowly as she traveled back to that time. "Even then, though, there were things that concerned me and took away from the purity of the experience..."

Dr. Savage looked at a clock only he could see on his desk, and announced that the time was up.

This shrink behavior infuriated Helen. She willed herself to hold her tongue as she immediately got up and turned to grab her cashmere jacket and designer purse.

"Here's my opinion," he said, as he reached for his prescription pad and began writing. "You are in what is known as a 'stage two depression.' This is the worst state of depression a person can reach. The only way out of this is to be put on medication to adjust your dopamine level by medically altering serotonin exchanges within the brain. It's possible that you really don't have any idea what day-to-day happiness truly is."

Helen managed to get into her jacket. She fluffed her hair out from under the collar, and adjusted her shoulders. "Really? I thought most people walked around with baggage, and I'm better off than most because at least I've got the physical comfort that only money can buy."

Dr. Savage handed Helen three prescriptions as he said, "Yes, well, we can talk about that next time. I've prescribed an antidepressant. I've also prescribed Valium and sleeping pills to help you remain calm and rested for the next couple of weeks until the antidepressant kicks in. These take about three weeks to infiltrate your system, and it's a hit-and-miss experiment, I'm sorry to say. There are side effects to all antidepressants, so what we'll be doing is finding the right combination for you. In the meantime, you should call me if you can't tolerate what I've prescribed."

He rose as he said this in what Helen felt to be a dismissive act. She responded by pretending to not be offended, initiating a handshake.

He studied her expression and suggested they meet tomorrow afternoon, at the same time—4:15. She replied OK, turned, and left before he could see her tears.

Helen had struggled through the wonder-drug maze four years ago and had no intention of falling back into the panicky black hole of trial-and-error drug combinations. Additionally, she'd made serious inroads into her type of depression and needed to reconnect with that self as soon as this week was over.

She needed to differentiate between types of depression, between her type and Max Shaw's. His probably would have been categorized as a disease, in which case medical attention might have prevented his suicide. Ever more clear, though, was the paralyzing Catch 22; only the right prescription worked positively. Otherwise, the medicine itself could lead a person to the act of suicide.

Arriving home, after a stop at the drugstore to fill her prescriptions, Helen threw her purse and jacket on the foyer floor, proceeding quickly into her bathroom where she grabbed her nail polish remover and cleaned the bloody color off the one nail. Her toenails always matched, so she paid them the same favor of erasing such a dastardly color. She scrubbed them clean and painted them with a clear polish. They now represented her challenge to find the path leading to calm, and clarity.

Through their marriage, Helen and her husband had developed a pattern of polite coexistence. Neither of them was prone to expanding the difficulties between them by harboring resentments. They just moved on. On some level, they were aware that this too had its own day of reckoning. But so what. Live in the moment. And for God's sake, don't make whatever the problem is worse.

It was in that spirit that they kissed each other hello when Steven arrived home that night. Later, while they made dinner together, Helen described an edited version of her appointment with Dr. Savage. She was well aware that an edited version could flip one day, that sooner or later, the real version might emerge. Could emerge. Would emerge? But she also knew that once in a while you could actually get to shore by frantically plugging the holes in the lifeboat.

She explained as much as she understood about her reaction to Max's suicide. She told him that she was forming a clearer perception of depression as a disease and that the doctor believed she might even have it herself.

While Steven was sympathetic, he couldn't accept this new medical information as fact; he suggested several times, in several different ways, that she was much too strong to resort to pills to get herself together.

This cavalier response from a man who refused to face his own demons so angered Helen that she lost her delicate composure and furiously slammed the salad bowl down. "That's exactly why people commit suicide, Steven," she yelled. "What you just said would be akin to saying that I'm much too strong to have developed cancer or to have a heart attack."

"Helen," began Steven…

She stiff-armed his approaching hug. "Let's just put in a DVD and watch it while we eat. I really ca…"

"Fine." He interrupted her and seemed relieved.

They watched Helen's choice, *Magnolia.* She loved the movie. Steven could barely tolerate its endless gloom and sadness. Helen loved it because she felt she was better off than the characters in the story, and therefore it cheered her up. Plus it did end happily in many ways, so there was hope. Hope was vital to Helen's emotional stability. As always, when her favorite phrase in the movie was declared, Helen laughed out loud. "You may be done with the past, but the past ain't done with you."

Afterward, Steven did the dishes and Helen eagerly prepared for the safety of bed. The hopefulness of the movie reminded her of a time in her early childhood when her parents had taken her to see the musical, *Annie,* and she and her mother had sung the showstopper for years…well, not years, about a year…It would have been a year at the most, yet, to this day, Helen found herself humming it once in a while. "Tha sun'll come up to-ma-row. Bet-cher bottom dollar, that to-ma-row (something, something). To-ma-row, to-ma-row, to-ma-row, to-ma-row…Izzzz onlyyyy ya day yawayyyy. Oh, oh, da DA da, da DA da, da DA da, da DA da…izzzz onlyyyy ya day yawayyyy."

She put on her coziest flannel nightgown, took two of her newly prescribed sleeping pills, grabbed her book, fluffed her pillows, and was reading with heavily lidded eyes when Steven came in to kiss her good night.

"So," he said, "need anything else?"

The drugs had apparently obliterated her optimism, as she took a sarcastic tone. "Anything else? What list am I unaware of?"

"...OK, Helen. Do you need anything? Can I do anything for you?"

"Apparently not," she responded.

Steven kissed her. She didn't move her lips, didn't respond at all.

"Is something wrong?" he asked.

"What could possibly be wrong, Steven? I'm tired. Let's not do this. OK? You're older, more mature, not physical, blah, blah, blah. Night, Steven." She went back to reading her book. He stood there staring at her.

"Helen, I'd love to get into your bed. I...I thought you were too upset."

"See, Steven, that's bullshit. I've told you on other occasions that I need to be cuddled when I'm depressed, but it just doesn't register with you."

"That's because I couldn't possibly think of cuddling if I was going through what you are."

"But, Steven, that's it in a nutshell. You think there's one tidy view for each problem. And there isn't. My view, my needs, are not at all the same as yours. And since I'm the one in pain here, wouldn't it make sense to try to imagine what I might need? Or, gosh, Steven, how about asking me, just straight out asking?"

"I just did," replied Steven coldly.

She turned hostile, slightly raising the pitch of her voice with each blurted remark. "Uh huh. Well too late. I'd feel pathetically needy now because you'd be doing it out of pity... It's so hurtful...And, you know what, I can think of...other people...who would be happy to lay next to me...but not you, not my husband, no, not the only man who's supposed to...

and to want to…to want to…Your indifference to my loneliness is cruel…I don't know how to be OK, and you don't care enough to help me."

Helen became painfully aware of exposing her longings, her loser side. She abruptly hurled her body around, switched the light off and faced her back toward her husband.

She lay there regretting her outburst. Embarrassed, she managed to silently catch her breath and speak evenly, "Good night, Steven."

He said, "I love you, Helen, and I hope you sleep well," as he turned, and just before he left, he said, "You know, Helen, I'm in mourning too. Max and I were forming a great friendship. I expected him to be around a long time." He cleared his throat several times to control his emotions as he left the room.

She went to get up, to give him a real kiss good night. To tell him she loved him too. But the sleeping pills had now reached their full potency and she fell back into bed. She fell asleep regretting her unkind behavior. Steven had loved her and cared for her for thirty-two years. She doubted that Max Shaw would have been up to the task. Yet Steven hadn't really been either. No one, and least of all Helen, had been up to the task of taking good care of Helen.

The pills were taking her away now.

She foggily remembered trying to keep Max Shaw centered. All the king's horses and all the king's men couldn't put Max together againnn…

Helen woke at 11:00 p.m. and, despite the sleeping pills, was wide-awake. She got up, brushed her chalky tongue, chugged two glasses of water, grabbed a book, and tried to fall asleep by reading. But the water swirled and gurgled in her stomach, and, after rereading the same paragraph three times, she surrendered to the subject that was sabotaging her concentration.

Why had she suddenly lost her ability to be civil to Steven? After all these years of accepting his ways, and he, hers, why was she furious? It must be the loss of the person who had completed her life in so many ways, and the knowledge that, once again, she would have to tolerate all that Steven held back from her.

Helen time-traveled back thirty-one years to the memory of Steven's recovery period, not a recovery as much as a reinvention of self: self together and self alone.

Because Camille's conception coincided with Steven's accident, Helen's miraculous pregnancy camouflaged and delayed the consequential marital damage. After her birth, Camille became their glue. In their shared love for her, they found an incomparable contentment. She was their love object, their joy, and their hope. Their connection with her innocence sustained them.

As the dust settled, however, Steven's loss of sexuality played itself out on the main stage of their union.

Helen's forced celibacy raised the question in her mind. Was this, again, her punishment for enjoying sex? Was forced celibacy the flip side of incredible sex?

During the first two years of Steven's recovery from the accident, Helen had been pregnant for nine months and nursing for the other fifteen. Despite her newly acquired motherhood, she had felt great compassion for her man and tried everything she knew to help him regain his sense of virility. Her sexual efforts were not only futile but caused him to feel unmanly. Anger became his passion and sports became an obsessive outlet.

Before she knew it, he had neutered them into a platonic relationship, avoiding Helen's needs altogether by claiming exhaustion at bedtime and moving to his own room. To assuage his inner turmoil over this cruel abandonment of his wife, he chose the path of what Helen later called 'pedestal crashing." To justify abandoning Helen's needs, Steven honed in on her faults.

In no time at all, Helen went from being adored to being abhorred. She recognized the escapist game of blame, having borne witness to her parents' fall from mutual grace in the same fanatical manner. Fixating upon her supposed defects, Steven began the crash by complaining that Helen swore, and that she drank and smoked.

Taken aback by these once valid, but now unwarranted criticisms, Helen's first reaction was shock and tearful defense. What? I do those things mildly and discreetly, Steven. Camille has never heard me swear. I don't get drunk, and she's never seen me smoke. I take my parenting obligations very seriously.

But when he retorted that she should just learn self-control, she spoke to the heart of the problem and replied that she was using all hers on her newly dictated celibacy. While that was true, the mistake in pointing it out was all he needed.

The man who had once admired his wife's stunning combination of humility and strength now saw Helen as altogether too self-assured and self-absorbed.

Once this convenient change of heart over his wife was under way, Steven was free to revert to the one-man show of his bachelor years.

Steven's new attitude was more easily accomplished when Helen wasn't with him. The very sight of her sometimes crushed his spirit, reminding him of his failure to accept the difficulties of their altered life, knowing he should be grateful for all that remained, but instead harboring huge resentment that his situation was so permanently damaged.

Marital maturity remained in Steven's future. But for then, his great escape became his work life, where he could pretend to be the same charismatic and much-applauded Professor Clark.

In her usual style of stuffing her feelings, Helen willed herself to believe that her long-suffering patience would see their marriage through her husband's apparent charade. Meanwhile, she privately employed her coping skill of amusement, viewing his behavior as his acquisition of yet another degree, "Bachelor of Marriage," which required extended field research for his "Desertion Dissertation." During the Clarks' extended cold war, Helen would add several reminders to her watch-your-ass list.

The human predisposition to mess things up cannot be overestimated.

Halfway through what would become ten years of this horrific nonsense, her loving tolerance unwittingly played into the age-old adage of give him enough rope and he'll hang himself. This took a heavy toll on her.

It took Helen several years to discover why Steven was gone so much and why he seemed content and patient when he was home. Most would say he was an exemplary father. He certainly viewed himself as such. But Helen knew from her own childhood that a father who neglects his child's mother is not a good father. She began to lose respect for him because of his self-deception, but still tried valiantly to put together some kind of normalcy for the sake of the family. After all, she loved him and felt empathetic much of the time, giving him many benefits of many doubts because of his mitigating circumstances. But it became evermore clear that his harsh judgments of her were based on convenience.

The appalling extent of Steven's hypocritical charade first came to light one frigid winter day when Helen stopped at their favorite Jewish deli to pick up some matzo and kreplach soups along with some chopped chicken liver and rye bread, thinking that would be a fun evening meal. She pictured Steven and Helen and little Camille sitting by the fireplace. For dessert they could roast marshmallows and make s'mores. As she waited in line at the pickup counter, picturing this coziness, she dreamily scanned the crowded restaurant.

When she saw them, her stomach flipped and she lost her breath. Her heart raced, but her body turned to stone and a rushing hum replaced her hearing.

There they were, holding hands and sharing a dessert of some kind. Her husband, Steven, was openly flirting with some woman.

Helen's fragile emotional stability simply snapped, and as if in a dream, she watched herself walk over to the table and see the look of surprised alarm on Steven's face as he withdrew his hand and put his fork down.

The women recognized each other. They'd recently met at a faculty gathering at which Steven had encouraged Helen to be "especially nice" to Lola because she was going through a bad time. Helen had been especially nice, and now she realized why Lola had seemed anxious and left early.

Lola looked into Helen's vacant eyes, as Helen told her to get up. Steven began to rise but Helen put her hand on his shoulder firmly forcing him back down. She never took her eyes off Lola as she told her again to get up. The shamed woman did as she was told. Helen grabbed her in a tight hug and whispered in her ear. "That's my man you're fucking around with. Third finger, left hand, sister. It's women like you who ruin things for the rest of us. Don't ever go near him again."

Helen let go of Lola who looked to Steven for guidance. He cleared his throat and suggested they all leave. "No, no," protested Helen, pushing him down again. "Lola has to go alone. She needs to research the meaning of sisterhood and loyalty. Maybe she needs to find a job at another university. That might be an appropriate result."

Steven told Lola he'd call her a cab. "No, no, no," said Helen. "I'll call her a cab." She looked at Lola. "You're a cab," she said. She giggled and then began laughing too loudly and too long.

As heads turned, the public embarrassment caused Steven to flush and stiffen. Humiliated, Lola grabbed her coat and quickly left. Helen sat down in Lola's chair and stared at her husband. He said nothing. Every couple of seconds, she let out another giggle until finally she took a deep breath and drank Steven's water.

Several minutes passed. Helen began asking her husband questions. At first, Steven refused to answer and announced he was leaving. She told him through gritted teeth that she would continue publicly humiliating him until he answered her. When he tried to call her bluff by muttering, "Fuck this," and backing up his chair to get up, she raised her voice and said, "I mean it, Steven."

Helen didn't care that people were surreptitiously eyeing their table, but Steven cared very much.

He sat still, defiantly locking eyes with his wife. After about five minutes of this, she said "Well?" loudly, and he realized there was no alternative. Public outbursts deeply embarrassed him, as Helen well knew. He said, "Well what?"

Helen told her husband that infidelity came in many forms, such as the one she'd just witnessed. Intimately chummy connections and flirtations were a form of cheating, because she, Helen, was being robbed of the very intimacy that Steven was sharing with another woman, or many women for all she knew. "No wonder you crave no attention at home," she declared. "I'm just now getting the whole infidelity thing. There's actually emotional infidelity. Now that I think about it, I'll bet that's the most popular type. It requires nothing but talking and flirting, so that no matter what kind of a lover you are or aren't, you never have to prove or admit anything. There's the illusory promise that you'd be great, and that intoxicating unknown probably goes a long, long way."

Helen was thinking aloud, figuring the matter out as she went along.

Steven was able to remain expressionless all but a few times. But those nervous reactions helped her know what he'd been up to. She saw her husband flinch a couple of times, and his complexion was several shades darker than usual.

Steven shifted in his seat and had the gall to deny any intimacy between him and Lola, let alone anyone else.

After a long silence, during which time he checked the room filled with people gradually rising and leaving, and looked twice at his watch, he became so infuriated at being held captive, never mind why, that he lashed out at the only woman he'd ever loved. He watched her trying desperately to keep control and wanted to hold her in his arms and stop all this, all of it. But instead he forged ahead.

He said he had every right to flirt with whomever he found attractive, since Helen no longer was. "Drunks aren't desirable," he said coldly. "I can't stand smokers," he added. "Neediness is a real turnoff," he announced. "You're a perfect example of a spoiled brat," he declared. "You have a talent you're not practicing, and that's lazy and shameful. You can do anything you want; yet you do nothing. Nothing. The women I spend time with are none of those—not drunks, not smokers, not needy, not bratty, not lazy. They're busy, bright, desirable women."

Seeing the look on Helen's face change by degrees at every new insult he threw at her, made him feel like killing himself, yet he didn't stop, and he didn't move. He sat there watching her sink, watching the color drain from her face, watching her lower her head, saw the tears drip down onto her pale blue cashmere sweater, watched her endlessly fish through her purse, finally locating her sunglasses and shakily putting them on. His heart was breaking for the very person he was devastating.

Helen's reaction was that of a bewildered little girl, wrongly accused, but needing to defend herself just the same, so she wouldn't be thought of that way. Her voice trembled as she slowly responded. "Why I. I'm in the prime of my life, Steven. I. I'm considered socially and physically attractive… desirable…I drink occasionally, and I smoke, but those are pleasures I allow myself because I don't have many others."

She squared her shoulders as she began thinking more clearly. "Let's try to minimize hypocrisy here, Steven. You don't drink because of the medications you're on. I'm raising a healthy, talented little girl who's being given every opportunity to eventually discover her life work. And, and…" (now she looked him straight in the eyes.) "I am painting. The new portrait of Mother is at the frame shop, and, as you well know, I'm currently painting Camille playing dress-up. Really, Steven, how DARE you turn this charade around and somehow blame me."

Helen managed to get up as she breathlessly spoke. "I'm stunned. You've…you've just graduated to vindictive. And I. And I will not sink to that level. I'm sorry for you, Steven. And I'm sorry for me."

Willing her knees to not buckle, Helen turned and found the door and then her car through blinding tears. She sunk into her heated leather car seat and into a sadness that left her numb.

Uniquely unfortunate timing allowed her to hide out. Her mother had gone to her home in Miami for the winter, and her best friend, Cate Taylor, had just moved to New York. Without her beacons, she had only to camouflage her depression for Camille, and that she managed. She forced herself to behave normally whenever Camille was with her out of pure loving protection for her innocent little girl.

But otherwise, Helen reacted to her discovery of Steven's emotional abandonment and his blatant flirtations by sleeping.

Because Helen loved Camille more than she hated herself, she was able to maintain a lovely, consistent balance with her, and with her only. It was simple enough to form a routine of hiding, yet sustaining her depression.

Steven was purposefully up and gone before Helen and Camille were awake.

She'd rise and shine with her daughter, hugging and kissing her, smiling and being playful with her, dressing both of them, watching Sesame Street together as Camille ate her breakfast and Helen drank her coffee, discussing their favorite characters, reciting the alphabet and numbers and colors: "Bananas are yellow and filled with protein. Orange juice is orange and rich in calcium…Cheers!—clink."

At three years old, Camille was enrolled in a Montessori school to experience the pleasure of other children, since she was and always would be an only child.

As Helen walked the love of her life to school each morning, they would typically sing: "Can you tell me what we do, what we do on Sesame Street…" and then recall what they'd learned from the show that morning.

After waving good-bye to her darling little baby girl, Helen would walk briskly home and immediately fall into bed, hiding out through sleep until it was time to rise and shine at two in the afternoon, shower her deadened, depressed self into a happy-mom state of mind, and gather Camille at three o'clock.

Back home, Mommy and daughter would have milk and cookies as they discussed Camille's day. They'd go into Helen's studio and paint for a while, or they'd read, or they'd write more of their ongoing story about the life of a little girl who lives in a big old home in River Forest with her mommy and her daddy, and her grandma lives there too, but only when it's warm, and the lucky little girl goes to Montessori School. Most days, Camille would change into a very fancy costume, and pose awhile for a portrait that Helen was working on. It was of Camille playing dress-up in her Mommy's clothes. This portrait would one day be famous, but neither of them knew that then. They were just spending precious time together.

Helen had a "play kitchen" for Camille in an area of their "real" kitchen, so the two of them would talk and cook together.

Steven would be home at 6:00 to eat dinner as a family. The one hour that Helen and Steven had to eat together and pretend all was well was horrible for them both. But night after night they got through it.

After dinner, they'd be free from pretense again, Steven giving Camille a long bubble bath, being silly together, interacting with her bath toys, and making up games, and Helen washing dishes as she listened to the NPR news of the day, then retreating to her studio to smoke and paint. The oil paint and turpentine covered the smell of cigarette smoke, thus protecting Camille from a bad example when she came in to kiss her breath-minted mommy good night. Steven would tuck Camille into bed and read her several stories before either slipping out to return to work or phone chatting, or watching television or reading. Eventually, he would come into Helen's studio and kiss her on the cheek. "Sleep well." was what they said to each other. Helen would climb into her own bed in her own bedroom and she would sleep some more.

Two months of this schizophrenic routine came to a halt the morning Helen was walking back home after dropping her little girl off at school when another mother came running after her, calling, "Mrs. Clark, wait up a minute, will you?"

The mother introduced herself as Helen Nevada.

"But what's your last name?" asked Helen, purposely throwing the woman off.

"Nevada."

"No. I'm not asking where you're from," argued Helen.

To her credit, Helen Nevada let it go. "Moving on," she said as they began walking alongside each other, "I've noticed you walking in my direction each school day and thought we might as well walk together."

The mom was obviously attempting to form a friendship, but Helen was immediately thrown out of her safety zone, and would have none of it. She behaved coolly, by telling this exuberant stranger that she needed to rush home each day to prepare for her job, but too bad, because, it would have been fun to become best pals.

Not only was this brash woman undaunted, but she looked almost amused, and announced that she liked to walk briskly—great exercise—and "what was Helen's job, by the way?"

Annoyed at this inquisitiveness, but aware of her crass conduct, Helen meant to switch tracks and play nice, but what came out of her mouth was the silly answer that she was a scientist.

"Really," exclaimed the other Helen. "What kind of scientist exactly?"

"So you're the other Helen," Helen exclaimed, dodging the question.

"You've heard of me?"

"Naw, not really, but I figured there must be another one someplace," she said, and turned down her street, only to discover the woman was still hurrying along next to her.

"Rocket," answered Helen.

"What?"

"Rocket scientist," said Helen adolescently. They'd reached Helen's home, so she said, "Gotta run," and turned her back to this pushy broad, further insulting her by hand-gesturing "good-bye" from behind her backside.

That was the morning that Helen Clark actually entered her home laughing a grown-up laugh. She was filled with adrenalin over being so merciless and instead of climbing into her escape bed, she made it.

Helen continued to get a kick out of herself for the next couple of hours, which gave her the time to gain perspective. She realized it was up to her to end her pity party, that she was only damaging herself by not rejoining the world around her. She used that bit of energy charge to make a list of activities that would help her climb out of her depression.

Later that night, when Helen asked Camille if she knew Other-Helen's daughter, Camille said no, that she'd noticed Lucy Nevada, who was a year older, but she didn't actually know her. But she did know Lucy's brother, Charlie. She said he was quiet and spent part of each day playing and learning by himself. The other part of the day, he was full of energy and very funny. He needed to be spoken to sometimes by Mrs. Karen, but always in a kind and private way. He was called the class clown.

"Charlie and I do water play together. He likes to wash dishes at the same time I do," she told her mother. "He's got lots of dark brown hair, and his eyes are green."

Such a cute and complete answer. And so innocent. That was her precious, charmingly precocious Camille. God, she adored that child.

The following day, Helen had wakened with a lighter feeling in her body and soul. Unbeknownst to Camille, her mother stayed at the school after they kissed good-bye, observing her class through the one-way mirror. There was darling little Camille, interacting with everyone. Helen spotted a little boy with thick brown curls and big green eyes who concentrated on numbers much of the time, glancing up to search out Camille every so often. And then, there was Camille at the small kitchen sink with Charlie right next to her, the two of them washing and smiling and talking nonstop. Charlie Nevada was Camille's first love. Such a tender sight.

She stood there watching these cherished children and realized that she was also God's child, assuming one believed in God, and she recognized that distractions such as humor and interaction with other moms could be her lifeline during this period of mourning. And so it was that Helen decided to give Charlie's mother, the "other Helen," a try.

Helen Clark held Helen Nevada responsible for cattle-prodding her back into normalcy. She considered her one of her personal angels, one of her best friends, and nicknamed her "Other." They walked and talked every day, shopped together, and threw parties together. Thank God for Other.

Nevada was her catalyst. No matter how rough the day was, Helen Clark remained up and running until bedtime. Who's to say what her life would have been without the companionship of such an intelligent live wire. Thank God for Other.

Because Helen had always been an object of desire, she really had no idea how to react to her husband's cruel emotional abandonment. To her utter astonishment, her discovery and confrontation had catapulted Steven in the polar opposite direction one might expect, as he spent more and more time at his office, forming an ever-stronger pattern of sexless infidelity. For so many reasons, Helen saw herself with no way out, left to tolerate her husband's egocentric withdrawal. Thank God for Other.

Clearly, Steven had chosen to assuage his loss of manhood by strengthening his female relationships. He welcomed the abundance of flirtatious women succumbing to his charms. He practiced a complicated form of infidelity, betraying his wife with a combination of emotional abandonment and degradation while using the always available other women to bolster his insatiably needy masculinity.

Steven's women knew that Steven was married to a beautiful woman, and that they had a daughter they adored, which made him that much more attractive.

Single/Married/Younger/Older—it didn't matter, most of his female students and fellow teachers were close with him, and many somehow managed the self-delusion of thinking their relationship different and more special than his others.

While enjoying any and all attentions, he preferred one actual "partner" at a time. Typically his coupling technique was to team up with a female for the purpose of accomplishing a project. This would require endless amounts of both face and phone time, steering them ever closer toward their eventual climax over the shared joy of successful completion.

They would bask in their glory for a breathless time, and then gradually Professor Clark's "teammate" would realize that he had no intention of ever piloting their flirtation into the physical. At first his women would see this as a challenge, but at this point in the affair, Steven would cleverly control his private boundaries by alluding to the physical passion he and his beautiful wife shared. He need only occasionally parade Helen at faculty gatherings or student lectures to prove his point. That would pretty much be that, although he did allow for "the fun" of occasional luncheons with his groupies "to keep in touch."

Meanwhile, Helen wore her fidelity like a badge of honor, knowing all about the keloids of adultery from her own childhood. Beyond the fact that she refused to emotionally scar her little girl, Helen knew that if she were to selfishly enter into an affair, it might be wonderful for a while, but the inevitable day of reckoning, that flip to the payback side would come around, and with her luck, hold far-worse consequences than that of enduring the bleak forecast of continued, unending Seattle rain from her detached husband.

Helen saw her glass as half full because of her unconditional love object, her precious daughter. Camille was her sunshine. Nothing came before Camille.

As it turned out, she fared far luckier during her winter of discontent. She had the daily blast of Other, the fun, funny, smart girl Helen might have remained herself, were it not for the black pearl of Max Shaw back in the summer of 1964.

And she had the mothers group that Other had gathered together, which Helen coined—Other's Mothers.

Other's Mothers were a link to the world. At the time when Helen Nevada was raising her babies, Lucy and Charlie, it was a rarity for white upper-middle-class children to have stay-at-home mothers. Mostly nannies accompanied their charges to the neighborhood gathering places—the parks and playgrounds and swimming pools and libraries and child-friendly restaurants. The nannies were sweet and loving, but spoke mostly Spanish. Helen Nevada did not, so even attempts at adult conversation with these bright Mexican women was not possible. The pot-of-gold at rainbow's end turned out to be the stay-at-home Montessori mothers, whom Nevada had discovered the previous year when her first child, Lucy, had entered the school. At the Montessori get-acquainted luncheon, she met four bona fides. By week's end, with baby Charlie perched on her hip, she had sought and gathered the unique four.

Desperate for adult companionship, the response of these intellectually starved career women-turned-moms was overwhelming gratitude. Helen Clark's inclusion a year later brought the group's total to six.

There were unwritten rules. The sharing of problems should be done in a general way. The six of them innately understood that no one should cross the comfort line of no return. Don't regret what you share. If in doubt, don't share your worst private problems. However, anyone who needed advice was absolutely welcome to command the group's attention.

Helen was by far the most cautious, having been taught from day one that family privacy and stoic behavior was the only acceptable way to live. She didn't share her problems, but helped her friends think theirs through. The unfortunate consequence was that the group thought of her as the perfect example of happiness itself. There she was again, appearing perfect, when she was just as confused as everyone else. But this time at least she was learning the valuable lesson that she was not the only one who made poor choices. Apparently everyone occasionally did. Still, she believed she'd win the Oscar for Original Sexual Misbehavior and Nonbehavior.

Helen would be sexually blindsided one more time in her life. Her final fateful life-altering tragedy waited around the corner of the next century. Counting the three weeks as a twelve-year-old, the thirteen months during her first marriage, the thirteen months and three weeks with her husband, Steven, the three nights it took to conceive Camille, and the last three months, Helen had experienced sexual pleasure for three out of the fifty-three years of her life. Her sex had apparently been too incredible. Forced celibacy must be the flip side of incredible sex. Sex was punishment, destruction, and death.

Did the Curse of Sex run in families, or was it universal? What was it like to be ordinary? Probably much more comfortable.

A rash of screaming, honking sirens jarred her into the present. Helen wrestled out of her twisted covers and padded to her window to see. At least the vehicles were whizzing past her building and stopping next door this time.

Her memories of the past receded and her present-day horror moved front and center. Awake and in the now, she was forced to face the latest addition to her life odyssey, in the "year of our Lord," two-thousand-and-seven, she thought irreverently.

Here we all are, twenty-five centuries after the Buddha offered us humans a workable plan for graceful living: Control your reactions. And do we? Naw.

Max hadn't and that was an undeniable fact.

Damn him.

That blood oozing out of his body onto the pavement, might as well have been nitroglycerin.

But then what was in her blood? After all, he hadn't gotten so messed up all on his own.

She tried to see a pattern in her life, because it seemed so alarmingly exaggerated, seemed almost out of control, seemed to need breaks put on it.

On the other hand, if she were to compare her life to the lives of other females, she wondered if hers would be just another story. After all, there must be darkly colored secrets buried in every family.

Also, most of her years on earth were filled with common events,—days and months of ordinary daily life that had been lived without incident. Those never popped into her mind.

Max wasn't in any of those.

Helen felt the injustice of possessing a punishing memory that forced her to relive only her weakest moments. *Groundhog Day*—one of her favorite movies—floated into her mind. Bill Murray had finally gotten it right. Helen embraced the hope that she might one day get it right herself.

Reality brushed the fantasy aside. This much she knew: Max Shaw would not be showing up in her future. The trip ahead looked to be calm—long, dry, and calm.

Helen tucked herself back into bed.

The sirens played background as she lay staring out her wall of window at the magical city lights.

Perhaps part of the human condition is such that ego defeats logic.

Destiny doesn't wait.

Shit happens and we react.

Destiny doesn't wait.

Cats land on their feet. Humans try, but there's no time for us to practice.

Destiny doesn't wait.

Shut the fuck up.

If only life could be lived in reverse, the beginning filled with all the accumulated knowledge of seventy or eighty years.

But no.

Helen dug into her survival kit and pulled out a brand-new coping variation. She held on to her brightly colored threads of sanity by cooking up a fairy-tale ending, in which she convinced herself that she was one of those people who lived life backward, suffering all the anguish in the first half and then things just got better and better. She'd read about people having experienced their lives in this way, and had actually met one such self-proclaimed foot soldier.

Her new scenario caused both relief and euphoria. It gave her hope that she might somehow allow herself to behave optimistically. She could wait. She would wait for the good part, the trustful part, of her life to begin.

The beautiful voice of Mama Cass Elliot singing "The Good Times Are Coming" entered her brain and calmed her.

She drifted off to another favorite, "Dream a Little Dream of Me."

*Bad is never good until worse happens.*
~ Danish Proverb ~

*I hate housework! You make the beds, you do the dishes and six months later you have to start all over again.*
~ Joan Rivers ~

# TUESDAY

Helen awoke Tuesday morning at nine to her trusted housekeeper, Francine, letting herself in. She threw on her robe and told Francine there'd been a tragedy and to please just go ahead as usual, no additional requests.

"I heard," said Francine, solemnly. "You knew him, didn't you?"

"Yeah, well I...we did, but let's talk about that later. After I've had some coffee, maybe."

"Right. Would you like me to do your room and bathroom last so that you can sleep some mo..."

Helen's eyes traveled to the grandfather clock in the foyer, interrupting Francine with a squeaky, "Oh, Jesus," as she turned back toward her room. "I've got an appointment with my gynecologist in forty minutes. Yeah, my room last, please. Thanks, Francine."

She arrived for her appointment showered and flushed, but on time. An hour and a half later, Helen was called in to see her doctor. She got into the God-awful paper gown and sat on the stirrup table for another twenty minutes.

During her forced two hours of downtime, she tried to read but kept interrupting her concentration with memories of other gynecological visits, punctuated by the occasional absurd thought: She could offer to paint Dr. Cole's portrait, and then have her wait two hours before each portrait sitting.

She could send Dr. Cole a DVD of the 1991 movie called *The Doctor*, starring William Hurt. In it he's flip-sided into becoming the impatiently waiting patient and gets a real education, at the end of which he's a changed man.

Why were these mandatory, demoralizing appointments called "visits," anyway? And why did so many of "the best doctors" not mind their patients having to wait so long? Didn't they notice how impossibly frazzled their patients seemed when at last they said hello, I'm sorry I'm running so late?

Dr. Cole walked in with Helen's chart and apologized as usual for being late. Helen surprised herself by blurting, "You always are. Always."

"Yeah, I guess I am," said Dr. Cole. "I really am sorry. If it makes you feel any better, I always give my full attention to each patient, so if I get behind, at least you know that even though there are many others waiting, when I finally do see you, I'll be thorough with you too."

Helen began speaking to her ridiculous logic. "One treatment precludes the other? You can't be on time and also treat us all thoroughly?"

Dr. Cole's eyes widened, as she looked at Helen straight on and without the slightest hesitation asked her what happened.

"Besides the fact that I rushed like hell to get here and then didn't see your face for over two hours?"

"Yes, beside that."

"Two days ago, I witnessed a man's suicide. He jumped from the forty-fifth floor."

"Oh," said Dr. Cole loudly. There was a look of repulsion on her face. "That's the angriest, most aggressive and hurtful way a man can take himself out. All he leaves is pain and sorrow for the people who love him. And a horrible vision of his bleeding twisted body. Men do that," she said aggressively. "Women just quietly take too many pills."

Helen was stunned. Other than Cate, not one person had raised that side of the suicide. She actually smiled. The doctor's outrage seemed oddly protective, which comforted Helen; really comforted her. She began to hold her nose.

"Don't stop your tears, Helen. You're traumatized and you need to let your feelings out." She whipped out her pen, wrote a sedative prescription and handed it to Helen. "Now you know I don't usually do this, and don't increase the dose. And do not mix alcohol with these."

"Thank you, Doctor," said Helen. Barely aware of anything but a fog of sadness shadowing her, it vaguely occurred to her to refuse the pills, but at this point caution was not a priority, and she easily blocked dreary thoughts of addiction and possible consequences. She'd been through drug rehab earlier in her life, and she knew she had an addictive personality. But now was now. Now was different. She was safe in the double protection of two drug sources, just for this one time. Just this week. Just this once.

"OK," said Dr. Cole. "Lie down and move forward, feet in the stirrups." She examined Helen as they continued to talk. Helen appreciated this. Appreciated the fact that a good gynecologist always conversed while examining, to get the patient's mind off the discomfort, for example, of having a cold iron tube stuck up her vagina and then widened to stretch the area for a better look. Ah, the combo of pain and humiliation…

"What else?" asked Dr. Cole.

"That's not enough?" Helen replied sarcastically.

"Yes. It is enough. But I can tell there's more. You've been my patient for a long time, Helen...When did you become sexually active?"

"Between my last visit and this one...Is...there something wrong?"

"Not here. Are you all right?"

"Yeah...God, that tube really hurts."

"I can recommend several psychologists."

Silence.

"OK." The doctor sighed. "So. Other than that, how have you been?"

"Um, I can't remember how I've been—how I was before. Before the suicide."

"How well did you know this person?"

Helen began to give her pat answer. "Oh. Um. That's the weird part. He's a neighbor. We haven't lived in the building all that long, so..."

"Now I'm doing a Pap smear," said the doctor. "This may hurt a bit."

"It does," said Helen as she launched into a more complete answer. "I. I've known him since eighth grade! We were, we dated for a while until..." she paused and gulped some air. "You know what, I...can't talk about this." And she burst into tears.

"All right. You can sit up. Look. You really do need to see a professional."

Helen struggled out of the horizontal stirrup position and sat up hugging the pathetic paper gown as she spoke. "Yes. Well, actually I did see a psychiatrist yesterday, Dr. Richard Savage, but...but I didn't really like him, or maybe I just didn't like the situation, because frankly I pretty much know myself, so how the hell is a veritable stranger going to shed light on complicated me? But anyhow, do you know him—he's affiliated with that Hyde Park Hospital, which I'm sure makes him a liberal Democrat, which, right off the bat there's a problem with us connecting because I abhor politics and especially when the attitude is one of 'power to the people.' We all know how that works out, but then the flip side of that belief is that the country or the world, for that matter, needs a leader like, like Thomas Jefferson or Harry Truman, and where are those leaders, I mean the capable people aren't willing to sink to the slimy art of politics to get elected and then put up with the everlasting bullshit of the egomaniacs in Washington, um, it's…what the hell's the name of that hospital…?"

"Saint Mark's," said the doctor, calmly noting Helen's rapidly accelerating rambling. "No. I don't know him but that doesn't mean he's not good."

"Anyway I'm forcing myself to see him again today," said Helen.

"Good. And in case you decide that you really aren't connecting with Dr. Savage, I'll write several names and phone numbers down and you can…here's how it works: You'll call each one and summarize your problem. They'll ask you some questions. After doing that three times with three of the best, you'll probably click with one. One will relate to you better than the other two."

As Dr. Cole was explaining this she was recalling and scribbling the names and numbers on a slip of paper, along with her private number and a reminder to take only the prescribed amount of the medication and no alcohol, underlined.

"And, Helen, I want you to call me at my private number if you need to, and I want to see you back here in a month."

"A month!…What's wrong with me?"

"You're severely traumatized. And I want to make sure you do something about it. I want to see you and hear how it's going. Otherwise, physically, you're in great shape as usual.

Get dressed and come see me. I'll give you some samples so you won't have to stop at the pharmacy for a few days."

Helen had an hour to kill before her appointment with Dr. Savage, so she ducked into an Asian nail salon and had her nails painted a clear noncolor, thankful the technician didn't speak English—no small talk, just tranquil music. Afterward she walked down Michigan Avenue, stopping at various store windows for the simple pleasure of seeing pretty things. About halfway through the walk across town, the day turned gray, and then it began to rain. She ducked into the nearest clothing store and bought an umbrella.

And so it was, that on a gray and rainy late-summer afternoon, a dampish Helen Clark was having her second session with "her psychiatrist," Dr. Richard Savage, who had just asked her to list her life traumas.

Buoyed by Dr. Cole's belief that Helen needed professional help, she entered into an uneasy alliance.

"Shall I list them chronologically, or in the order of their importance?" asked Helen.

Dr. Savage studied her. Her voice was sarcastic and her body language defensive and rebellious, but she was connecting. "Which would you prefer?" he asked.

He waited through her silence.

Helen cleared her throat. "The only sensible way to examine my life would be chronologically, in the sense that one thing leads to another."

"Fine."

"Well why didn't you clarify the appropriate order?" she asked.

"Better if you do," he said.

(Was he smirking? Did it matter? Christ, calm down and peace out. That's what Max Shaw would have said, "Peace out, sugar." Oh, God...) She sucked in her cheeks and sat very still for a moment.

He watched her collect herself, preparing to remain calm and keep her voice level.

Helen took in an athletic breath. "Let's see. My memory is that the first ten years were great. My parents were in love. We had a happy, traditional household. My friends and I used to lovingly tease my mother about emulating the two famous television moms: Donna Reed in the *Donna Reed Show,* and June Cleaver in *Leave it to Beaver.* In fact, she liked that comparison so much that they probably were her actual role models. She was beautiful and always perfectly groomed. She was a wonderful cook. We baked cookies together. She kept the house in perfect order, kept me in crisply ironed clothes and freshly polished shoes, and encouraged my friends to come over any time, day or night. I called her Mrs. Housewife. My dad was funny and handsome and made a lot of money. I called him Captain Businessman...What are you writing?"

The doctor cleared his throat. "I've begun a list of your traumas."

"What trauma? I haven't mentioned one yet."

"You indicated that things went bad after the tenth year. My notes are not the focus here," he said, reestablishing order.

Helen plowed on. "So moving forward, I'm barely thirteen and manage to become pregnant."

The doctor stopped writing to watch her.

"I can't speak about this if you watch me," she said tightly.

The doctor wrote and Helen continued.

"The boy was fourteen. We were not allowed to communicate. My mother handled the abortion. My father wasn't told.

Long silence.

"Did you want to keep the baby?"

"Yes, I did." Helen's voice cracked. She rubbed her temples to stop herself from becoming emotional. "I believe that the angels frown upon one of their own being murdered. I've always believed that.

"Back in 1965, middle-class America considered abortion a better choice than giving birth out of wedlock…Also, my mother claims she saved me from a horrible destiny by insisting on the abortion. Believe it or not, I really didn't quite understand sex, but she found that impossible to believe. I was quite developed for my age; actually my body hasn't really changed much since then."

Helen fell silent as she remembered her wonderful thirteen-year-old self.

After a minute, Dr. Savage asked what she was thinking.

"Well I've time-traveled back to that summer. Isn't that what this therapy is all about?"

"In many ways," he answered. "So, what are you remembering?"

Helen's face softened, which caused her to look like a vulnerable little girl. "I really did love that boy. We had a connection I have never come near to duplicating."

Silence.

"What happened to him?" prompted the doctor.

"His parents sent him off to a boarding school in the East three days after my abortion. I thought he had simply abandoned me, but Mother told me years later, on my wedding day as a matter of fact, that she'd intercepted his letters and phone calls.

"As for me, my mother sent me to my room for a couple of weeks, and then kept me in the house reading, pretty much for the rest of the summer, except for certain public appearances, like church or grocery shopping or a movie or a meal out—always with her, though, and always wearing outfits that showed how flat my stomach was, so people wouldn't wonder about me, gossip about me."

Now Helen was on a roll. She was back in the late sixties, living out the time left under her mother's authoritarian roof.

"Because of my outstanding grades, my wealthy, well-connected, fiercely determined mother was able to push all the bureaucratic buttons to get me into high school. So instead of staying with all my pals, I skipped eighth grade and went to high school with no friends, but after what happened, I was way beyond an eighth-grade mentality anyway.

"I guess I haven't really fit in since then. I've felt out of step ever since. At the time, I wished I could have been one of those regular kids…I missed lots of transitions…I even missed acne."

Doctor and patient smiled together at this absurd witticism.

Uncomfortable with his familiarity, Helen fished through her purse for her reading glasses.

"I didn't know you wore glasses."

"I wear them for reading or to hide behind…It's much safer with armor."

Savage wrote something in his book and then said, "Helen, tell me why you didn't try to contact the boy, and why you kept the secret from your close friends."

"Well, Doctor," began Helen, "since I was at the mercy of my mother, those would have been pretty stupid moves. At that time, I thought of my mother as a dominating person."

"So you managed to get through school pretty well, then?"

Helen sighed. "Not really 'well,' because I was now an adult in certain ways. I was no longer the class 'wit.' Nothing struck me as very funny anymore. I just told everybody that my parents had informed me it was time to really bear down on my studies, to focus on remaining at the top of my class all through high school so that I could literally get into any university in the country."

"Weren't your old friends a little confused, since you'd been so social, earned great grades, and been funny just the year before?"

"Yeah, they were. But it's not all that hard to fool kids entering puberty. Their heads are up their asses most of the time, because their hormones put them in such a foggy state, that, well…it's easy."

"Always adjusting," commented the doctor.

"Yep. My coping skills are really quite amazing, as you said yourself. But that's probably because I've had so many wonderful, fun-filled opportunities to hone those skills."

"And your cynicism—that works well for you," he said.

"Uh huh."

"What about your father? Where was he in all this?"

"Let's see," said Helen, "I learned years later that my pregnancy was responsible for more than I ever knew. In my thirteenth summer, my father was going through a change at work that caused him to need even more of my mother's attention. But my mother felt it her duty to not only keep my 'mistake' from him, but to concentrate almost totally on me. So my dad sought comfort elsewhere and found it in the form of a secretary at work, who remained his mistress until his death. My mother reacted to his absence by drinking a lot. He spoke of this mistake on his deathbed."

Helen crossed her arms in front of her chest. Her voice choked. "Thirteen summers later, I find out that not only did I seriously mess up my life, but also did irreparable damage to my parents' lives and our happy family. My behavior caused a disastrous chain of events, resulting in my father's infidelities that led to my mother's alcoholism. The whole thirteen years, I thought of my mother as my enemy and treated her that way. Then I find out she sacrificed her life so I would have what she hadn't had. And why was she so vehement about this? Because she had to marry my father straight out of high school, because of me. This abruptly ended any chance she had of self-discovery."

With an increasingly crazed expression, Helen continued. "After a while, he, for some reason, told me he had a mistress with whom he actually had a home. I of course didn't know how to react. He seemed so happy, and that caused me to be happy for him. Then he began taking me over there sometimes and I'd play card games with them. The deal was that I could spend time with my dad if I didn't tell my mother where we had been. I didn't mind lying to my mother because she had literally erased love and trust from my life and killed my baby."

"Why are you grinning?" he asked, as he added more notes.

"Because it was so fucked up. I had to cover up for him in order to be with him more often. My mom's biggest push was to get me to college. I lied to the one person who was devoting her life to creating a good one for me. Of course I didn't put all that together at the time. But I got perfect grades for my mother, and boy did that make her happy. And I lied for my father, which seemed to make him happy...don't you want to write that down?"

"I already have."

"Really. I'm impressed, Doctor. You figured out what I was going to tell you beforehand. My, my."

"Well, time's up," said the doctor.

This really burned Helen. She really did not like to be dismissed. So she went on.

"I'm wondering, Doctor, what you have determined about me. Do I, in fact, really need depression medication? Because my husband thinks I should be able to keep it together without chemicals."

"My opinion remains the same as yesterday, Mrs. Clark." He opened his calendar and studied it. "I can see you tomorrow at my Skokie office, at..."

"That's the funeral. The funeral is tomorrow," interrupted Helen.

"Oh." He looked over his appointment book again. "Well then, Thursday in Skokie..."

Again Helen interrupted him. "I couldn't possibly begin to find your office in Skokie. I'm really not up to locating highways and streets and office buildings and offices. No. I can't drive anywhere. The convenience of your office is half the reason I came to you." She realized that last comment was discourteous, and backed up. "No. I came to you because my best friend told me you were the only good psychiatrist she'd ever known, and because your office is down the street from me."

The doctor smiled at her civility and suggested she would probably need to see him in two days. He was concerned that the funeral was tomorrow, and they'd only had two sessions. "How does eight o'clock Friday sound?"

"Morning?"

"Yes."

"Way too early. I don't even get up until nine."

"What about this office, same time, then, Friday afternoon, at 4:15?"

"Fine."

He stood up abruptly, so she did too and quickly threw her jacket on, so she wouldn't feel so demeaned by his dismissal. Then she "coped" with these feelings by shaking his hand and giving him a nice wide smile.

"That's quite a smile," he said. "First time I've seen it."

Helen immediately dropped the smile. She couldn't stand manipulative compliments. She dropped his hand. "Thank you, Dr. Savage, for seeing me on such short notice." She grabbed her purse and umbrella, and walked out the door, and the other door, and the other door. Although they were obviously "privacy" doors, she thought of Lewis G. Carroll's hallucinatory doors that he had Alice going through in her strange wonderland.

She passed the restaurant where Max had arranged to throw the gang's last Halloween party. Ah, the coping skill of a good time recalled: He'd reserved a private circular room that had a round table just big enough for the twelve of them. He decreed that all the gals were required to wear blond wigs, and everyone must come bearing a good Blonde Joke. Dress accordingly, they were told.

Everyone came gamely dressed and shared their jokes, which led to other jokes, one of which caused Steven to laugh so uncontrollably that Max later baptized him with a splash of Cognac back at the Clarks' place at one in the morning. "Steven Clark, I christen thee, 'Two Dogs.'"

During the last year or so, Helen was newly able to retain jokes. Desperately in need of lingering in past laughs, she remembered those of last Halloween's party. In this way, she managed to keep her grief at bay during the remainder of her walk home, ironically appearing as a happy citizen strolling home as she grinned and smiled at each joke's recall.

*The Halloween party, six wives in blond wigs, all twelve friends half drunk and laughing hysterically, telling each other jokes. Max had created his wife, Janet's, costume. He dressed her as Marilyn Monroe and instead of telling a joke, she played the tape of her singing "Happy Birthday, Mr. President" (the point being she WAS the joke, as was Jack Kennedy that night). Later in the evening (sometime in the early morning), Helen and Steven had both opined to Max that it was in the worst possible taste. Max had disagreed, stating his position: "Wasn't that the point of blonde jokes, or most jokes for that matter?" The only criterion, in his mind anyhow, was that the joke be clever.*

Two blondes are on opposite sides of a lake.

One blonde yells to the other, "How do you get to the other side?"

"You are on the other side," the other blonde yells back.

How do you keep a blonde busy? (see below)

How do you keep a blonde busy? (see above)

How does a blonde turn the light on after having sex?

She kicks the car door open.

A young ventriloquist is working a small-town club. With his dummy on his knee, he's going through his usual dumb-blonde jokes when a blond woman in the fourth row stands on her chair and starts shouting, "I've heard enough of your stupid blonde jokes. What's funny about saying blond women are dumb?"

The ventriloquist begins to apologize when the blonde yells, "You stay out of this, mister! I'm talking to that little jerk on your knee!"

An American Indian boy reaches his thirteenth birthday. A special bonfire is built to honor his ritual rites of manhood. He's told that he may ask any questions of his father, the chief, as part of the celebration.

"I do have a burning question," he says.

"Go ahead my son. Don't be shy."

"Well," says the boy, "I've often wondered how the parents come up with the names of their children."

"Ah," says the father, and offers the answer. "At the time of his wife giving birth, the husband awaits protectively outside the birthing tepee. At the moment he hears his infant's first cry of life, he looks straight ahead, and the first thing he sees becomes the name of the baby.

"For example," the chief continues, "here is your friend, Doe Running, who sits next to you. At the exact moment of his birth, his father looked up into the moonlit night and saw a doe running across the prairie.

"Another example would be your friend, Black Eagle. Again, the father looked up at the exact time of birth and saw a black eagle soaring in the wind.

"Another would be your sister, Beautiful Yellow Flower, born in the daytime of sun in the spring of the year."

The chief turns to his son and says, "But why do you ask, Two Dogs Fucking?"

Home again, and temporarily basking in the silly memories of jokesters telling jokes, Helen unlocked her front door to find Francine, putting her coat on to leave. They laughed at the timing.

"I already got my money," she said, holding up the cash and there's nothing else to…oh, we need Windex added to the grocery list."

"OK," said Helen, politely scanning the area.

They went through their weekly routine of Helen telling Francine everything looked great and Francine blushing and saying she hoped so.

"Oh, and I found this under the rug here at the front door."

"Not again," said Helen. Six months earlier, her carpenter had mistakenly cut the entrance door an inch too high and Helen had remedied the situation by buying a thick oriental throw rug to fit slightly under the door, leaving the impression that the door had been purposely cut to accommodate the gorgeous rug.

The flip side of this clever cover-up was that the building management often slipped informational notes under the owners' doors—notations of meetings, of window washings, of sprinkler system checks, of board meeting dates. Now, at the Clarks' unit, half the time these messages ended up under the throw rug, which Francine then came upon each Tuesday when she rolled back the rug to wash the floor.

Francine started to grin as she reminded Helen of the time a notice for the window washers had gone under-rug and unread. Helen had walked out of her bathroom naked to get some clothes from her closet. She'd almost killed herself banging into the side of the closet in her hurry to hide. "The window washers had a good time that day," Francine said with a laugh. Helen laughed too.

But as the door shut behind Francine, she wondered why she always seemed to have a recent story like that to laugh about. Actually, she knew it was just a part of who she was.

Still holding the letter, she finally examined it. This letter looked different somehow. It was addressed to Helen Clark—House Committee, but it was sealed. With her summer jacket still on, and still holding the mail, she studied the letter and noticed something else.... It had just the faintest scent of Old Spice.

She held the letter as she threw the umbrella and the mail onto her bed and wriggled out of her jacket. Now she fished through her purse and took a "sample" tranquilizer. Her heart was visibly pounding. She could actually see it pumping beneath her blouse. Helen sunk into her red leather armchair. She grabbed a cigarette from the end table and studied the envelope. Please don't have this be a letter from Max Shaw. Please. She wasn't exactly praying, but rather hoping that the letter was not from him.

She used her letter opener to very carefully slit the envelope. She knew in her soul that this would be a letter she would be keeping for a long, long time.

Helen finished her Fantasia as she studied the view from her bedroom window. She saw Lake Michigan with its boats moored in the deep blue water and Grant Park with its tennis courts and its playground where she often imagined she would someday take her grandchildren. She saw glorious Millennium Park, of which she was a board member. She saw Michigan Avenue. And she saw the Art Institute, where she'd studied as a young girl and now computer-tutored once a week. She watched some neighbors walking uphill toward home, some walking down, and some stopping to talk—maybe about the suicide and tomorrow's events.

She walked around her home holding the unread letter, seeing nothing but beauty, inside and out. Surrounded by beauty and beautiful herself, she realized that, even though her childhood had taken a tragic turn, it wasn't over. She was destined to experience more tragedy to balance the splendor she had experienced and enjoyed.

Helen lit another Fantasia, this one almost the bright deep blue color of Max Shaw's eyes and those of Camille. The letter was folded inside a formal announcement for house committee members. The letter, the actual letter was from Max Shaw. He'd never done that before. Helen barely breathed as she studied it. The date was six days old. This meant it had been delivered three days before his suicide.

Thursday, September 20, 2007

Dear Helen,

I need to see you even though we agreed not to again. I have to see you privately. I've come up with a plan that might somewhat normalize our situation.

No one asked for this, Helen. It's not as if we've purposely wound up together again. We need to feel all right about where this whole situation is headed. Or just what to do with all these emotions flying around the place whenever we're forced together socially. I'm surprised no one has noticed the electricity between us.

I'm in hell.

Please come over anytime today, tomorrow, or even the next day. Janet will be out of town for three days.

Please, Helen.

You know I'll do anything for you. You know that I've proved that. You know I've always loved only you.

Yours forever,

Max

Helen barely made it to the toilet before throwing up. Next came dry heaves, mixed with tears. She ran a steaming bath, quickly undressed and climbed in.

The letter had landed on the bathroom floor. She picked it up and read it over and over again. There was a ringing in her ears. She had dry mouth and kept dipping her face under the water to drink. Finally, beet red, she dragged herself out of the bathtub and slipped into some flannel pajamas, socks, a robe, and a shawl. Still she shivered. She put the letter in her bathrobe pocket.

She took a Valium. It seemed to remove her from such emotional intensity, to distance her from the horror. She focused on getting her act together for the service and eulogy tomorrow. She began locating black clothes and shoes to put out for her and Steven.

After obsessing over and completing that task, she took the phone off its cradle and put it under her mattress, got another blanket and curled up in the fetal position in her bed. She was asleep within minutes.

Helen awoke around 9:00 p.m., slowly gathering her wits. She realized that it was evening and that her door was shut, so Steven must be home. She could hear the television, and she didn't want to see him, so she got out of bed to pee and didn't flush the toilet, then propped up her pillows and crawled back to bed.

Safely in the warmth of her bed and the darkness of night, and knowing she would not be interrupted; she lay on her back sorting through the loss of Max Shaw. Forever. Helen enveloped herself in the magnificent memory, the beauty of them together, their story.

She recalled the very first day they laid eyes on each other. Max was fourteen, a grade school graduate. Although Helen was only thirteen and entering eighth grade, she looked and acted like she was in high school. She had already entered puberty and developed an exceptionally curvy body, which she camouflaged the best she could. Other than being leered at, Helen had a good and fairly easy life. She had an inordinate amount of self-confidence because she was pampered as an only child. She was also witty and a bit bored that life was so easy and predictable. She was on the verge of becoming a daredevil.

It was the middle of June, school had just gotten out a week ago, and the YMCA was busing several groups of middle-school students to a nearby lake to enjoy a day of swimming. Helen and her schoolmates were sitting in the middle section of the bus, generally making fun of each other. The bus driver had become more and more agitated as all three groups of kids became more and more boisterous and had begun bonking each other with objects such as M&M'S and sticks of gum. So, as a well-raised class leader, Helen rose from her seat and bumped and swayed up to the front of the bus. She took out her gum and said something to the bus driver. He smiled and said, "Go for it."

Helen faced the busload of kids and chewed her gum awhile until she'd gotten everyone's attention. Helen then took on the posture of the prissiest teacher in her school, pursed her lips, and, in a high-pitched voice, said, "All right now, class, we need to have some quiet time. This is NOT the time to be having fun, for the love of Pete," hands on hips, pretending to push her eyeglasses back into position. At this point, one of the boys made farting noises from his armpit and Helen played along by squeezing her buttocks together and saying, "Whoops." Then she switched to her own voice. "Really, guys, the bus driver is getting agitated and we could really help him out here if we could quiet down and stop lobbing things at each other."

The center of the bus, filled with Helen's schoolmates followed her advice. The class at the front of the bus followed. But the class in the back became rowdier still. This annoyed Helen. She bumped and swayed her way to the back of the bus and used her tough-guy talk. "Awright! Who's your best class clown?"

Without hesitation, everyone pointed to a smirking boy with the most beautiful eyes she'd ever seen. For the rest of her life, when Helen traveled back to that time in her memory, she would always feel the stomach-flipping jolt of their eyes meeting for the first time on the YMCA bus. Max Shaw's bright turquoise-blue eyes appeared to be lined in black, but that was because of his short thick black eyelashes. He had a mop of curly blond hair and was more muscular than most of his peers.

The boy met her gaze and grinned. He'd never seen such big dark eyes in his life. She wore loose clothing but he was already wondering what she looked like in her bathing suit.

Helen cleared her throat. "What's your name, clown-boy?"

“What’s yours?” he asked.

When she didn’t respond, he tried another tack. “It’s I. P. Daily, but let’s not stand on formality. You can call me I. P.”

This produced lots of laughter.

Helen also grinned. “OK. Well, listen, I. P., here’s the deal. If our driver here has a heart attack, then we won’t be able to swim today. And, now follow along with me on this, I. P., then you’d miss your golden opportunity of dunking me a bunch of times like you strong boys love to do to us weak little girls. So,” Helen concluded, “It’s up to you. Your call. Do you want your fun now, maybe never, or for sure in just about half an hour?”

Max Shaw had his arms crossed, but hadn’t taken his eyes off Helen once, not once. “That’s compelling. It’s well put. And I choose box number three.” His boyfriends laughed at his intended double meaning that none of the girls understood. “I’ll just take a little nap and wake up to our wonderful bus driver announcing that we’ve arrived.” He then closed his eyes to slits so that he could still see through his eyelashes. He watched this feisty school leader smile and go bumping and swaying her way back to her seat.

Once everyone disembarked the bus, they all ran directly to the sand, hooting and hollering, peeling off the clothes over their swimming suits, and running into the water.

Helen swam out quite far to get some exercise after being confined in the hot, sweaty bus for over two hours. Then she swam the backstroke halfway to shore, whereupon she was suddenly lifted out of the water and thrown back into it. She surfaced only to be picked up and tossed out toward the deeper area of the lake. This caused her to giggle. She managed to get a look at the person who was on the attack. It was I. P. Daily.

She saw his strong tanned arms and watched him dive under her and throw her up again. Next he twirled her.

Then he pushed her into the water and held her face down for what seemed like a minute. She surfaced, spitting water.

"That last one wasn't funny," she squeaked. She threw her whole body on his head and held him down by locking him between her arms and her chest. And what a chest it was.

Max licked her neck as he surfaced and then picked her up over his head, placing her on his shoulders, her legs on either side, her crotch on his neck. He walked farther in and cried, "WAR TIME," very loudly. Other girls climbed onto other boys' shoulders, and everyone began attacking everyone else, playing Water-War.

In the end, Max and Helen won. Quite the team as it turned out. Exhausted, Helen slid off Max's back. He turned quickly around and launched her one more time. As Helen was thrown, she experienced her first orgasm. She had no idea what it was, just that there was a powerfully rigorous itching throbbing feeling going on in her crotch that made her arch her back and close her eyes. She inhaled and left her mouth open as the throbbing continued, and finally she sunk underneath the water. She was still so aroused that she touched herself to examine the feeling and her hand felt the throbbing subsiding.

Max lowered himself to her level in the water and kissed her mouth. They both came up for air breathing deeply, Helen feeling as if she was going to faint.

And now there was a whistle as the lifeguard motioned them to come in. They saw that everyone else was already getting their gear together, heading for the bathhouse to change.

Overcome with physical desire, neither one spoke as they came ashore, and when they split off to go to their girls' and boys' bathhouse entrances, Helen pretended to act cool by nonchalantly saying, "Well, see you on the bus, I. P." Max muttered, "You'll see me a lot more than that," but she didn't hear him.

That was in early June. By late July, Helen discovered she was pregnant. Max offered to pay for an abortion. Helen was devastated that he could be so cavalier. Max was confused. There were endless discussions about what to do, but still, they couldn't keep their hands off each other.

Finally, one early afternoon, Helen decided to ask her mother if she would help her raise the child so that she could get through high school. And that was the end of Max and Helen. Three days later, Max was put on an airplane to an Eastern boarding school and Helen was lying on a gurney in an abortion clinic, feeling excruciating cramps, and so, so sad. She could not stop crying.

Her mother was barely civil to her on the ride home, and as soon as they arrived at their house, she yanked Helen out of the car and up to her room. "There," said her mother. "You've got your own bathroom, and I'll bring you food at mealtimes. You will not be answering the telephone. You will NOT be talking to that boy again. I'm locking you in your room. Now drink plenty of water with these antibiotic pills, and sleep for a few days. You'll get over this, Helen, but you will pay for your actions too."

Years later, Helen's mother would finally explain why she'd been so ruthless—after Helen was safely married to an educated and well-respected man of means, and after the reception on her wedding day.

What a wedding that was. Everything was "custom" this and "special" that. She was their only child and her parents spared no expense at showing Helen and Steven's friends and family the grandest of times. Harold and Miriam Hemingway reveled in the glory of showing their world of friends what a fine young lady their daughter had become.

The night of her wedding, as Helen was changing out of her white lace bridal gown into a tailored pink suit with matching high heels, her mother's eyes shined. Filled with pride and love for Helen, she said, "See, precious, how much better off you are. You're off to the right start. I'm so happy for you."

Helen had learned long ago to be silent if she had any difference of opinion with her mother. So she said nothing.

She'd worn her mother's double strand of pearls on her wedding day to represent the "something borrowed" and now she was taking off the pearls to return them.

Her mother stopped her by holding her arms. "No, darling, you keep them. I want you to remember you and me—always—as you wear those pearls. The first strand has a pearl for each year you were a child. The thirteenth pearl is a black one representing the wicked year when your childhood took a deep turn into adulthood." That's how Helen's mother had always referred to her abortion—"when you became a young lady," or "when you reached adulthood," or "when I saved you from a lifetime of sadness," or "when that boy's parents got him out of town."

"Sometimes people have their tragedies early, darling. There aren't too many people who get to start over, the way you and that boy did," she finished tearfully.

Helen was quietly crying, thinking, I'm in hell. Please, God, just let me go out to our guests, to Steven. I'm Mrs. Steven Clark, now. Please let me get away from this woman.

But the "talk" her mother had obviously planned was not quite finished. She said, "There's something you should know, Helen. I would do anything for you. I loved you, Helen, the minute the nurse handed you to me. I loved you through all the years you blamed me for your loss. I'll always love and cherish you. You are a complete person, Helen. Now you can finally understand why I was so tough with you. You do, don't you, darling?"

"Mother, really. Let's just take our champagne and go join our guests. My husband's waiting for me. I love you, Mom. I forgive you. OK?"

Her mother's eyes blazed. "Forgive me. Why, Helen, you've missed the whole point. You should be thanking your lucky stars I saved you from the kind of life I was forced into."

Helen looked up toward the cathedral ceiling of the chapel dressing room. "Thank you, lucky stars. Thank you, Mother, for sacrificing so much for me." She knew the only way to get out without further unwanted knowledge was to satisfy whatever it was that her mother was after.

Her mother smiled smugly. Helen let out a breath of relief. She was about to be freed of this woman.

But her mother wanted to finish the pearl story. "The second strand represents the many lucky years you were given because I saved you. Eleven years of education, Helen. Your three years of high school with honors classes in everything. Your seven years at Berkeley, continuing on for your master's degree, where you met the love of your life. And every year, Helen, at the time of your…at the time when I saved you from a lifetime of frustration, I've added a pearl to represent the grief I've spared you.

"And now, that second strand of pearls has caught up to your first ten innocent years. I've added this year's pearl a little early because you'll be on your honeymoon on the date of the yearly pearl celebration. This is a very significant pearl, Helen, because it represents having outlived your mistake and you've got the rest of your happy, educated life ahead of you. Look, darling." Her mother guided Helen up close to the mirror. "I had our jeweler attach a diamond next to the last pearl, showing how very special it is to have outlived your mistake."

During this last speech, Helen had been holding her nose to stop her tears. She swallowed hard, grabbed her mother, and hugged her tightly. "Thanks for everything, Mother. The pearls are beautiful. And the diamond! It's just gorgeous. Thank you for everything, Mother."

Her mother beamed as Helen took her hand and said, "Come on now, Mother, let's join our guests."

Taking a certain pride in herself for loyally enduring her mother's skewed rendition of past events, Helen picked up her honeymoon suitcase, put on her actor face of joy, and led her serene mother out of that room.

Some things are better left unsaid, was what she thought. And when she saw Steven, his face shining with love for her, his eyes taking in the beauty of her, she let go of her mother's hand, walked up to him and gave him a long, loving sexy open-mouthed kiss. The guests hooted and clapped as Mr. and Mrs. Steven Clark waved good-bye.

But nothing is that simple. On his deathbed, her father told Helen facts about her mother that would cause Helen to understand and accept her on a very different level, and they would enjoy and like and love each other for the next fifteen years before she died.

And now, the fifty-four-year-old Helen Clark was drifting off to sleep, safely, out of harm's way until morning, her brain hearing Norah Jones softly singing "Don't Know Why."

*Sometimes I think it would be easier to avoid old age, to die young, but then you'd never complete your life, would you? You'd never wholly know you.*

~ Marilyn Monroe ~

*Since everything is in our heads, we had better not lose them.*

~ Coco Chanel ~

# WEDNESDAY

Helen sprang awake at her usual God-awful two o'clock in the morning, which she had been doing ever since rehab, four years ago. She'd developed two tricks to put herself back to sleep: She could throw on a bathing suit and go up to the pool to swim laps; after that, the sauna, and back to dreamland. But door number one wasn't going to work anymore, not with what had recently happened up there. No, she wouldn't be swimming laps and doing the sauna at two in the morning for a long time, probably never.

She got up to execute the drowsy/pleasure trick: Reading while eating three cookies with a small glass of milk for dunking; then back to bed and concentrate on a recent accomplishment. The cookies (actually it was the milk) made her drowsy, and the good-girl memory gave her pleasure.

This time, she settled on the fact that she'd managed to sidestep a potentially crippling depression by allowing herself professional help. Good job, she told herself. You're not alone. It's not that she thought anyone, trained or not, could advise her helpfully. No one ever had. Her hope lay in the fact that she was helping herself. That Helen was honestly trying to figure herself out was huge.

And how was that going? What had she learned?

During her two sessions with Dr. Savage, he'd asked her about her mother, and her answers were eye-opening. She'd never before pondered the depth of the revelation at her father's deathbed and the resulting life changes because of his untimely death. What went down that year and the next impacted her reality, changing her view, altering her attitude, molding the future.

Now, she time traveled back to her father's heart attack, thirty-two years ago.

Her first recollection was of her father's mistress, Betsy Black, probably because she'd made the call.

Betsy Black.

Helen had never been treated fairly by her father's mistress because of the woman's nasty jealousy. As a young girl, this had confused Helen. Their relationships with the man were so different. Why would a savvy adulterer think she needed to compete with a sad young teenager? Their attentions toward a man they both loved didn't compare.

But of course it had to do with resemblance. Helen began to look more and more like her beautiful mother, so that when she spent time with her father and Betsy, her mere presence was a constant reminder of the woman who would never be left and always come first in the eyes of Harold Hemingway.

Betsy Black was quite the multitask master, juggling hidden spitefulness with open accommodation. She took every opportunity to even the score of her third-place ranking by keeping Helen as off-balance as she could while pretending to be good to her in front of Harold.

Still tender, Helen didn't fully understand emotions like jealousy or hatred, but she loved her father dearly and believed that he was lonely and sad, though why she couldn't quite grasp. Convinced that she could help by doing as he wished, she spent time with him at Betsy's place without her mother's knowledge.

Harold Hemingway expected his daughter to enter into his deception. He chose not to see the harm of it. He wouldn't understand Black's nature for years, didn't understand her intention to replace his wife and discard his daughter.

Young Helen sensed this truth, but couldn't possibly think it through on that adult a level. To temper her dread of this horrid person who hated her and had been thrust upon her, Helen took to the private comfort of conversing with her selves, calling Betsy by her last name. Black was such a wonderful name for a mean-spirited person, a she-devil.

This much Helen knew: Black was immoral. Helen couldn't bring herself to think of her father that way and settled on clueless. Her father was clueless.

The relationships continued in one form or another for twelve years.

It reached its apex of sorts on The Day of The Call.

*It's 1975. Helen's new husband, Steven, has been offered a position at the University of Chicago. The newly married Clarks are persuaded to spend two weeks with Helen's parents at their rambling estate in River Forest. Because Steven is so delighted with them, Helen sees her parents in a new light and is shocked to discover she actually enjoys them as adult friends. The Clarks extend their stay, Steven is taught how to play bridge, and they settle into an unforgettable summertime of fun.*

*Both the university, and Harold and Miriam Hemingway concentrate their considerably persuasive powers on Steven accepting the job offer, and after marathon discussions, Helen and Steven Clark decide to go for it.*

*It's the last Friday in August and Helen Hemingway Clark is preparing to meet up with her mother, who's at Marshall Field's getting her hair and nails done. Her father and husband have spent the morning at the University of Chicago campus, going over Steven's teaching contract. The plan is for the four of them to meet for lunch at the Walnut Room. Helen is halfway out the door when she gets The Call.*

"Drat," she says as she runs to the hall phone, "Hello."

"Oh, Gawd, I'm glad it's you who answered…," came the unmistakable voice of Betsy Black.

Pin-prickly shivers of alarm traveled through Helen's body. "What is it?" interrupted Helen.

She was chewing gum and sniffling. "Your father's had a heart attack. He's in a private room over here at the University of Chicago Hospital, and he just keeps asking for you. Do you think you'd have time in your busy schedule to come…"

Helen interrupted, "How is that possible? He's with Steven. What are you saying?"

"Yeah, he was…but then he decided to stop by and see me, and Steven went on ahead."

"What the…"

"Your dad lost his temper," sobbed Betsy. "He, he just came apart when I refused to…"

"I'll be there as soon as possible," Helen heard herself say.

"Oh! There's no rush."

"Right," said Helen. "Bye, Black" (bang). She quickly located her mother's personal phone directory by her kitchen desk phone and found the number of Field's beauty salon. After a great deal of shuffling, her mother was handed the phone, and gave her a peppy, "Hi, dearie, What's up? You running late?"

"Mother, there's an urgent situation."

"Yes." Miriam's voice was now stoic.

Helen and her mother had an unspoken agreement to always refer to Betsy Black as "ThatWoman." Helen said to her mother, "ThatWoman just called from The U of C Hospital. Dad's stabilized, but he's had a heart attack and is in a private room in the Intensive Care Unit."

"N…No," said her mother.

"Yes," said Helen. "Here's what needs to happen: You should go find Steven where he's probably waiting for us in the Walnut Room, and the two of you should meet me over at the hospital. I'll head over there right now. ThatWoman is such a moron, she probably isn't handling this well."

Mrs. Hemingway didn't respond.

"Mom? I know you don't want to meet her, but if I were you, I'd go over there and take charge. He's your Goddamn husband, and besides that, you hate gossip, and ThatWoman might enjoy causing some over this. Personally, I say the three of us get there quickly and take over. It's your chance to point out—in person—that he's your husband, and that's that."

Since Helen's mother was still tongue-tied, she patiently instructed her. "OK, Mom, this is such a shock. I'm going to run upstairs and pack a pair of slippers for you in case it turns into a long vigil."

"Yes," said her mother. "Good. I'll, I'll change out of this salon robe and go find Steven. What else should you pack?"

What a role reversal this was, thought Helen. "Um, let's see. Uh, I'll pack your Mary Baker Eddy and whatever novel is next to your bed. And a notepad; I know you'll want to make a list. And, and…maybe a nightgown and your toiletries. We can take turns staying overnight with him if it comes to that. OK, Mother? We should hang up now and get going. All right, dearie?"

"Yes, darling. Very good. Thank you," came her mother's strong, businesslike voice.

Helen entered her father's private room, caught off guard by his fragile appearance. She went to his bedside, kissed him on his cheek and then tenderly stroked his head.

Betsy Black entered the room. She talked in her sing-song way that had always driven Helen mad. "Oh, Hel-len, Hi-E. I thought you'd never get here."

"What in the hell are you talking about, you called less than an hour ago," whispered Helen.

"Really? It seemed like it took you ages. I called my cousin, Ned, to keep me company, because I had no idea when you'd come, being the busy bee you are."

Helen was silent while she thought about the reaction she was having to what Black had just said to her. (You canNOT choke her.) And, in a monotone voice, she calmly said, "Well, that's good, because then he can drive you home."

"Home! I can't just leave him here all by himself."

Helen took a breath. "See, now, that's the thing, Black, I'm here, now. And my mother's on her way."

Black's eyes dilated. She stopped her gum chewing.

Helen finished, "The rules in ICU are strictly 'family only.'"

"Well, I'm not going anywhere," said Black angrily. "Maybe your father and I aren't married, but we might as well be."

"I don't think so. 'Might as well be' doesn't quite make the cut. I'm guessing the list of rules probably doesn't read, 'doctor,' and then 'might as well be doctor' either."

"Look, Helen," said Black, between clenched teeth, "You shouldn't have called your mother in the first place."

"Oh, please. You know they will always be husband and wife. Just because he spends a lot of time with you doesn't mean he would ever marry you. He has never asked my mother for a divorce."

"What? I happen to know he's been asking her for one ever since he met me."

"You've really been given a line of bullshit, Black, if you believed him in the heat of the moment as if he ever intended to honor your adultery by marrying you.

Just for starters, he'd have to respect you to actually marry you. I must have underestimated your stupidity."

The gloves were off. Helen was filled with a wondrous sense of relief as she released years of pent-up dialogue. ThatWoman could cause no more harm than she already had. Helen and her mother had made room for Betsy Black and now Betsy Black was going to learn exactly what that place was.

"Save it, Helen. I know what I know. He wanted a divorce to marry me, and the bitch refused. Simple as that."

"Ah, the most oft used line in all adulterous affairs," said Helen. She faced Black head-on and spoke in a cold monotone. "Never. Not once did he ever broach the subject. In fact, I asked him one time why he saw you, and he said, and I'm paraphrasing…that means that, entirely for your benefit, I'm restating what he said in a simpler way, so that you can understand it. He said, 'Helen, life is complicated. Different people satisfy different needs. I will always be your father. I will always be your mother's husband. That's because I love you both. And that's that.'"

Black furiously straightened the already straight covers on Harold Hemingway's bed. "Yeah, right," she said, scrunching up her bitter face and chomping on her gum.

"Look," said Helen. "You can leave, because you should, or you can stay and be humiliated. The problem with choice number two is that it might upset the patient, and that, Black, would definitely not be cool."

Betsy glared at her and crossed her arms over her chest. "I'm staying."

"Yep," said Helen. She walked out to the nurse's station and asked about her father's present condition.

The nurse began to explain that his doctor was the one to ask, when his doctor showed up.

Helen flashed her "we're comrades" smile, and introduced herself. The doctor smiled back, and introduced himself as they shook hands. He explained that her father had had a coronary and that they had a chance of repairing his heart once he was stabilized. "But for now, Mrs. Clark, we'll continue monitoring him all night long every fifteen minutes. He's been sedated and probably won't be awake until morning. And your mother is in there keeping an eye on things."

Helen blanched, but she hid her contempt well, drawing from her wealth of practice. "Well, therein lies yet another problem, Doctor," Helen said. "That's not my mother. ThatWoman is my father's mistress, and my mother is on her way over here. Isn't the rule 'family only' in ICU?"

This clearly annoyed the doctor. He frowned and said, "These matters are not my concern. I'm a heart specialist, not a therapist or a mediator. This situation has arisen before. It isn't the first time, believe me."

He sighed as he saw the embarrassment on Helen's beautiful, sad face, the innocent daughter of a problem the patient himself had created. He took pity on her in spite of himself. "But I will tell you that, yes, the rule is 'family only,' and since he won't waken for hours, it seems you and the others might use that time to sort this out, the whole night long." He finished this last part sarcastically to toughen himself back up.

The doctor went into Harold Hemingway's room. Soon Betsy came out. "No one's allowed in there while he's examining the patient," she said to Helen. She cracked her chewing gum.

"Uh huh," said Helen, trying to keep her temper. Even as her father lay in mortal danger, this egomaniacal idiot was seeking center stage. She inwardly appealed to her various personalities: Keep it together, girls; you can do it. But they couldn't. "Go fuck yourself," muttered Helen.

"What? What did you just say to me?" Betsy asked loudly.

"Shhh, not so loud. I said, fuck you," Helen replied quietly, all the while smiling sweetly to whomever walked by.

"Listen, Helen," managed the red-faced Betsy, "You should thank your lucky stars I got him here in time."

"Thank you, lucky stars," said Helen, looking up at the ceiling. "They get a lot of thank-yous," she said to no one.

Silence.

"On the other hand," continued Helen, "You shouldn't have been with another woman's husband in the first place."

Black locked her arms over her chest, looking around to make sure no one was overhearing these insults. But Helen told her not to worry, that she wouldn't humiliate her publicly. That wasn't her style.

Actually what Helen was accomplishing was twofold: She was freeing herself of holding in all that she'd wanted to say to this albatross for a long, long time. And as a pleasantly surprising side benefit she was so thoroughly rattling Betsy Black that Black might be tongue-tied when her mother, Miriam, arrived. Miriam had been raised to be a lady at all times, and to turn the other cheek. It was not in her nature to be confrontational on her own behalf. But Helen knew this could be as cathartic for her mother as it was turning out to be for her. She wanted her mother to seize the moment and confront the woman who'd made her life heartbreakingly complicated for so many years.

"So, Miss Black, there's actually a bigger picture here," continued Helen. "I see this as an issue of gender-loyalty. If female traitors, like yourself, weren't available to the temporarily confused husbands who should be home working out their problems, those men would have no place to run and hide out, so they'd go home, and they would work out their problems.

"In a perfect world, all females would honor their sisters by considering husbands as untouchable. Married men—off limits. And you know something, that adage, 'What goes around comes around,' is true. Look around. Read. You cunts just don't get it."

Black was a purplish color, but the witch was still in the game. She said, "Your precious daddy loves ME, not your mother. Miriam's too goooood for him."

"Mrs. Hemingway," corrected Helen. "Call her Mrs. Hemingway...So, yeah, well, I don't know much about these things, thank God. But I've heard that there are lots of men out there in our crazy, funny world who fantasize about having a vagina and a maid all wrapped up into one bleached blonde."

Smoldering silence.

"Also," continued Helen, "I would bet the house that Mr. Hemingway's wife wasn't into blow jobs."

"Shut up, Helen."

"See, the thing is, Black, Mr. Hemingway had exactly what he wanted all these years. You know he's French on his mother's side, don't you? His family spent a lot of time in France, and the French notoriously have a wife and then a mistress later on. Generally French women accept this as inevitable. It's easier to understand why he would behave that way when you consider his background. He has his intelligent, respectable, and beautiful wife at his side for all public appearances, and all social events. They have an active life, a group of very close friends, and they really have good times together. He gives his wife an elegant negligee every anniversary." (This was an especially good one. Black actually flinched, which led Helen to expand.) "He loves her and, by the way, they are very sexual. They also have the greatest bond a couple can have, their child. Moi." (Here, she smiled.) "The three of us had a life together all those years you thought that he'd, what, disengaged himself? Did you really think he'd leave all that for a cheater? I saw how he treated you. There was absolutely no respect there."

Betsy was now breathing heavily. "How dare you speak to me like that."

"How dare you play with another family's well-being. You're a traitor to the sisterhood of American females. We stand today as the women who've gained the most from our men. We American women have more freedom and respect than women from anyplace else in the world. Only idiots like you join the ranks of the whores who sabotage what we've accomplished."

"I don't know what you're talking about," said Black foolishly.

"I believe that you don't. It takes a bigger brain to have character."

At this point the doctor emerged from Mr. Hemingway's room, saving Betsy Black from further chastising. He looked only at Helen as he spoke, apparently having decided to help her with her family problem after all.

"Mrs. Clark," he began, "I'm going to speak frankly because I think you can handle it. If I were you, I'd remain with your father tonight. There's a fifty-fifty chance, he'll wake up later on, have a lucid hour or so, and then…unless you request life support, which he himself declined, according to our files. It would be good for your mother and yourself to be with him. I'll let the staff know that you and your mother are the only ones allowed in his room, unless he requests otherwise."

"And the other 50 percent chance, Doctor?" whispered Helen.

"The other is that he'll stabilize during the night and wake tomorrow morning in good enough shape for us to perform surgery later in the day," he answered.

"And the odds of his surgical procedure are?" asked Helen.

The doctor studied Helen briefly, and answered by inhaling deeply and telling her that, "again, there's a fifty-fifty shot of him surviving. Either way, it's good that you're here and that his wife is on her way." He touched her arm for comfort. "I'll be back making rounds again later."

"Thank you, Doctor," Helen said, as she shook his hand. "I so appreciate your compassion and honesty."

He glanced at Betsy, smiled at Helen, and left.

As Helen absently looked down the hall, pondering how to get rid of ThatWoman who had the stones to still be there, she saw Steven and her mother step out of the elevator and walk briskly toward them. Her eyes teared. Only then did she realize that she hadn't had a chance to react to the possibility of her father dying.

"Shit," said Betsy.

Helen's mother looked stunning. She'd dressed for what she'd expected of the day, wearing a navy-blue knit dress with a starched white collar and the matching fitted jacket with white cuffs at her delicate wrists, pearls at her regal neck, the picture of refined elegance in her simple beige hose and navy-blue high heels and purse. As always, she was handling herself in an appropriate manner, her expression one of controlled concern.

Too late to move and keep any remaining dignity, Black stood there in her three-inch heels, tight Capris, and low-necked sweater, dumbly watching their rapid approach.

Helen spoke. "Boy, did you get here fast!" Her voice shook as her mother hugged her, patting her back in a comforting way. "Here's the current situation." Steven was next with a kiss and protective embrace. "He's out cold, completely sedated, so we have time to regroup."

All three of them turned their attention toward ThatWoman.

Helen said, "Mother and Steven, this is Bitsy Black."

No one shook hands.

"Betsy," corrected Betsy. "Betsy Black." She chewed her gum vigorously.

"Charmed," said Steven sarcastically.

Mrs. Hemingway nodded her head and said, "Fluffy." She saw Helen's wide-eyed surprise and her subsequent smirk, which egged her on.

"Betsy," corrected Betsy, a little too loudly.

"Oh! Ballsy," said Helen's mother.

Helen was now stifling laughter, and Steven coughed to keep control.

Helen called a halt by repeating the doctor's information, the fifty-fifty chance for the fifty-fifty shot at the 50 percent possibility if Daddy stabilized, odds being equal.

Everyone was aware of Betsy not exactly belonging there, but what to do begged discussion.

"Bitsy," chirped Helen, "why don't you go see about your cousin or something, while Steven is getting everyone coffee, so that we Hemingway gals can have some private time to sort this out."

Helen's mother could not get the teeny tiny but definite smirk off her face.

Well, thought Helen, if that's all it takes to keep Mother feeling OK, then we'll just keep putting ThatWoman in her place. Helen was feeling strangely protective of her mother in a way she hadn't in…many years.

"I'll walk with you, Steve, to help you carry the coffees," said Betsy, boldly joining the ball game.

He studied her briefly, the audacity to think he'd walk with the enemy. "Thanks anyway, I'll get a tray."

She turned and left, saying, "Don't get excited, I'm not leaving, just going outside to have a cigarette."

"She's claiming the right to stay here," said Steven as he cleared his throat and left, saying he'd…"be back with coffee and perhaps a Snickers Bar for ThatWoman."

"Let's go in," said Miriam, as she took her daughter's hand.

There he was. The tall, handsome man who'd loved them and paid their bills for twenty-three years.

"Oh, my," said his wife, as she walked to his bedside and took the hand that wasn't hooked up to tubes. She kissed his hand and said, "Dear? It's me, dear. Helen and I are both here with you now. You just rest and stabilize."

Helen surrendered to the moment. Her eyes teared as she looked at these two characters that had managed to raise their little girl to womanhood despite all their own idiosyncrasies. She joined them at the other side of the bed, ducking the mass of tubes attached to the various machines. The three of them had loved one another, as only they knew how. How else does anyone love?

In fact, as her father lay on the hospital bed unconscious with all those tubes in him, she wanted to somehow create a peace between them, to ease their disappointments and regrets.

Helen considered the possible scenarios to the night before them, and after a while, whispered across their man, "Mother, what do you want to do about ThatWoman?"

Mrs. Hemingway's face changed from an expression of tenderness toward her husband, to one of scorn. "What I'd like to do and what the right thing to do are probably light-years apart."

Helen whispered that these two options might be compatible if they put their minds to it. She gave her mother a blow-by-blow account of her previous "discussion."

The two women did, of course, hold Harold Hemingway accountable for his relationship with Betsy Black, and they knew that at the time this whole mistress thing began, if there hadn't been a Betsy Black lurking around the corner with open arms, he would have returned to Miriam Hemingway. They would have sorted out their needs and straightened out their problems.

When Steven returned with the coffee, his wife and his mother-in-law told him of their plan to simply speak their minds, no holds barred.

Meanwhile, Betsy had formed a plan of her own. Helen had humiliated her and she wasn't about to let it go. She returned quietly to the room and rubbed Mr. Hemingway's feet. "He always did like to be rubbed," she said with a smile.

Poker-faced, Helen said, "Yeah, we rubbed his back a lot, but in your case, didn't he prefer the open-mouth-rub-thing?"

Three pairs of eyes grew wide with what she said.

Helen feigned surprise and affability. "What? Can't we talk freely among quote family unquote? Apparently Betsy here believes she's part of the family and therefore allowed in Dad's ICU room, so we might as well amuse each other."

At the same time Betsy was saying she "didn't have to take that shit," and Steven was saying, "Helen," Miriam was saying, "Well, I'll have to admit that I found that amusing."

"I'm afraid that's what this family does when we're in the throes of fretting. Now, for example, as we anxiously wait for our man to recover. It passes the time. But you should leave if this is too much for you. Just pretend you never met him. I know that's one of my fantasies."

"Mine too," said Helen.

"I'll have to agree there," said Steven. "Your relationship brought heartbreak to others. Tell me, Miss Black, have you ever read, well no, heard expressions like: 'Bad karma' or 'What goes around comes around,' or..."

Betsy interrupted. "Have you heard the one that goes, 'Butt out'?"

A nurse entered the room to do the fifteen-minute check. "Oh this can't be going on," she said. "Only two at a time allowed and only blood relatives. Right now, though, you all need to leave the room so I can check Mr. Hemingway's vitals."

All four filed out, hotly debating.

"Well," Steven said to Betsy, "resorting to reason, blood relatives leaves us out."

"The hell it does. I brought him here. So I belong here. And I'm staying here."

"See, though, the thing is, you shouldn't have been with him in the first place, so, logically, your bringing him here is negated," said Mrs. Hemingway. "You don't belong anywhere near him and you never have."

"Says you," Betsy responded.

Mrs. Hemingway said, "Well, says me, and says the Bible, and says all of us who believe in loyalty and honesty."

"That would leave out Harry for sure, wouldn't it now. So I guess since we were partners in crime, we might as well stick it out to the end," Betsy shot back. She was getting the hang of this in her own limited way.

"Harry," repeated Helen and her mother at the same time. No one had ever called Harold Hemingway 'Harry' in his life.

Steven held his hands up, palms out, as a "stop" gesture. "All right, let's..."

But the nurse came out and interrupted him. "He seems to be stirring, and mumbling something...sounds like... Miriam? Is there a Miriam here?" Mrs. Hemingway beamed as she put up her hand.

The nurse said, "OK then, you should say what you want to say while he's coherent…I'm going to look the other way so I can't see how many people are in that room."

They all mumbled, "Thank you," as they filed back in.

Mrs. Hemingway went to his free hand and held it to her cheek.

The others stood at the foot of his bed and watched.

"Miriam? Is that you?" His speech was slow but clear.

"Yes, dear," she said as she gently stroked his forehead and hair.

"Oh, thank God you're here. You mean everything to me, dear, dear Miriam…and Helen? Is Helen here?"

"I'm here, Daddy," she said as she walked over to stand with her mother.

"You're such a wonderful daughter, Helen. You light up my life. Always have. Whenever you think of me, know that I loved you with all my heart."

Tears streamed down Helen's flushed cheeks. "You're very young, Dad," Helen pleaded. "There are so many possibilities of future goals and satisfactions. Daddy, please! You…have…a good chance, the doctor says."

"I'm dying, sweetie. But it's OK. Be faithful to your mother, Helen. Her whole life has been about us, you and me, and now she'll have only you. You and Steven. And the beautiful grandchildren to come. I'll be with you in spirit, Helen, with you all. I want you to be happy. That's what I expect. And, who knows. Maybe you're right about spirits hovering near their dear ones. You've certainly described it often enough. Maybe I'll be around. Maybe you can call upon my soul in grave times. Who knows?"

And with that, he drifted off.

Helen could not let herself be the last person Harold Hemingway talked to. It had to be her mother. So she bent down and began kissing him awake, just the way she had done for the first ten years of her life. She kissed him on his forehead, on his temples, on his cheeks, and he smiled and stirred. Helen made way for her mother to step up to his head and hands, and as she did, he opened his eyes and said, “You smell so good, Miriam. You always smell so good.”

His wife smiled sweetly. “The Shalimar you’ve always bought me,” she said.

“It’s not just the Shalimar, dear. You always smell so clean and wholesome.”

“How are you feeling?” asked Mrs. Hemingway. She looked so soft, so vulnerable. “Tell us what happened, if you have enough strength.”

He slurred his answer. “Simply put, I was nefarious and this is my punishment. I don’t expect to make it past tomorrow. I owe you an explanation about my…other life. After a while, I felt that I…just couldn’t measure up to you. You need to know that even though I was twice as educated, you were the more intelligent one. Not only that, but you seldom did anything that wasn’t nice. And not only that, but you educated yourself.

“Our marriage began harshly because I impregnated you. I felt like I stopped your life before it officially got under way. No college experience at all. I knew you would have loved college, yet you never once complained about your loss. And you were a good mother, Miriam. Helen became a real handful, and you sure gave it your all.

“So your question would be, what did I do to drive my husband into someone else’s arms. Wouldn’t it?” he asked.

His wife was thinking that he was beyond doped up. He really was going to die. He had never in their lives together talked so intimately, or been so frank.

Helen looked at her beautiful mother who had been sad about her husband’s affair for twelve years. “Go for it,” she whispered. “How many people get their moment of truth?”

So she did. "Yes, Harold, that is my burning question. What in God's green earth did I ever do that wasn't in your interest? I worked hard to achieve all that you've mentioned. I was eager to please you in all ways."

"That's it," replied Mr. Hemingway. "You were practically flawless. That left me in the impossible position of returning your perfection with my own. And I tried. I really...well, I succeeded most of the time. But after about twelve years of that kind of effort, I just became tired. Also, it seemed like, all of a sudden, you shifted your attention to Helen that summer."

With a sinking heart, Helen understood that it was she who had caused her mother's problems. Jesus, thought Helen, if I hadn't been conceived, my mother would have had her college experience. And if I hadn't gotten pregnant that twelfth summer, my mother would have paid more attention to my father's restlessness. And there would have been no Betsy in their lives.

Mrs. Hemingway thought about Harold's words for a while, saw that Helen looked like someone had just hit her, and then she spoke. "That's just not enough of an answer, Harold. From what you've just said, Helen and I are responsible for your affair."

Helen appreciated her mother's courage.

Harold spoke up quickly. "No, really, that's not what I meant. I'm saying I felt I was never quite good enough for you, so I purposely went for a mistress who was your polar opposite. She wasn't great looking—bleached blond hair, too much makeup. She swore, she gossiped, something you never put up with. She'd do anything I wanted, things I would never think of asking you to do, and she liked sports and she belched. That alone meant that I could be basic too, as earthy and disgusting as I chose.

"You have no idea how many times I've regretted ever starting up with her. The only defense I could claim is that

I'm half French. My father had a mistress, his father had one. They all do. Their wives know about them, and it seems that it doesn't bother them."

"Oh come on, Harold," said Mrs. Hemingway. "We don't live in France. This is America, home of the free, where you can do just about anything you want. But here, we believe in cause and effect. We believe in retribution. We believe that what goes around comes around. Are you at all familiar with 'bad Karma,' because you and your selfishness have created a bunch of it." Her eyes were blazing and she was breathing heavily. This was Miriam Hemingway at her angriest.

"Good. This is excellent. Just let it all out, Miriam," said Harold.

"Oh no, you don't. This isn't confession time and then Saint Peter opens the pearly gates. I do not forgive you for your adultery. And if you think that's the worst, I have an even lower opinion of your whore. She took another woman's husband, which makes her a traitor to her gender."

Helen was stunned to hear her mother talk this way to her father. She had figured the game out pretty much as Helen had; in modern American society, Betsy Black was the lowest of the low. She looked at Black, who was sitting in an armchair, chewing her gum and staring straight at them, not even having the decency to look away. She looked at Steven who was sitting on the sleeper couch at the windowsill. He returned her gaze with one of compassion, and mouthed, "Should we leave Mother and Dad alone?" Helen shook her head no.

Mr. Hemingway was sweating profusely, so Mrs. Hemingway prepared a cold washcloth in the corner sink and applied it gently to his forehead, patting him on his head. "I've always loved you, Harold. You're a good man in so many ways. So thank you for encouraging me to free myself of this hatred I've carried around for all these years. It's so tormenting to both love and hate the same person."

"You're the one. You're the only one. You've always been the only one," he said softly, as his eyes closed. Helen and her mother immediately looked over at the heart monitor, and let out relieved sighs as they saw the signals playing strongly across the screen.

Harold Hemingway would awaken one more time, in the middle of the night, and ask for Steven. And when he did, Helen padded out of his room in her slippers to find Steven who was sleeping in a nearby waiting room.

"Steven," said Harold. "Take my hand, my son. I wanted you to know how very much I respect you, and that I've enjoyed you as a son-in-law more than I could imagine. Is there anything you want to ask me, Steven?"

Steven was crying. Helen had never seen him so emotional and she suddenly realized that this was really it. Her father was saying good-bye.

"I love you like a son, Steven. Don't cry for me. I've had a full life, and shared it with some very special people," said Harold. "Ask me your question."

"Advice," Steven managed to say. "Give me your best advice, Dad, because I respect you in so many ways. And I love you too."

"You don't need any, really," said his father-in-law. "But, all right." A minute or so went by as he gathered his thoughts.

"My best advice is to be faithful to the woman you love. Honor her, be her buddy, her best friend. And keep no secrets. Never go to bed upset with each other. And if you need something that Helen isn't providing, you need to be up front. Just tell her. And ask her what she needs, that you're not aware of. For God's sake, learn from my tragic mistakes. Helen is a treasure. She's been through a lot of heartache, and she's still smiling, still being nice. So when she acts out, be patient. Peel away her veneer of self-confidence, and you'll find a twelve-year-old girl who needs a lot of tender reassurance. And Steven? Helen feels safe with you, which is the single most important part of love for her."

That morning, Mr. Hemingway died holding Mrs. Hemingway's hand to his mouth as a farewell kiss.

Funny how things work out. Harold's death was such a blow to all three of them, that Helen and Steven changed their minds about the loft they'd found in the city, and had their movers reroute their belongings to the Hemingway mansion in River Forest. Their intention was to continue living with Miriam until life calmed down for her.

So there they were. Mother and daughter living in the same house once again.

Question: What's wrong with things going right?

Answer: The better they're going, the worse the turn will be.

Momentum reverses in on itself, and then flips.

Let's take what happened to the Clarks, for example. Here they were, newly married.

True, Helen's father, Harold, had died suddenly, but they were adjusting.

Steven had taken the job Harold had helped arrange before his death, that of professor of economics at the University of Chicago, and they remained living with Helen's mother on what was to be a temporary basis, but almost immediately took on a permanence.

The adjustment had been amazingly simple and actually therapeutic, since both women were keen on reinventing their relationship by forming a different kind of bond.

Mother and daughter realized successful accomplishment of this magnitude would require them to reestablish boundaries within the household. The women used this transformation as a healthy way to grieve in a positive and, at times, fun way because they both understood and enjoyed interior design. They went about redesigning some of the rooms to abolish bad memories. Miriam, for example, took the two guest bedrooms on the first level, as her new suite, leaving the entire second floor for Helen and Steven. What had been the Hemingways' master bedroom suite became Helen's studio, Helen's girlhood bedroom became Steven's study, two of the guest rooms were combined into one glorious suite for the newlyweds. The other was cleared for the baby that Steven and Helen were actively engaged in trying to conceive.

Miriam and Helen were in that future nursery, studying paint chits and fabric swatches when the call came.

*A doctor something spoke into Helen's ear, telling her that Steven was in the Emergency Room of the University of Chicago Hospital—car crash, trucks involved, critical condition.*

*Miriam drove the Eisenhower to Lake Shore Drive to Forty-Seventh, west to Cottage Grove, and south to Fifty-Seventh, while Helen used the car phone to contact Steven's primary physician, her father's personal physician, and two other influential family friends.*

*At the hospital, the women immediately were brought into Steven's private room where a myriad of top physicians were conferring. His heart is good. The rest of him is traumatized. Give him a kiss. Give him your prayers. We're taking him in.*

*Three days of surgeries followed. Miriam went home at night, back in the morning. Helen stayed.*

*On the third day, there was news.*

*The good was that Steven had suffered no permanent trauma to his upper body, his head, his heart, and his arms. Amazing.*

*The bad news was that his lower body had been mangled and might be partially paralyzed.*

*The good was there were new procedures and therapeutics that could possibly correct most of this.*

*The worst news was that Steven probably would be impotent.*

*His reaction to the impotency part was utter devastation. Helen had never seen anything like it. His face went slack; his eyes went dead. He was a stranger. He shut down in every way and would not speak. He was quickly sedated and out for the night.*

*Helen walked the corridors not noticing anything for hours. It was close to 10:00 p.m. when she turned one of those twilight zone corners. The place was being locked down. Visiting hours were ending.*

She didn't look up when she ran headlong into some man who uttered an apology and then stood staring at her. The man bent into her to make sure and then said, "Helen?"

"Yeah. That hurt. That really hurt," said Helen.

The man grabbed her and hugged her in a way that completely calmed her. She felt weak in the knees from the power of the hug and surrendered to the tenderness. She remained locked in the embrace, but backed up her face and looked into the turquoise-blue eyes of Max Shaw.

Max Shaw!

How was this possible? Why was he here? What did this mean? Don't let me go. Hold me like this.

Max whispered "What's happened to you, Helen?"

"Me? I..."

He led her into a darkened corner where they sat on a corridor couch.

"What's going on, Max? Did someone call you? Who would have done that? Why are you here?"

"Helen, I'm here because my wife, Janet, is six months pregnant and she's having some spotting, so she's being observed for a couple of days. I was just locating the room her doctor said I could sleep in. But you, why are you here? What's happened?"

Helen related the story. The end part, the part about not ever being able to have a baby with Steven moved Max to tears. She was so surprised at his reaction that she backed out of his embrace, held him at arm's length, and said, "What a reaction!"

Taken aback, he said, "What are you talking about? Are you implying that all those letters and phone calls and letters and flowers and letters meant anything other than how sorry I was about us not having our baby?"

"What phone calls? What flowers? What letters?"

"Oh my God. You didn't get any? Any of my attempts to reach you?"

She spoke in a zombie voice now as this news sunk in.

"Not one."

They stood facing each other, staring into each other's wounded eyes, unable to move or speak.

He was working his jaw, clenching his teeth to gain composure.

She was trying desperately to breathe without collapsing.

"Tried." He began, stopped, continued. "For the next four years, I tried. I tried until you went abroad."

"Abroad? I went to Berkeley."

"Berkeley! The word around town was that you went off to study in Paris and seldom came back."

"I skipped eighth grade, went straight into high school, and then went to Berkeley when I was sixteen."

"Christ. Berkeley. I was in Berkeley a couple of times during those years."

"We probably passed each other in the street."

"No. No, Helen. I would have felt your presence. I…just like tonight. I was restless because of Janet. But there was something else at play. I felt completely unsettled, just kept taking wrong turns trying to locate the room my doctor buddy said I could use to sleep a little. I…must have been finding you."

Helen was speechless. She'd just been told by the man who'd broken her heart that he hadn't done it purposely. In fact, quite the opposite. He thought she'd been the one to reject him.

The first love of her life firmly took her hand and quickly located the hospital room his doctor friend had suggested he use. Once inside, Max and Helen came together as if no time had passed at all and nothing had happened in the meantime to keep them apart.

At first he began kissing her to stop the tears. Then it was for love. And then they simply responded to each other like they had that one summer long ago.

She was ovulating. Touching her made him crazy—They were hot, cold, prickly, dizzy, desirous of one another.

Some things cannot be undone. In a way, though, some things seem to have a life of their own and almost exist despite convention.

Such was the fate at some point during the next three days of random stolen hours when a second conception was the result of Max and Helen's fierce love for each other.

They belonged to each other. Now that they were clear on that fact, Max convinced Helen that he could make up for all their sorry years of separation by giving her the baby she so desperately wanted. Helen and Steven had made love the last two nights before his accident with the purpose of beginning their family. It was uniquely possible for them to have conceived a child before Steven was rendered impotent by his tragic accident.

A simple plan. What were the chances?

By the end of the week, Max and Janet were back in New York. A month after that, Helen guaranteed Steven's emotional sanity by announcing that she was pregnant.

Camille was Max's compensation to Helen for all the years of torment she'd suffered over their unborn first baby. This would be their secret forever.

And this time around, when Helen became pregnant, her mother was overjoyed. The irony. The unbelievable irony was that Helen was, once again, pregnant with Max Shaw's baby. For Helen the deception was at times delicious and at others, the saddest tale in the world. What had really changed? Once she carried Max's baby and her mother forced her to abort it. The spirits of Helen and Max, and her mother and father had been wounded in the aftermath of that aborted baby. Now here they were again, she and her mother and Max Shaw's baby, but this time, instead of Harold Hemingway, the man of the house was Steven Clark. And Steven Clark believed the baby to be his.

This time, everyone wanted the baby.

And this time Helen was not relegated to her room or to extra studies. She was treated like a princess, pampered and cared for as the carrier of the most precious baby on earth. Knowing that this would be the one and only child in the family was impossible to ignore, so everyone just rose to their best selves for the nine-month gestation. After the treasured infant, Camille, was born, Helen nursed her for one year. Helen did not smoke or drink during those twenty-one months, and after that, she really didn't have a need to.

At 7:00 a.m. on this particular Wednesday in the year of 2007, it was Steven who woke Helen. He woke her by kissing her softly all over her face, and when she smiled and turned to take him into her bed, she was quite obviously startled and confused to see him. In her dream, she had been with Max.

"Whoa! Didn't mean to startle you, beautiful. But it's seven o'clock and we're meeting the Vertels in the lobby at nine thirty."

In a flash, the whole of yesterday infested itself into today "and probably all my tomorrows," thought Helen. She opened her arms to her husband and he bent down and hugged back.

"Want me to bring you some coffee?" Steven asked.

"No. Can't we just stay in bed all day...all week...all year?"

He kissed her on the cheek and moved back toward her door. "Coffee coming up."

"Yep," said Helen sarcastically. "Just another day to tolerate."

She hadn't finished brushing her teeth before Steven returned with her coffee and set it on her vanity. Helen looked at him coldly. "Exactly what does this day mean to you, Steven?"

"A day to get over. It's going to be rough. But by next week, most of us will be too involved with our own difficulties to put much thought into the deceased Max Shaw."

"Yep," said Helen again. "And what about his widow, Steven? How does she get on with her life?"

"Listen, Helen, don't go after me. I know you're taking this very hard—more than normal, I'd say..."

"What's that supposed to mean?"

"Well Jesus, Helen. He was a goddamn neighbor—a nice guy—a very nice guy—who obviously had major problems. I'm not all that surprised, to tell you the truth. The guy was a heavy, heavy drinker. And why would that be? Because he lacked coping skills, I'd imagine."

"Oh my God," yelled Helen. "Get out of my bathroom. Your thoughts are so condescending. As if you've never fucked up."

Steven tried to respond, but found himself being shoved out of the bathroom, the door slamming in his face. "Helen, for God's sake..."

"Look, Steven, just fuck off. Thanks for waking me. I'm going to take a really long shower and calm down and get dressed. And I'll see you at our front door at nine thirty."

"Well, actually, nine twenty-five," said Steven. "It'll take a few minutes to get down to the lobby. I imagine a lot of people in the building are going to this because Max was so well liked and..."

"Get away from my door, you moron," screamed Helen.

Helen took a tranquilizer from her sample pack, noticing she had another five left, which should certainly get her through the day, seeing as how the directions instructed taking one every four to six hours, which meant that, let's say, she took them every four, that would be: 7:00 a.m., 11:00 a.m., 3:00 p.m., 7:00 p.m., 11:00 p.m. That should do it, plus she had a prescription for thirty more from Dr. Cole, and she'd filled the Valium prescription from Dr. Savage, plus his other antidepression medications—but she wasn't about to start that whole thing with its "side effects" until all this horror was over. She would need to bring a bottle of water in her purse, which she better get while she was thinking about it—plus she needed more coffee anyhow.

She came out of her room and quietly entered the kitchen. Bad luck; there stood Steven. He glared at her. "Don't do that," she said. "I'm sorry I'm having a bad reaction, Steven."

"Helen, you needn't raise your voice. I can hear you, and so can everyone in the building probably."

"Stop it," she screamed as loudly as she possibly could. With shaking hands, she grabbed the water bottle out of the refrigerator, found a tray in the side cabinet and three mugs. She filled the mugs half with coffee and half with milk. She then took a deep breath and picked up the tray evenly, not sure she could manage bringing it all the way back to her bedroom desk. But she managed. Then she locked her door and began preparing for a day of torturous hell.

At 9:25, a beautiful woman named Helen Hemingway Clark emerged from her bedroom. She wore a black silk high-necked, capped-sleeved dress falling properly right below the knee, with a matching coat, pale stockings, and black patent leather high heels with a small matching purse. Wearing very little makeup and only her gold wedding band as jewelry, she was the picture of appropriateness.

Steven was waiting in the foyer. He watched her walk down the hall, smiled, and said what he meant as a compliment. "Well, hello, gorgeous. Your mother would surely be proud of her perfectly groomed-for-a-funeral daughter."

Helen stopped in her tracks. She held her nose to quell the onslaught of tears.

Steven looked crestfallen and went to hug her. She shrugged him off and fished for her sunglasses. "Steven, you don't tease a person who's distraught," she announced. "Let's go." And with that she brushed past him, opened the front door, and held it for him.

"Sorry," he said.

The elevator door opened to the disconcerting sight of a full load of black-clothed, grim-faced neighbors. In a heartbeat, the Clarks viewed the scene, gathered their stunned wits, and entered the elevator picture perfect, dressed to the nines, and softly smiling, uttering a quiet hello to all the others dressed in black.

As the elevator descended and stopped for more neighbors dressed in black, Helen finally noticed Steven. Steven looked his most amazing in black with his engraved white, white shirt, because of his black hair and black/brown eyes. He had a natural grace about him, perhaps partly because of his looks, and the assurance six feet gives a male.

But his charm also had to do with his attitude that life deals blows, and you soldier on. He held Helen's hand protectively. She took several deep athletic breaths.

Helen was flabbergasted at all the people in the lobby, but not Steven. Peter Vertel already had a cab waiting. Christy was chatty in the cab, Steven, responsive. Helen's best effort was to utter a polite uh-huh every once in a while. Peter quietly handled the cabby's directions and payment.

The church was near overflowing. Again, Helen was shocked. Christy managed to find a partially empty pew halfway up. The people in the church were muttering about how the priest would handle Max Shaw's death, since strict Catholics believed suicide could be a mortal sin. This meant that Max's soul could be in hell for eternity. Helen overheard a yapping neighbor in the pew behind them say, "Limbo." She turned around indignantly to tell her "wrong, Max was baptized," but Steven grabbed her hand firmly. He whispered sage advice into her ear. "She's ignorant, Helen. Let it go."

Helen turned to her handsome husband—the only man, now, who knew her well enough to talk her off the ledge. She whispered in his ear, "Whisper something else—that feels so good."

Steven smiled proudly and whispered, "Hey, baby, if you've taken any drugs, you really shouldn't drink at the luncheon today."

Helen immediately pulled away, furious at his patronizing coolness, his hypocritical ways. If he only knew the personal torture she was experiencing. She should have told him years ago. But now? What would be the point? She reached into her purse and located another sedative, coughed as she put it into her mouth and drank from her water bottle, just a little, so she wouldn't have to pee.

Now the newly widowed Janet Shaw was being supported by two of her nephews as they led her to the first pew. Helen's voice caught as she let out a little sob. Steven took her hand, back sliding his fingers in between hers, linking them, claiming his wife. He had no idea that the sob came from spotting Max's sister, Ruth, who was the only one, now alive, who knew some of the truth—the original Max-and-Helen story. And even she knew only half their story.

Now they were at the luncheon. They'd arrived ahead of almost everyone because of Peter's gift for hailing cabs and "getting the hell out of crowds." Max's widow, Janet, wasn't there yet, but her best friend, Patty, was. This was exactly what Helen wanted, someone who smoked and drank. She walked up to Patty and gave her a tender hug, telling her how sorry she was for her, and that Janet was lucky to have such a wonderful friend.

"How did the service go?" asked Patty. "I've been here making sure everything was set up properly."

There was a full bar right behind them. And ashtrays. Helen suggested that since everything was under control and Janet wouldn't be coming for a while (you should have seen the line of people waiting to hug her), that they might as well have a drink and a cigarette before the onslaught, and then she could answer all Patty's questions.

By the time Steven had used the men's room and had stopped to talk to several neighbors, Helen was on her second glass of wine and third Fantasia. He wore his blank expression to cover up his…what? Helen wondered. Was he angry or sympathetic?

Steven hugged Patty politely, and suggested to Helen that they get a table and then go talk with Janet who'd just arrived. Helen put out her cigarette and slid off the barstool. She gave her glass of wine to Steven to carry to the table for her, because, everyone knew that a lady does not walk with a drink in her hand.

Patty went immediately to Janet. The Clarks claimed a table and Steven drank most of Helen's wine so that she wouldn't. Helen didn't care because she saw all kinds of wine on all the tables. Patty and Janet were both heavy drinkers, so of course that would be covered. But so was everything else. Lovely centerpieces of Max's favorite flower, orange poppies, graced each of the fifty round tables of eight all draped in white linen. Four hundred people were expected. The food was extraordinary, but Helen had such a lump in her throat, she could barely swallow the wine—besides which she couldn't digest food comfortably when she was chemically altered.

The luncheon was truly impressive. Max's favorite nephew took the master of ceremony's role. There was no particular order to who spoke when. Person after person walked up to the microphone and told funny Max stories. He'd apparently never stopped being the class clown, nor had he retired his wild ways. His best friend since kindergarten, Buzz Shafer, spoke of Max, the little boy whose mother, rest her soul, had always encouraged his funny side because she got such a bang out of him. But after eighth grade, Max's dad—we hope he made it to heaven—just kidding—had sent Max to an elite boy's school in the East. His intention was to tame Max. But Max didn't see it that way (knowing laughter).

Many of his Eastern schoolmates had flown in to pay their respects, to tell story after story. Almost everyone had funny stories about his crazy side, about the mischief that got his friends grounded or campused but left him free to walk away laughing. The thing was that no one had ever minded because he was so much fun so spirited and just a nice guy. Funny as hell. One after another, his Princeton schoolmates came to the podium to tell charming stories about Max-the-scholar, who'd actually managed to get his BA degree. Max, though, he liked to call it his BABS degree as in Bachelor-of-Arts-Bull-Shit. It took him six years, because, well, just because he was Max and wanted to enjoy the ride of his youth.

Present-day colleagues came to the podium to laud Max. And loved ones tearfully said their good-byes.

At some point, Helen switched to water. She'd learned she could control her highs by stopping right before she was about to fall off the edge. Usually she chose to not control her highs, but only in small private gatherings with other drinkers. This was much too public a place.

Max Shaw's law firm partners spoke of his legendary abilities to mediate and arbitrate "in a fun way." He sometimes told people that he "redesigned" for a living. He "redesigned pandemonium into pleasure."

The condominium president also spoke of Max Shaw as the great mediator, the guy who could charm anyone into ending spats with their neighbors, could arrange for better deals for the upkeep of the place, the man who always seemed to be around to solve situations amicably.

The widow Janet rose from her family table and came to the podium, seeming to be in perfect harmony. She thanked everyone for honoring her Max so thoughtfully and beautifully. She said she loved the humor, because that was Max.

She began to thank her best friend from college for flying in from her office in Spain to be with her. Gracias, she began, apparently beginning a sentence in Spanish, but her voice cracked. The same two nephews who'd escorted her to her pew seat rushed up to escort her back to her table. And when she was seated, she turned to her friend and hugged her for a long time.

Afterward, Peter was the first to rise, as if to tell a joke at one of their memorable dinner parties. Everyone sat at attention, quietly waiting for his remarks, but Peter was obviously using self-control and needed to avoid losing it publicly. He rose, red-faced and sweating, and said, "Well, time to go."

That seemed to jostle the others out of their weariness and they began pushing back their chairs and rising too. Steven had been casually eyeing his watch for a good hour already, so he jumped at the chance to announce that he needed to get back to work.

Helen was wide-eyed. "You're going back to work?"

He looked at her and knew she needed him, but he was furious with her for drinking so much, even though she hadn't said or done anything inappropriate. So he said, "Yeah. Well some of us have to make money."

"No one I know," said Helen. "We can both be nasty if that's the game," she whispered, as she excused herself and took another tranquilizer in a stall in the ladies' room. She put on some lipstick and her serious expression.

By the time she came out, Peter was wiping his eyes, and her group had decided upon their course of action. The Vertels were going to walk home. The biggest drinkers at their table were going to drop Steven at the Union League Club for his meeting and had already invited several others to their place for "after" drinks. This was great news for Helen, who was doing everything she could to avoid thinking about her personal trauma—her history with Max.

Helen put her hand on Steven's back. "Steven, we've got to say something to Janet before we leave." He agreed and while the drinkers got their car, the Clarks approached Janet's table as she was getting up. She grabbed Helen and rather fiercely hugged her as she whispered in her ear, "Come over for a drink in an hour or so. I'm just inviting our favorites, and the family will be there of course." Helen breathlessly agreed as Janet let her go and was now giving Steven a less intimate hug.

She said, "Max liked you, Steven. I recall him saying that to me after the Randalls' dinner party. He said he thought you were stalwart and—how did he put it—sensibly loving to your family."

Steven was puzzled by this compliment but responded in kind. "Well, it's obvious from today that everyone liked Max. You take care of yourself," he said, and kissed her gently on the cheek. "We'll be in touch."

Helen suddenly realized that Janet Shaw would never ever be getting another kiss from the man she obviously dearly loved…And neither would she. She wiped a tear from her cheek, and managed a bleary-eyed "see you later," as she and her husband walked away together. She couldn't help herself from tearing, and now she needed to stop and blow her nose.

Steven reminded her that the car was probably waiting by now.

Helen fished a tissue from her purse and blew her nose as she spoke, "Did you want me to just keep walking with my nose running?"

Steven took hold of her upper arm firmly and, smiling for anyone watching, said, "You need to go home and sleep, Helen."

Helen patted Steven's hand that was leaving a vicelike mark on her arm, smiled the same kind of social smile her husband had put on, and whispered, "Fuck you, darling. You shouldn't be going back to, quote, work and leaving me alone."

She was clearly out of hand, but Steven thought that she would be even if he stayed with her, so why put himself through some kind of ordeal?

The three o'clock, sunshine hit Helen so harshly that she stumbled backward. She grabbed her sunglasses as Steven said, "Perfect."

Helen spoke aggressively. "What, Steven? What did you say, precious?"

The valet was holding the door for Helen to climb into the drinker-friend's backseat and Steven was on his way around to the other side to get in, when Helen spotted an empty cab and spontaneously hailed it.

"Hold on a minute," she called to her husband, "Let's take this cab to have a little private time." She leaned into the car. "Listen, we just need to be alone for a few minutes. You people go ahead and we'll meet up with..."

Steven interrupted her, "Look, I'm already running late," and got into the car.

Aghast at his insensitivity, Helen nevertheless waved the cabby away and allowed the valet to help her into the car. Humiliated, she pretend-listened to her phone messages to recover her dignity, while the others commented on the amazing job Janet had done.

When Steven got off at the Union League Club, he kissed Helen on her cheek, reminding her that she had her exercise class that night. Using a jokester voice, he said to the drinkers, "Now don't go getting my wife drunk before her class."

Ha, ha, ha from the drinkers.

That was it for Helen though. She said, "Why, honey, I was planning on getting really fucked up. So now, you just go about your crucial business and don't worry your pretty little head about this here grieving stuff."

The drinkers snickered. Steven gave Helen a withering look and then said, "See you later, smarty-pants. Thanks for the ride, Fred. Bye, Maggie."

Helen grabbed the door handle on her side and quickly shot out of the car. "See you back at the hood," she yelled to her friends.

Steven looked momentarily appalled, then quickly caught up with his wife at the club entrance and held the door for her.

He ushered her into an unoccupied sitting room and they faced each other in overstuffed chairs.

It's me again—just me, thought Helen. Once upon another life ago, two men loved me: There was Max who could have helped me through this tragedy if only he hadn't ironically caused it, and there was Steven, who, in the interest of himself, just attempted to ditch me.

We are truly—all of us—alone in this world.

Helen began their conversation. "Who leaves their mate on their own at a time like this?"

"You did," said Steven. "You already left by boozing yourself up like that."

Wide-eyed by his lack of civility, she clenched her teeth, desperately trying to not be hurtful back.

"Where is Helen?" taunted her husband.

"Listen, buddy," said Helen, "There is no moral high ground here, not on my end, but certainly not on yours either."

Silence.

Helen said, "Look, Steven, I can't just be abandoned. I know I've put up with that before, but it's not right of you.

"When was that, pray tell."

"When was *that*? After your accident you shut down to everyone but Camille. You emotionally abandoned me all those years, confusing your inability to make love with your refusal to behave lovingly. I might as well be your sister."

His color had risen as he watched her speak. "There's no helping you when you're like this..."

"Like what?" she interrupted. "What am I like? I'm in a heightened state of mourning. I'm trying to get through this as best I can. I..."

He interrupted back, "What exactly is it that you're so upset about, Helen? Christ, you act as if you've lost the love of your life."

She caught her breath.

He watched her become numb, become ashen, become still.

"Oh," he said.

Two minutes went by.

"Here's what I'm going to do," she said. "I'm going to tell you what I need from you and you'll either finally end the suppression, or you won't."

"Suppression?" he repeated hotly. "That's what keeps me going. If I stopped to analyze what I'm missing out on by not being able to, to perform..."

She interrupted. "To perform? To perform? Maybe that's the problem right there, Steven. Lovemaking is not a performance, Steven. It's being loving. Making love. It's not just physical. It's mental. There are so many ways to express tenderness. What about hugs and cuddles and kisses? The other night, Sunday, last Sunday night, you came up behind me at the kitchen sink and hugged me and kissed me so tenderly, and I just melted. You haven't done that in years. It felt so good..."

"Well I won't do THAT again," he said. "Wouldn't want you to get used to being pampered..."

"What the...why would you say that? Why are you behaving so adolescently?"

"Why are you?" he asked.

"I'm a mess," she said. "But right now, in this conversation, I am trying my damnedest to clear us up, to normalize us as a couple."

He said, "Last Sunday night I was caught off guard, Helen. My tenderness, as you call it, was an instinct. It was after the girls left for O'Hare, and you'd tried to figure out how to not call Max's death a suicide. I've never seen you so irrationally upset. I felt confused, and, and protective. I guess I was drawn to your vulnerability..."

"So what are you saying? That you don't feel tenderness toward me? That instinct just took over at that moment and really doesn't count?"

"I'm saying that I am not capable of feeling physically loving toward you because all it does is frustrate me. And I cannot live my life wanting what I am incapable of having."

"Nor can I," she said. "So that's it, then? We are forever platonic, and that's that; best friends but no touching? No touching at all? And that's fair to me—how?"

"Fair to you? Fair to YOU?"

She cleared her throat to calm herself. "Yes, Steven. What about me? I still have a healthy libido. So I live with the desire to be physical. You have conveniently shut yourself down and medicated yourself right out of the ball game."

"I CHOSE to do that?"

"Yes."

"What's this really about, Helen?"

She thought this through for a minute. "My need for attention and, um, tenderness. I need that, and you owe me that. Whatever else this is about may not be discussable."

Steven looked at his watch.

"Look," she continued, "I know you don't have a crucial meeting here at the club today. I know you can just appear in one of those dining rooms upstairs and some friends or other will beckon you over to join them. I know that's one of your escapes. And it really troubles me that you would abandon me at a time like this. It's so selfish..."

"Here we go," said Steven. "Now I'm selfish."

She stared at him.

He glared at her.

A few minutes passed in this way.

"OK, I tried," she said, rising with her purse in hand. "I guess I'll see you back at our place sometime later."

He rose to escort her.

She now looked determined. "Well, I'll say this, Steven. Our conversation may not have solved much, but it has somehow grounded me a bit, perhaps just to speak openly about my loneliness..."

"Poor you," he said.

She remained motionless, so many possible retorts swirling in her mind.

She smiled sadly. "Yep. Poor me, for sure. All the tea in China."

She leaned up to kiss her man on his cheek. "I do love you, honey."

"Is this it, then?" he asked hoarsely. "Are we done here?"

She stared.

"Sure," she said, and turned and left.

Helen cabbed home, breathless with relief that she'd been able to voice her feelings and, despite her husband's belligerence, to end in a nonaggressive and loving manner. She considered continuing this maturity by going home, but found herself escaping to Fred and Maggie's—sipping wine in no time.

Fred was opening a second bottle of wine when Christy Vertel opened the door, saying, "Knock, knock." He pulled up a chair for her and poured her some wine as Christy explained that Peter wouldn't be joining them because the day was very rough on him and he needed some alone time… couldn't seem to get hold of the fact that Max Shaw took his own life.

Helen burst out sobbing. Maggie was sitting next to her on the couch and immediately patted her shoulder, saying, "Oh dear, aw, there, there."

"I'm sorry," said Helen. "I just don't understand why Max…why really good, extraordinarily nice people, who try their hardest, have to go through the kind of internal agony that would lead to…"

The other three couldn't quite hide their astonishment at this sudden outburst and looked at Helen as if to say, what planet are you from. But they quickly covered their city cynicism by comforting her.

Maggie softly said, "I know," and rubbed Helen's back for a while, and Fred said, "How about it," as he refilled Helen's glass.

Christy looked at her watch and said, "Wow, look at the time. We should probably go on up to the Shaws'—well,

Janet's place. She did invite all of us particularly, so we should..."

"Yes," agreed Maggie. "Absolutely."

The Shaws' place was filled. Helen checked her watch. Then she hiccupped. "Good lord," she said. "I'm supposed to be at my water exercise class in forty minutes!"

A friend came over with glasses of wine for both of them.

"Thank—hiccup—you," said Helen. "—Hiccup—Christ, I haven't hiccupped for years—hiccup—" She could feel someone staring at her and turned to see Max's sister, Ruth. They locked eyes as Ruth approached her.

Helen hiccupped. She put her wine down and gently hugged Ruth. They were both quietly crying. Ruth didn't seem to want to let go. "God, am I glad to see you," she said as she broke away at last. "I'm so drained. So tired of the pretense."

Helen hiccupped. "What—hiccup—do you mean?—Hiccup—"

She put her wine down and grabbed a bottle of water from one of the ice buckets. She twisted off the cap as Ruth rubbed her foot and slipped it back into her high heel. They meandered into a corner of one of the doorways for privacy.

"Helen...I've wanted to talk to you so many times," said Ruth.

"Every July, I'll bet," said Helen. "—Hiccup—"

Ruth rubbed her other foot. "Well, yeah. And all the times Max begged me to find out where you were."

Helen said, "Ruth, honey, change your shoes, for God's sake. Put on some flats—hiccup—"

"OK, but please don't move. I'll be right back."

Max's best friend since kindergarten approached Helen. "Helen, you look wonderful," he said, kissing her cheek.

Helen kissed him back. "Well so do you, Buzz."

Buzz said, "You always were gorgeous. But you sure look sad..."

Helen burst into tears and began hiccupping again. "Well, for God's sake, Buzz. So—hiccup—do you—hiccup—"

Buzz whispered in her ear, "You know he never did get over you, Helen. Did you know that?"

"—Hiccup—Let's not go there, Buzz—hiccup—"

Ruth returned. Now Buzz turned to Ruth and said, "I was just telling the beautiful Helen that your big brother never got over her."

Ruth blushed and said, "We've all been drinking since noon, Buzz. It would never be appropriate to say that to anyone else, or have anyone overhear you. Least of all Janet."

Helen hiccupped.

Buzz shrank a bit and apologized. "Jesus, I...I'm so upset."

Helen glanced at her watch and hiccupped. "Oh my God, I've got ten minutes to get into my suit and be upstairs for my water exercise class—hiccup—"

Ruth looked crestfallen.

Buzz said in her condition she'd probably sink.

Helen said to Ruth, "I'll be back, honey. The class is only an hour."

Ruth looked doubtful. Her eyes were so, so sad. They hugged once more, knowing they'd probably not see each other again.

"Gotta go," she said to people she passed on the way out. "Exercise—hiccup—class."

Helen rushed into her unit, throwing her clothes off as she grabbed a bathing suit and made it to the toilet, where she peed for what seemed like an hour. She multitasked by putting her hair in a ponytail and rubbing her tongue with toothpaste while peeing. She pulled up her suit, threw on her long white terry-cloth robe, stepped into her rubber wedgies, grabbed a water out of the refrigerator, and was upstairs in the pool only five minutes late.

Her fellow classmates made various comments about not expecting to see her. She responded by hiccupping and asking why. "I'm drunk," she announced, "so just don't let me sink to the bottom—hiccup—"

Having been a varsity swimmer in high school, Helen could not help but be competitive in the water, so even though she was filled with drugs, tobacco, and alcohol, she managed to not only keep up but also talk and hiccup at the same time, keeping her class amused and herself from thinking about Max. Helen Clark had figured out many strategies to keep from thinking about Max Shaw, but still, when she died many years later, her very last thought would be of him, and of them. Max and Helen. Helen and Max. And she would hear the beautiful achingly clear voice of Whitney Huston singing, *"I will always love you."*

*Normal day, let me be aware of the treasure you are.*
*Let me not pass you by in quest of some rare and perfect tomorrow.*
~ Mary Jean Irion ~

*Men and women, women and men. It will never work.*
~ Erica Jong ~

# THURSDAY

At 2:00 a.m. on Thursday morning, Helen woke hungover and confused about the boozy end of Wednesday evening. At first, she thought she was back in the 2:00 a.m. of months earlier—the night that ended any question about what was leading where.

She smiled with excitement at the memory.

*Having completed her laps, she climbed the pool stairs and saw him sitting at the deep end, dangling his feet in the water, watching her in that way that made her blush.*

Sharp breath intake. "You. Startled me."

"You amaze me," he said.

"What are you doing here?"

"Being amazed. Being utterly turned on," he said.

"What're you lookin' at?"

Big sexy heavy-lidded smile. "Nothin'," he said.

"Mmmmmmm."

"What?" he asked.

"Um. Well." She sank back into the water. He dived in and was at the shallow end embracing her within seconds. She didn't even think about refusing him.

They reenacted their very first swim together. That first innocent encounter could not be duplicated. But water play performed by mature adults who still had the same insatiable desire for each other lengthened and heightened their pleasure.

When they finally went to the sauna to calm down, it reminded them of those hot summer days of long ago in Max's garage, leading them to further exploration, intensified by experience. Their timing and their moves prolonged the pleasure and brought it to a whole new level. Max said, "Peace out, sugar," just as he did that long-ago summer.

From then on, their 2:00 a.m. rendezvous became the focus of their day.

"Here I am, lookin' at you lookin' at me."

"Blue skies, baby."

This delirium occurred every Monday, Wednesday, and Friday for about three and a half months, until Camille came home on holiday the Friday before last.

Thoughts of the now rushed into her brain as she peeled off the covers, and dragged herself into the diner/kitchen where the remnants of wine and cigarettes sat on the counter under the Neon EAT sign. She did herself the favor of erasing the evidence (the morning would be bad enough) as she consumed the required cookies and milk. Afterward, she padded back through the darkness, never really dark because of the magical city lights, where she sunk back into bed, safely tucked under her heavy velvet quilt.

Since Max Shaw's eulogy was on her mind, the eulogy she'd given her mother seventeen years ago came to her. Back in 1975, when Mr. Hemingway died, Mrs. Hemingway began handling his investments from his office on LaSalle Street and continued up until her death in 1990. All but her best friends and family thought of this as a surprising outcome if there ever was one. Who would have thought, in a million years, that Miriam Hemingway could possibly take over her husband's work, the peripherals marveled.

But of course she did: She was intellectually challenged for the first time in her life. She thrived on it, blossomed, and showed great humility whenever anyone complimented her accomplishments. She attributed her vast knowledge of stocks to having been raised in a family of stock traders, coupled with her husband's habits of twenty-three years: Harold's joy was to come home after work and relax with his wife over a cocktail or two, describing his day in minute detail, basking in the attention of Miriam, who not only actually understood what he was talking about, but had been raised to listen attentively, and converse appropriately. In short, Mr. Hemingway's daily confidences became a wealth of knowledge for Mrs. Hemingway, and she put it to good use for the next fifteen years.

Ever since her husband's death, Miriam Seymour Hemingway had come into her own, showing her strength and originality.

And ever since her father's deathbed revelations, Helen had become close with her mother.

One time when they were up late, drinking and smoking, Miriam raised the issue of her funeral. Helen objected, but her mother insisted, because she had definite requests. They ended up planning and goofing around until 5:00 in the morning.

The next day, over morning coffee at noon, Miriam asked Helen to keep all the notes she'd taken because even though it had been fun and silly cooking up "the plan" last night, those really were her wishes.

Helen drew strength from her mother's life story. Miriam Seymour Hemingway came from a long line of men whose business was the Chicago stock market. Every Sunday, there would be a family gathering at the senior Seymour mansion. Cocktails would begin at four. Her grandfather, her father, and her father's brother would gather by the fireplace in the den to discuss the market. The three wives would be in the kitchen, drinking wine and sharing news while preparing the meal.

Even as a little girl of eight, Miriam felt detached from the kitchen talk.

So she figured out a way of gaining acceptance in the den with the men and their wild talk of stock market numbers and changes and politics and the resulting impact on Chicago, the country, and Europe. She'd wait until the men were settled into the den and carefully walk into the room carrying a silver tray of hors d'oeuvres, which she offered each man in turn as they remarked on her grace, and then she would quietly sit down. She was a good listener, and a darling little girl, so she was allowed to stay.

At ten she worked up the nerve to ask one simple question, which her grandfather thought so clever that he answered it at length. This encouraged her to ask other simple questions of how they did whatever it was they did, and this developed into a bonding experience for everyone involved. All the men, Grandpa Luke Seymour, Uncle Ben Seymour and her father, Henry, got such a kick out of little Miriam's retention of not only rudimentary facts, but basic lingo, that soon they were sharing their "tricks of the trade."

Amassing this knowledge enabled Miriam to excel not only at math, but more importantly, critical thinking. This, coupled with her awareness of local and national affairs, caused her to surpass her peers in school. But, partly out of humility, and partly at her mother's prompting (never appear brighter than the rest if you want to be accepted among them), Miriam learned to keep a low profile.

She was a tomboy because of the only-child-spending-time-with-your-dad-who-sometimes-wished-you-were-a-boy thing. She played endless hours of catch with her father in their backyard, and he taught her how to golf. Back in Miriam's day, only swimming and archery were offered for girls in high school, so she excelled in those.

Miriam fit the profile of traders being ex-athletes, of trading being, in many ways, a sport.

Nine years later, the men in her life introduced seventeen-year-old Miriam to the new kid on the block, and a favorite of theirs, the handsome thirty-five-year-old trader, Harold Hemingway, and soon after that, he too was welcomed into the Sunday ritual. Harold Hemingway married Miriam Seymour seven months later. Helen was "prematurely born" six months after their wedding. This shocking turn of events tamed Miriam's high spiritedness into submission, where it stayed for a long, long time.

*It's 1990 and Helen enacts her mother's explicit eulogy plan. Since neither Miriam nor Helen had much connection with organized religion, the plan was for Helen to eulogize her mother in the old Board of Trade room, which had been dismantled and painstakingly reassembled in a custom-built addition on the east side of the Chicago Art Institute by a highly financed group of history and architecture lovers.*

*And, now, there stood Helen, on the very stage behind the very desk in the very room where her mother's young grandfather had begun his career, never dreaming that generations of his family would follow in his footsteps, most especially not a female.*

*Helen took the liberty of changing only one part of her mother's wishes, and that was a one-minute reflection on Miriam's accomplishments.*

She looked at all the friends who filled the round tables with combination centerpieces of white tulips, daisies, and roses, on crisp white linen tablecloths. Most people looked sad, so she smiled. "Good evening, friends," she said. "Two days ago, I lost one of my best friends, my mother, Miriam Hemingway." Helen paused to control herself. "She died in her sleep, a happy, fulfilled woman, loved by many and cherished by her family."

She swallowed past the lump in her throat and continued. "Miriam Hemingway was a complicated woman who believed she'd been lucky enough to have two amazingly fruitful adult lives, one as a wife and stay-at-home mother, followed by the other as a strong businesswoman. She appreciated having the inner strength to explore her worth as a young widow.

"What we see and do tonight is what she herself, decided was the way a funeral ought to be, for her anyhow. So we've gathered in the reconstructed Trading Room of the old Chicago Stock Exchange Building on North LaSalle Street. It was designed by Adler and Sullivan, erected in 1894, demolished in 1972, and now is replicated here. This room is symbolic of generations of Seymour traders, including Miriam Seymour Hemingway herself, after her husband died.

"When my father died, fifteen years ago, I was grown and had just married my husband, Steven. It was as if, in one year, Miriam not only lost the love of her life, but also all her jobs. She was pretty much done mothering, done planning and executing my wedding, and then she was no longer a dedicated wife.

"At thirty-nine, she was still plenty young, but certainly old enough to realize that if she surrendered to the depression of a kind of 'forced retirement,' it would be a long hard climb out, so she acted on that wisdom. Because of her background and her evening discussions with her husband, it took her less than a month to learn his office procedures and take over.

"Now at this point, Miriam would want me to stop talking and get on with the show. She'd probably say, 'Less is more,' or use her favorite line, 'Never complain, never explain.' But she's not up here...But she's not here, so I will explain, because she should be recognized for her achievements.

"And now, what I want to do is simply tell you what she meant to me, after which we will get on with the show.

"My mother was a stoic. When she became a wife and mother at the tender age of seventeen, she set her mind to enduring life with spirit and attention. She did whatever was necessary to care for and protect her loved ones. My dad and I tied for first place.

"She told me once that because she was married and a mother at such a young age, she and I sort of grew up together in many ways. She could be so wonderfully childlike. And even after years of living, she was still able to get silly and play and giggle with her cherished granddaughter, Camille. My mother was loving and funny and stern and serious.

"It was the serious Grandma Hemingway who set up an account for piano lessons for Camille's fourth birthday present. Little Camille felt so grown up and important that she herself reacted very seriously. She became the teacher's little darling as she earnestly paid attention at lesson time, and she practiced religiously.

"Miriam and her son-in-law, Steven, blew all the negative stories and jokes about 'the mothers-in-law from hell' clear out of the water. The two of them enjoyed each other's wit and wisdom from the first.

"Miriam was a true feminist, never a martyr, and unwilling to be victimized, she quietly and gracefully learned to achieve her goals alongside the men and mostly without struggle. She didn't see the point of trying to 'get even' with men for centuries of oppression by belittling them. 'They just needed to get the picture and proceed in a less threatening manner' was what she told me.

"I watched her behave in that genteel way many times, and very few men responded negatively to her civility. Miriam believed that men and women are very different creatures. She applauded and enjoyed those differences, and, because of this, they always treated her with great respect.

"She didn't whine. We all have our share of traumas, and she handled hers with loyal dignity. She didn't cry. She simply hunkered down and did whatever it took to handle whatever was happening. If her choice was an unpopular one, she rode out the protests, determined to handle her responsibilities and achieve a good outcome. My dad was one of her good outcomes. I am another.

"And now, dear friends, I ask you to fill your glasses with Miriam Seymour Hemingway's favorite wine, a 1961 French Bordeaux, and enjoy what she requested be your final memory of Miriam in all her glory with all of you."

Helen descended the three steps on stage right as Camille ascended the three steps, stage left, and walked a few feet to the grand piano. Camille smiled at their guests and sat ready for the performance. The lights dimmed as a spotlight followed a Kate Smith look-alike who walked on stage and stood to the side of a projection screen that was being lowered over the famous wall clock at center stage, between the two original Trading Room blackboards. In big, bold letters, one blackboard read, "IT'S NOT OVER" and the other, "TILL THE FAT LADY SINGS."

The screen began running slides of Miriam, beginning with her childhood home, the Seymour estate in Lake Forest.

In all her large glory, "Kate" bowed slightly to Camille as they began their performance. *"God Bless America,"* Kate belted out.

*"Land that I love."*

*"Stand beside her, and guide her"*

~ A slide shown of Miriam as a baby, being cuddled by her mother.

*"Thru the night with a light from above."*

~ Miriam as a happy little girl posing with her friends and parents at her Montessori school picnic.

*"From the Mountains, to the prairies,"*

~ Miriam sitting on Santa's lap with her parents lovingly watching.

*"To the Oceans, white with foam"*

~ Miriam with her best friends at their grammar school graduation.

*"God Bless America, My home sweet home."*

~ Miriam working with her classmates as the high school yearbook editor.

*"God Bless America,"*

~ Miriam posing with the chess club.

*"Land that I love."*

~ Miriam as a beaming high school graduate.

*"Stand beside her, and guide her"*

~ The tender bride, Miriam, posing with her husband, Harold.

*"Thru the night with a light from above."*

~ The young mother, Miriam, happily holding her sweet baby, Helen.

*"From the Mountains, to the prairies"*

~ The three of them, smiling away, Miriam and Harold, with little Helen in the middle.

*"To the Oceans, white with foam."*

~ Miriam with her book club friends.

*"God Bless America, My home sweet home."*

~ Miriam and Harold with their bridge club friends.

*"From the Mountains, to the prairies,"*

~ Miriam throwing a surprise birthday party for her husband.

*"To the Oceans, white with foam"*

~ Miriam with her volunteer group at the hospital.

*"God Bless America, My home sweet home"*

~ Miriam baking cookies with seven-year-old Helen's Brownie troop.

*"From the Mountains, to the prairies,"*

~ Miriam and Harold all dressed up for New Year's Eve.

*"To the Oceans, white with foam"*

~ Miriam as the room mother of Helen's fourth grade class.

*"God Bless America, My home sweet home."*

~ Miriam and Harold teaching Helen how to golf.

*"God Bless America, My home sweet home."*

~ Miriam, surrounded by family friends, presenting the twelve-year-old Helen with her birthday cake.

*"Gahhhhd"*

~ Miriam and Harold with Helen and Steven at their wedding.

*"Blessssss"*

~ Miriam and a very pregnant Helen, holding hands at Helen's baby shower.

*"A-me-ri-ca"*

~ Thirty-nine-year-old Miriam dressed in black at her husband's funeral.

*"Myyyyy home"*

~ Forty-year-old Miriam dressed in a crisp navy-blue suit, at work in her late husband's office.

*"Sweeeet home."*

~ Miriam with her Helen and Steven and Camille, posed in front of the River Forest family estate they shared.

Helen awoke later Thursday morning in such tender spirits that all she could do was cry. She missed her mother. She missed her father. She missed her best friend, Other. She missed her so much that she found herself foolishly wishing she'd never met her, because the flip side of having best friends is the possibility of losing them.

Helen recalled when that flip had begun.

*It was on a Friday, back in 1985, that Other casually told Helen she'd be gone for the couple of weeks of spring break, and that the worst part was she'd be missing the next Girls' Night In. "One of the others can play my part," she suggested.*

Helen said that no one could do it like Other. "How could I possibly get into that silly state of mind without my best friend?" she complained.

Other said, "Nonsense. Everyone's replaceable."

But no. They're really not.

When Lincoln School resumed classes that spring, it was Other's husband, Ted, who dropped off Lucy and Charlie, and it was Ted who collected them after class, both times in his car. He gave Helen and Camille a smile and wave, but didn't stop to talk.

And when Helen called Other, Ted answered. He said something about the nasty flu that Other might have picked up in Mexico. "You know how she is when she's sick," he said.

Helen told him that no, she didn't. She'd never even seen Other sick, let alone bedridden.

He got off the line by telling her Other would call her back as soon as she was up to it.

"Up to it," said Helen. "She can't talk on the phone?"

"She's on heavy medication and sleeps most of the time," was Ted's answer.

Helen had Other's favorite flowers (birds of paradise) delivered.

Charlie delivered a "thank you" note to Camille, sent by his mom to give to her mom. The handwriting was uncharacteristically messy, but the message soothed her tremendously.

"I miss you like crazy," said the note. "I shall call as soon as I'm up to it."

Up to it. A week went by, during which Helen became more and more agitated as each day passed with no call from Other.

Over bananas and milk, Helen asked Camille how Charlie was doing these days. Camille was thoughtful. Her face was sad as she answered that she thought Charlie didn't want to be her friend anymore, because he mostly sat alone.

"I sit with Polly and Madison at lunchtime, but I miss talking with Charlie a lot."

"No more of those earnest conversations?" asked her mother.

"No more," whispered Camille.

With dread, Helen walked up to Ted's car the next day as he waited for school to get out. "Ted," she said, "I know how private you guys are, and I respect that. I mean Steven and my mom and Camille and I are the same way about our problems. But, Ted, don't you think it's time to let me help you with this 'flu situation'? I mean, I haven't laid eyes on my best friend or even heard her voice for almost a month."

Ted told her that they appreciated everyone allowing them to close ranks and get over this privately.

"What kind of flu is this?" asked Helen sarcastically. "I miss her. And I'm concerned, really, actually consumed with worry, even dread."

Ted responded with an annoying near-lecture about how his wife would be appalled at the notion that anyone was giving off "bad vibes" about her.

"End of the line here, buddy," said Helen. "She's my best friend. Tell her I'm coming over tomorrow when the kids are at school."

They were both clearly out of their element. Ted thought he was protecting his wife. And Helen knew she had a right to help her dearest friend.

Helen told Ted that love wasn't just a matter of receiving, that the giving was just as important to the soul, and that she needed to help.

"Please consider that," she said.

As their kids approached, their parents both smiled widely, sparing the innocent.

Helen gave Lucy and Charlie hugs and kissed them lovingly on their tender cheeks, and she and Camille joined hands for their walk home.

That night, Helen received the relief of Other's phone call. She said she was finally getting better, though her shaky voice betrayed her. It would only be a week or so before she'd be up and about. But hey, why didn't Helen come on over and visit tomorrow when the kids were in school. Say around noon.

Helen appeared with a dinner for the family to enjoy later. She handed it to Ted as she kissed him on the cheek. He grabbed her arm and told her to brace herself. She ran up the stairs to Other's room. What she saw before her was a much thinner Other, radiant with the help of an IV running fluids into her body. Her eyes were huge and sparkling, her skin translucent.

Helen barely managed hello. She entered the room as if in a trance and moved in a kind of slow motion to the untangled, tubeless side of the bed.

"This is me dealing with my second bout of cancer," Other whispered. "I completely recovered from my mastectomy, and was supposedly 'cancer-free' when I met you four years ago."

"I see," said Helen, as she bent to gently kiss her friend on her damp forehead.

"This time though. This time I think it's 'blinds,'" whispered Other.

Helen smiled and said that it was not curtains. She walked to the window and blew her nose. "It's not over till the super-size-me lady sings."

"The fat lady is gonna sing," said Other. "I'm on a bagel here."

"No," said Helen. "You're not on a roll. Your performance is too exaggerated."

"I'm not being melodramatic," Other insisted. "Confront the information."

"I won't face the facts," said Helen.

Helen and Helen got as goofy as they could manage.

Helen insisted that Other let her help Charlie. "He wears his serious face almost all the time," she told his mother. "He's obviously upset. He's not even playing with Camille."

Other agreed immediately.

"Well, why didn't this come up before?" asked Helen indignantly.

"Now is now," said Other.

"Better late than later," said Helen.

"The early bird misses some sleep."

"Wake up and smell the water."

"Why put off today what you can also put off tomorrow."

And they were off again.

Bolstered by lightheartedness, Other allowed Helen into her last days. She was up and running for about a month before her system began collapsing upon itself. During that last good month, she and Ted made the arrangements for his and their children's life without her. She told them over and over how she knew they would pull together and find many joys in each other. She told each of them privately how much love the father and daughter and son shared, how very much they respected each other. She hinted that the future could hold some wonderful woman to complete their family, thus granting them the freedom to love again.

She spoke to Helen about her talent. She made her promise that she'd never go more than a day or two without working in her studio.

One day Helen persuaded the other Helen and Ted and Lucy and Charlie to dress in their favorite clothes and pose for a slew of pictures. She flanked Other with her two men and her little lady, all smiling in their love.

Then she began a portrait of the four of them, using the photos so they wouldn't have to sit and pose too often. She worked on the portrait night and day, so that Other would get to see it.

Ted hung the portrait on the wall facing his wife's bed, and every night when it was bedtime, Other would ask her little lady and her big and little men if, just this one night, they could all cuddle in bed and sleep together. They'd fall asleep talking and looking at their beautiful portrait.

The best friends had several heart-to-hearts. Other encouraged Helen to find her own happiness apart from the sacrifices she made for her little girl and her husband and her mother. She broached the delicate subject of sex with a story on herself.

"Ya know what? The best part of my radical mastectomy was that the nerves in my breasts were severed. I've always had such sensitive nipples that, before that, I was in an almost constant state of arousal. I missed that at first, and then one day I realized that the whole thing probably normalized me. I wasn't on fire every time anything brushed up against my breasts. I honestly had a great couple of years of feeling less like a nymphomaniac, before the cancer returned.

"We've never shared this kind of talk," she told Helen. "But I'm fairly certain you have needs that aren't being met."

"Yeah, well, that's life," said Helen.

"Uh, uh," countered Other. "A lot of couples have good consistent sex as a normal healthy part of their lives. It's a craving that needs to be satisfied, just like hunger and sleep and cerebral stimulation."

"No one's ever said that to me," replied Helen.

"Well, I'm so very surprised," said Other sarcastically. "I wish I'd said something sooner. Then I could have had the joy of watching you connect with a lover. Ah well."

"Well I'll tell you this much," said Helen. "You wouldn't have watched me do that, so don't go up there thinking that. Nope. It would take mountains to move me in that direction."

"Maybe I'll become a mountain for a couple days, then," teased Other.

"Don't you think though," said Helen, "that part of our charm was not trying to fix the past or the present, but just making it a little more fun? Our charm was that we refused to be stuck in our past traumas, refused to even share them, but instead, we created and shared all the gaiety we could."

Other tearfully agreed.

"And you, Helen Hemingway Clark, you've enriched my life in so many ways I can't even begin to count them. You know anyhow. Once or twice in a lifetime, you find a sister who connects with you, dearest best friend. The pleasure we've had with one another is rare, and I thank you for letting me into your very private life. We were best pals from the day we met…four years of the friendship of a lifetime. Four years more than many people ever get." She grimaced in pain, and pushed the morphine button.

Helen kissed the best friend she'd ever had good night, which turned out to be a kiss good-bye.

The last thing Helen remembered before sleeping through the rest of Thursday morning, was the famous Helen and Helen fight.

*It was a Tuesday, grocery day, so they were in Other's station wagon, bound for Treasure Island, and Helen was going over her perfectly printed grocery list, when, in a crabby voice Other said "Who organizes food groups on a list according to the aisles of the grocery store."*

"Pardon me?" said Helen.

"I said, who makes a perfect shopping list for God's sake? You must think you're just perfect."

"No, I don't," said Helen.

"Yeah, right," said Other. "Well I'm sick of it. You, and your good moods, and your effortless beauty, and your ability to do anything you want."

"Give me a break, Other."

"That's the last thing you need. Your whole life has been a holiday. You pull off this living thing so effortlessly."

"It takes more effort to be me than you could possibly grasp," said Helen darkly.

"Poor baby," said Other.

They came to a red light. Helen grabbed her purse and jumped out, slamming the door behind her. "This, I don't need," she said. "Ba-Bye." She seemed to be walking easily down the street, when in fact she was trying not to shake as she headed home.

Other pulled to the side and was watching her in her rearview mirror. She got out of her car and yelled, "What are you doing?"

Helen turned around and yelled, "Getting away from you, you nutcase." They began walking toward each other as she continued. "You think you're so together you can lecture me? Well, sister, I've just drawn a line in the sand. Get back on your side."

Other fished through her purse. "OK. Sure. But before I get back on my side, here's our lunch money, since it was my turn. You can eat for two like you usually do but still don't gain a pound. What are you, bulimic?" She threw some bills and change in Helen's direction. The coins made it to Helen's feet, but the bucks blew back into Other's face and one stuck to her lipstick.

They both giggled.

Helen threw her entire purse at Other. "Here. Not only do I not want your money, but you can have mine too."

Other caught Helen's purse as she threw hers at Helen.

"That was stupid. Where's the fair trade?" she said. "In this case, you'd be America and I'd be China."

"Oh! Good one! But let's examine your stuff, China," yelled Helen as she dumped the contents of Other's purse onto the sidewalk. "Following your dense analogy, China, wouldn't you want to take my stuff and also keep yours?"

She bent down, scooped several items back into Other's purse, and began sorting through the wallet as she said, "I'll play my American part by keeping your credit cards for binge shopping, ensuring that I stay in debt by never paying off the balance. You'd better keep your driver's license though, China, since your country is a stickler for papers." She studied Other's picture and smiled. "How does one manage to look sexy in their driver's license picture? In fact, come to think about it, how does the worst driver on the planet manage to get one of these? Was it sexual favors?"

Other smirked, though she fought against it. "Sexual favors," she repeated. "What century are you from?"

During this "showdown," it was slowly dawning on Helen that Other was playing some kind of game.

Other confirmed this by saying, "Well, finally some proof that you're human. You're temperamental just like everyone else, but you never show that side of yourself. Show it more often, tight-ass." And she grinned her famous sarcastic grin.

"Also," she continued, "now we're even for what you put me through that first day I tried to be your friend. God, were you merciless. And funny. So funny. I couldn't stop laughing once I realized the number you played on me that day."

By this time both women were laughing so hard that Other had to hold her hand over her chest to calm herself down and get some air. And Helen was crossing her legs so she wouldn't wet her pants right there on North Avenue.

The memory caused Helen to have to get out of bed to pee, and, for some strange reason, when she fell back into bed, her memory began tracking all the baby stories in her life…maybe because a key scene occurred right after Other's death.

*First she remembered 1965: Helen is twelve years old, and pregnant. Miriam is twenty-nine years old, and her mother.*

Twelve-year-old Helen Hemingway began what was to be her final plea to give birth to her baby. "This couldn't be the only case of a young girl getting pregnant, Mother. Other families must have coped with this, she pleaded. Couldn't, couldn't you and, couldn't you and Daddy raise my baby? Couldn't that somehow work? I mean, I could help a lot, all the time. I could do all the work. We would just live with you. But I'd do all the work."

"Anything's possible," her mother answered. "But you're too young to see the complications down the road. You're too young to understand even if I did tell you all the reasons why this wouldn't be in your best interest, and why I shouldn't get involved."

"Involved? Where's…where's God's involvement?" asked the confused young girl.

"Where was he in the first place?" was her mother's reply.

*Next she remembers 1985: Helen is thirty-two. Miriam is forty-nine. Camille is nine. Helen's dear friend, Other, has recently died, so she's unusually sensitive to losing her loved ones. Helen's mother, Miriam, is aware of her daughter's anguish and is trying her hardest to somehow help her through her grief. Miriam has the bright idea of each of them renting one movie as a conversational tool to make sense of their past.*

Helen popped the corn and melted the butter as Miriam made the martinis.

"So what movie did you choose, Mom?"

"*Chinatown*," she announced brightly.

For some reason, this annoyed Helen. "*Chinatown*! How in the heck is that relevant to our evening of enlightenment?"

"You'll see."

Together, they prepared the silent butler. Miriam filled the upper tier with the mixings for Martinis and Helen slid the tray of movie snacks into the second level as she spoke. "I've seen the movie, Mom, several times. It's a Roman Polanski classic, for God's sake."

"Well if you're so knowledgeable about the film, Miss Movie Buff, then you should easily be able to figure out why I chose it."

Helen wheeled the silent butler into the TV room and placed the contents of the tray on the coffee table as she pondered her mother's movie choice.

Miriam followed, balancing their first round of prepared drinks, while also carrying the video and her cigarette case as she too wondered about her bright idea.

"Here's a thought, Mom. Since I've seen it and you've seen it, maybe we could cut to the chase and…"

Miriam had that look of obstinacy, but Helen plowed on.

"…discuss it, discuss its relevance to us, without the two-hour downtime of watching the whole movie."

"Do you honestly remember it all that well, Helen?"

"Yes. I do. Basically, John Huston gives a stunner performance as evil, playing to Faye Dunaway's marvelously skittish victim, and Jack Nicholson gives a flawless performance as the detective who uncovers the hideous but fascinating web of secrets that ultimately brings down the whole sorry house of cards. Brutal ending. There are no winners. The film is brilliantly written by Robert Towne, and directed by Roman Polanski, who also has an acting part. *Chinatown* is a masterpiece. It's a horribly depressing story of manipulation and victimization."

Miriam said, "It's the last scene that speaks to my point. When Nicholson, who's become Dunaway's lover, can't stand not knowing her secret and follows her to Chinatown. There he watches her interact with a teenage girl who turns out to be the result of Faye's father having raped her when she was a little girl, which produced the unbearably bizarre situation of Faye being both the girl's mother and her sister—additionally, her fierce protector. Remember the scene, Helen? Let's just watch the one part where the secret is divulged."

Helen sank into a corner of the chenille couch and sat in stony silence, much the same as she had during her teenage years, when she'd been forced into silently bearing Miriam's domination.

Miriam inserted the video and sank into the opposite corner, using the remote control to fast forward until she found the scene. They watched Nicholson slap the truth out of Dunaway. "She's my sister. She's my daughter. She's my sister. She's my daughter. She's my sister AND my daughter."

Helen's stomach was in knots and her chest so constricted that she had to inhale several huge gulps of air. She set her jaw for what her mother was about to offer.

"Remember when you asked me if your father and I could raise your first baby, Helen?"

"Sure, Mom. I remember. That baby would be twenty-one right now."

Miriam drank half her Martini. "I had no idea you even thought about that baby."

"Didn't know you did either," said Helen, lighting two of her mother's Camels and handing her one.

"Well, but here it is though, a perfect example of what happens eventually down the road."

Helen glared at her mother. "Eventually means down the road, Mother, so that's redundant."

Miriam assumed the armor of self-protection in the form of a deadpan expression.

Helen's voice steadily rose as she continued. "And as far as comparisons go, yours is absurd. Dad wasn't deranged, and he didn't father my baby."

"No, you're right. I've gotten ahead of myself. The point of this movie is that secrets don't stay secret and can have horrific results."

"Christ," said Helen, grabbing a fistful of M & M'S. "I hope this leads to some semblance of reality."

Miriam downed the remainder of her martini.

"Yes, well, listen to this parallel," she said. "About a year after making Chinatown, at the age of thirty-seven, while on the set of *The Fortune* directed by his pal, Mike Nichols, Jack was called to the phone to speak with a hometown newspaper reporter who had accidentally uncovered a secret while writing Jack's biography.

"Was it true, the reporter asked, that Jack had been raised by his grandmother, who claimed to be his mother, and that the person he thought to be his older sister was actually his real mother. By this time, both women had died; nevertheless, facts had been found to corroborate this discovery.

"Imagine his shock. Imagine finding out you'd been deceived by your family your whole life long. All humans suffer and practice deception, but hardly ever this dramatically."

Helen crossed her arms. "That's not a parallel, Mom. It's more of an insane coincidence that a movie plot point would somewhat mirror his personal life…and if you want to travel down Coincidence Road, you could make a case for his next movie mirroring his reaction to his secret past being unearthed—*One Flew Over the Cuckoo's Nest.*"

Helen couldn't help but laugh at her own wit.

Miriam laughed too, at her cleverness, which she'd often gotten such a kick out of.

"OK, there, Miss Clever. Let's stay on point here. It's my movie choice. You'll get your chance. Oh, and by the way, did you know that Jack and I are the same age? Well, he's a year younger, but still. He and I were both seventeen when we decided to postpone college. He went to Hollywood and I had you. Neither of us ever did go to college."

"Okeydoke," she said. "I'll tell you why your point is actually mine."

"I'm listening," said Miriam politely as she rose to make drinks.

"So Jack Nicholson was raised by his grandmother, I think her name was Ethel, who he believed to be his mother. So he grew up believing that his real mother, I'm pretty sure her name was June, was his older sister. So what? From what I've read, he had a happy childhood. Seems to me that young Ethel and even younger June managed to raise a real good boy. I mean, look how well he turned out."

"What about the shock factor?"

"Mom, don't you see that your example belongs on my side of the scorecard? Your example says, yes, let's keep that baby because, eventually down the road that baby will be a star."

Miriam tried to collect her original thoughts. "Consider this," she said. "Chinatown depicts the deception surrounding a child conceived out of wedlock. Then Nicholson's own revelation is so shocking, and by the time he's told of it, both women are dead, so he can't even ask any questions, so, see, It's relevant in several ways..."

Completely exasperated, Helen interrupted. "The biggest relevancy, as I see it, is that you and Daddy had to get married because of me..."

A bug-eyed Miriam said, "Who told you that?"

"I figured that out the night Daddy died."

"I see."

Miriam suddenly looked so small and fragile to Helen that she reversed her assault at once. She scooted down the couch and put her hand gently on her mother's.

"Listen to me, Mom. What you should know is that I understand why you handled my pregnancy all those years ago the way you did. That's not to say there aren't better ways of handling it, but I do understand that you were trying to save me from a life you knew all too well as incomplete. I know that you could have gone on to become anything you chose—well, anything you chose within the choices men allowed back then—but the point is, you loved learning and not only did you miss out on college, but then Daddy put his foot down about you going back to school or even getting a job outside the house, because of his false sense of pride, the manly man whose wife doesn't ever have to work.

You were Martha Stewart under house arrest all those years that Daddy and I got to pursue the mental stimulation of working and learning."

"But I embraced my role, Helen. And your father truly appreciated the lovely way I managed us three. I liked those years, Helen. I loved those years."

"Yeah, well, maybe the first stage. Maybe until I managed to get pregnant at the age of twelve."

"Well, but you didn't mean to…It was that horrid boy."

"You know what, he wasn't horrid. He just…We really didn't quite know what was happening. Even all these years later, Mom, I can't explain…"

"Honey, there's no need to. Now you know…well, apparently you've known since your father died, that if anyone should understand the innocent mistake of conception, it would be me. Not Harold, though," she snorted. "He was thirty-five, for God's sake.

"I was the victim of a man who did what he wanted and a mother who didn't tell me the facts of life in enough detail. And, see, that's what really threw me about your situation. I had every intention of making sure you knew exactly what was what in that department, which, by the way, I have never forgiven myself for, and why I never told your father. I was the one who failed. It was I who didn't nip the…whatever, the…"

"Flower," said Helen.

"Yes, the flower in the bud, by telling you all that information sooner, because then there you go and proceed ahead without me and my planned whadya-call-it, the bee and bird talk."

Helen let out a giggle. Miriam tittered. They broke into laughter. All these years later, it was almost as if the two of them were bonding at the similar experience of both being impregnated too early in their lives.

Miriam caught her breath. "See there? I still even have trouble with the phraseology." She pretended to work her mouth with her hand. "Facts of Life." She blushed. "There, I said it."

Helen wasn't smiling. "It's funny, and it's not—you know what I mean? There is victimization about these conception stories…"

"That's a pathetic word, and it begs sympathy, which is the last thing..."

Helen could see her mother was gearing up her tough-gal persona and wanted her to stay vulnerable for a while longer, so that she'd answer some questions and perhaps open more doors of understanding between them.

Miriam felt the pull herself, and bravely submitted for the same reason.

"So, what did your mother say when you got pregnant at seventeen?"

"My parents...they..."

And all the pain of that time in her life came rushing back right along with the memory.

"They saved face by throwing a fancy wedding at our Lake Forest mansion. My father wrote out a huge check and gave it to Harold. He told him he expected that to cover the cost of getting settled in a Chicago suburb other than Lake Forest. He said he could keep his position at the Board of Trade, but to stay out of his sight. He told him to buy a house, buy it outright, and let me furnish it any way I wanted. And he said he didn't expect to be seeing us. And...my mother... my mother kept saying, 'How could you do this to me,' and then, after the wedding, she just stood around sort of staring, as I packed up and left."

Helen enveloped her mother in her arms as the two broke into sobs.

Miriam withdrew first from the embrace. She blew her nose, and up she got to freshen their drinks. "Do not pity me, please," she said crisply. "I've had a good run, as good or better than most. We bloom where we're planted. We screw up, we take our lumps, and we go on."

"Yes, well, chipper attitude and all that, Mom, but you got screwed in more ways than one."

Miriam began to protest, but Helen put up her hands.

"Please let me finish. The video I brought as my little contribution for tonight's getting-to-know-you party is *The Days of Wine and Roses.* After we watch it, you won't be surprised that my chosen subject for tonight's marathon group therapy session centers around the seduction of alcohol."

That morning when nine-year-old Camille padded down the hall toward the kitchen, and breakfast, she heard her grandmother and mother talking in the front room. They didn't hear her coming but what she heard made her stop and catch her breath.

Her mother was telling her grandmother that she forgave her for treating her so harshly when she got pregnant in grade school and then her grandmother told her mother that she never ever thought of her mother as ruining her life at seventeen when she'd gotten pregnant with her.

So astonished was young Camille that she did something she'd never have thought to do before. She sat down in a corner of the room and eavesdropped. She sat quietly watching her two role models stretched out barefoot on the couch, facing one another, sipping coffee, munching toast, and telling secrets.

"The truth of the whole matter, Mom, is that most mothers cherish their daughters—and sons, of course, but we're speaking of daughters right now because of the reproductive aspect. They love them dearly and would do anything for them. And they *do* do anything for them. The sacrifice is thorough and ongoing, relentless, really. And, what do you think, because I personally believe it's just a shame we can't postpone our reproductive years until we're educated and have gotten the work-world under our belts. The security and wisdom of a long childhood with a properly thorough education and then a good solid fifteen years of working at a chosen profession would make for such a much more sensible preparation to the approach of motherhood in all its glory and sacrifice."

"I simply couldn't agree more, when you put it that well, darling. I felt the hole in my life all through those years, but now that I've had the pleasure of a rewarding career, I actually have the tools for comparison. I couldn't imagine my life without you, and I would never choose my career over you... but I do so love having both."

"Thank you, Mom, for trying your hardest to prepare me for a complete life. I do so love my work, my painting. And Camille, well she's my treasure. I love having both too."

"Both," thought little Camille. "I want to have a baby, and I want to have a career. And I can't have an accident, or I won't maybe get to have both at the right times. Wonder what an accident is."

Back in the twenty-first century, Helen's eyes popped open at the sound of her phone ringing. She let it go to voice mail and listened to Christi asking if she and Steven wanted to do a quiet barbecue and talk about this whole thing some more.

Christ, thought Helen. She made her bed as she recalled the fateful barbecue of...was it only last June?

Coincidence would be an understatement. Destiny would be the proper description for what occurred at the Clarks' first condo barbecue.

Living in her mother's house after Miriam died in 1990 had been sad for Helen. When Camille left for university, things only got lonelier. It was sometime in 2004, about a year after her detox, by the time Helen finally decided they needed to move to the city, and began the daunting task of relocation, which ended up taking almost a year.

In the end, Helen and Steven bought two condominium units near Millennium Park. The remodeling necessary to combine the two units, with an additional challenge of a two-floor space for Helen's studio, took the better part of a year to accomplish. During that time, Helen gradually broke up the River Forest estate, placing half of its content in storage for Camille to have someday, whenever she decided to settle down and get on with her adult life.

It was 2006 by the time they moved. Camille came home for a two-week semester break and helped her parents settle into their condominium. The move-in and placement of artwork ended up taking the whole two weeks, during which time the Clark women basically didn't go out of their unit, concentrating their excited energy on fine-tuning their new home.

Steven's duties were relegated to what he enjoyed. He went straight to work to teach his classes and manage his faculty, then shopped for groceries, and prepared the evening meals. After dinner, he continued organizing their considerable book collection into the custom shelves throughout their new home.

At 9:00 p.m., they would quit for the day and walk through Grant Park to Buckingham Fountain to have their treats—ice-cream cones, and the eye candy of their glorious magical city of Chicago. It was a shared time of wholesome change and calm cooperation. They were a healthy American family.

All three Clarks were captivated by the change in location and lifestyle, and enjoyed their teamwork, while keeping their inquisitive neighbors at bay.

*As it happened, the family was officially settled right before the annual summer barbecue, and so, at the urging of flyers slipped under their door, and not wanting to appear antisocial, Helen whipped up a fruit salad, and the three Clarks went to the party to meet their new neighbors.*

*It was a beautiful, sunny, Sunday afternoon in early June, and they were warmly greeted as the new kids on the block. Camille stayed for an hour before politely excusing herself to join a bunch of friends for drinks in Old Town.*

There was an air of anticipation that the Condo King and his wife were expected home from their place in Hawaii late that afternoon, so Helen and Steven were encouraged to stick around.

They'd discovered a couple, Christi and Peter Vertel, who played bridge and were in midsentence of arranging a bridge date, when Helen felt a strange rush of adrenalin.

"All right," exclaimed Peter, who saw him first. "Our Main Man is back."

"Don Ho has returned," announced Christy.

Steven smiled at the approaching stranger.

"The party has arrived," said the unmistakable voice.

Helen turned around to meet the amazed gaze of Max Shaw. There was nothing to do but shake hands as Peter introduced them. The minute their hands connected so electrifyingly, the game was on, as they feigned indifference.

One neighbor brought Max a drink, several others gathered for handshakes and hugs. Max shook hands, drank his drink, kissed the ladies, and never lost sight of Helen's gaze. He launched into an airplane joke as neighbors fawned over him, freshening his drink, bringing him food.

Christy asked where Janet was.

He cleared his throat and waited a beat.

"We're not speaking," he said.

At this, everyone chuckled, knowing he was about to tell a joke, because it wasn't in Max's nature to argue. He never needed to.

"We had an argument yesterday, so we were giving each other 'the silent treatment.' I didn't want to break the silence first, so last night before bed, I left her a note by the bathroom sink to wake me at five a.m. so I could finish packing for our early morning flight. 'Please wake me at five a.m.' So I wake up at seven this morning to a piece of paper by the bed, which said, 'It's five a.m. Wake up.'"

It wasn't the joke itself that got the laughs, but the charismatic way he held everyone's attention, coupled with the goofy way he told it.

"Yeah, YOU try arriving at Kona International in your pajamas."

"So? Where is Janet?"

"Janet's upstairs taking another airborne," he announced. "She thinks it's a cure-all and even safeguards against jet lag. But, hey, if she thinks it works, then it does. Am I right?"

"Absolutely," said Helen, before she could stop herself. They might as well have been in a room alone, because from then on whatever they were saying within the group was simply to amuse each other.

Here they were: Meeting up by mistake for the third time, hadn't seen each other in thirty-one years, and still, with all that had gone down between them, they instantly reconnected.

It was Steven, though, who threw her. He was just as drawn to Max as everyone else. Somehow, she couldn't wrap her mind around Steven and Max becoming buddies. But that's what happened.

Max made sure of that.

The circle made room for Janet as she entered. Max held a charming hand out to her and announced her entrance. "And the beautiful and talented Janet has arrived, sans jet lag," he said. She smiled at everyone and allowed kisses on her cheek. She politely shook hands with the new Clarks.

Helen saw that Janet had little spunk, possibly because Max used all the spunk airspace. She was perfectly groomed and at ease as the women purred over her stunning new Hawaiian necklace, black pearls mixed in with jade beads, from their Honolulu jeweler.

Helen tried to pay attention to the neighbor speaking to her (something about a committee she should join) but couldn't help checking out "the beautiful and talented."

Max watched the love of his life watching the wife of his life, as he probed Steven. "Where was he from? What did he do? Kids?"

"One"

"Really...how old?"

"Thirty-one. And you?" asked Steven. "How many kids?"

"None," said Max. "We wanted children, but it just didn't work out for us."

Steven was sad for Max, knowing he was lucky to have fathered Camille before he was injured.

And for Max, the news of such stolen happiness almost leveled him. Here he was, the lucky bastard who'd spent the last thirty-one years with his love and his child, *his* love and *his* child.

As the evening wore on, Helen and Steven were aware that they were being courted by the condo's inner circle. It was to be expected. People had always gravitated toward the Clarks, but this time the Condo King was after them. He had settled on them as the ninth and tenth members of his court, and that was that.

Max was always one foot in the moment, the other foot one step ahead.

He took Steven's drink to refill it, but only so he could take Helen's glass, could touch her hand as he did so, could share another bolt of lightning.

In the months to follow, whenever the Shaws and Clarks were in town, this became part of his routine, one of his many plays. Another was to manipulate the group into heightened activity—more get-togethers—more chances to be with Helen: bridge and dinner, charades and dinner, theater and dinner, sailing and dinner. All eagerly looked forward to by Steven.

Steven was a happy man. And Helen? She knew this was wrong, but she wasn't going to stop it. It just wasn't possible. It was only a matter of time.

Steven and Helen Clark had quickly become the new darlings of the condo in-crowd, regulars at the Sunday dinner parties. In truth, both the Clarks got a huge kick out of Max, and Janet's lack of humor was counterbalanced by her knowledge of the business world, since she was an international litigator. Max was a low-profile, highly connected political adviser who worked mainly out of his home office with local power-lunches and the occasional trip to the Capitol. He was obviously a "player," but skirted any intimate details with the old joke about having to "kill you if he told you."

That year, the Clarks spent Thanksgiving and Christmas in London with Camille.

Home for the Shaws' famous New Year's Eve Party, an intoxicated Helen allowed herself to be propelled into the guest closet filled with the sensuality of fur coats. When she realized the pusher was Max, she closed the door and welcomed him into the brand New Year with a long, deep Happy New Year kiss, involving tongues and nipples and excruciating, aching desire.

The following Saturday the coincidence of spousal trips came out at a dinner party the Clarks were hosting for their "new best friends." They were sitting around the table enjoying desserts and cappuccinos, bantering on about mostly mundane condo issues, when someone asked Janet if she was off to any foreign port of interest. She said yes, in fact she was leaving early Tuesday morning for O'Hare to catch a flight to Beijing, something about unmet international trade agreements. Steven piped up that he was making a rare trip himself on that very same Tuesday morning, back to Berkeley to present a three-day lecture series. They agreed to share a limo.

Max shot Helen a stomach-flipping we-just-got-insanely-lucky look. She blushed and passed the dessert tier around again, aware that sometime in the future that coincidental trip could be targeted as the point of no return.

Helen threw up later that night.

*Max prepared methodically, arranging for a smooth sixty-three hours together. Helen prepared emotionally, behaving like an infatuated schoolgirl, consumed by her naked body and fun ways to partially cover it.*

Early Tuesday morning, Helen and Steven kissed: Bye, honey—safe trip—love you too.

Max and Janet kissed: So long, doll—see you soon—love you too.

Max and Helen were between her sheets before the limo hit the Kennedy Expressway.

Helen and Max celebrated their temporary union for three days and two nights.

They ventured out only once, for dinner and martinis at Keefer's, which led to their one mistake.

It was on their way home that the actual mistake took place—only the one mistake, but it turned into a whopper: Caught on camera blowing a red light while kissing.

This photo, along with a traffic ticket would arrive in Max Shaw's mail after he was dead. Janet would open it. She would not mention it to Helen. In fact, Janet would seldom see Helen after Max died. Janet would not be the one to put an end to their relationship. Rather, it would be Helen who would become more and more reclusive, and finally withdraw.

But for those three days, those three honeymoon days with the love of her life, Helen could not have been more electrifyingly alive, and Max kept the pitch turned up.

Nothin' but blue skies, baby. Here I am lookin' at you lookin' at me. And I am in heaven. Helen, we were made for each other. Oh, God, how did you just move your hips like that? Who kisses like that? Only you, sugar. You're the one. It's only ever been about you.

Helen was five five. Max was five ten. They fit into each other perfectly. He loved to point that out at just the right moments. Everything he said to her seemed to compliment her, to make her feel even more desirable, to make her move in ever more sensuous ways. Max Shaw was simply larger than life. And that should have been the tip-off. How do you sustain "larger than life"? Well…you don't. You can't. It's not possible.

Even drunk, especially hungover, aching from constant physical pleasure, they kept up the pace for their exhausting three-day-marathon, sleeping briefly, eating scrumptious foods they prepared together, wearing only the aprons Max had custom ordered. Hers said, "This Belongs Souly To Max." His said, "This Is Only For Helen." She remembered wondering when he had placed that order, and the other personalized gift, her beautiful gold 'MINE' lighter. They watched parts of their favorite movies between rounds of lovemaking; sometimes slow, sometimes fast, but always tender.

Max began a new game; Let's pretend we'll be together forever—They entered into intoxicating smoke-and-mirror conversations about the delirious future that could be theirs. That was a serious mistake. For Helen, it was momentary pleasure, but for Max, the anything's-possible-guy, their talk fueled his need to possess her.

Helen tried to keep more perspective than that. At her insistence, the Shaws left for their winter home in Hawaii on schedule. This meant they were out of contact for the rest of January until the beginning of June. They had four months to get over themselves.

They did not.

The annual condo barbecue had never seemed so appealing. Never were two people more eager to be there.

A few months more of their unnerving "kill-me-now" 2:00 a.m. pool/sauna trysts followed their barbecue reunion. How far they'd come in one year's time. From barbecue to barbecue, with no turning back.

And now the beautiful two of them truly had no tomorrows.

How could he, she thought.

She'd targeted the wrong source of trouble all along. The real threat hadn't been being caught by spouses, by friends, by others. Not at all. It had been their fatal attraction. Max was the threat all along.

And Helen?

Look in the mirror, little girl.

Even still, even now, all it took for her to become totally aroused was the memory of Max playing his favorite Sting song over and over again.

"Every Breath You Take."

*Life isn't about waiting for the storm to pass, it's about learning to dance in the rain.*
~ Vivian Greene ~

*I don't exercise. If God had wanted me to bend over,*
*He would have put diamonds on the floor.*
~ Joan Rivers ~

# FRIDAY

On Friday morning, Helen partially awoke from one of her recurring dreams. Still half asleep, she decided to try to reenter the dream and attempt to conclude it.

Helen returned to the dream in her semiconscious state.

*She's standing in a pure white hallway, facing a glass door on which is printed: Wives: Research & Development.*

She opens the door to a pristine laboratory of white-coated technicians holding Lucite clipboards and space pens. They're bent over at their various tasks of notating and discussing the activity of tiny caged creatures.

She sees that the adult-sized white-coated technicians have poor posture, and that the tiny caged creatures seem familiar. But as her vision adjusts to the harsh fluorescent glare, she sees with a chill that the laboratory crew and caged research creatures are reversed; the white-coated technicians are human-sized rats standing hunchbacked on their haunches as they work, and the tiny caged creatures are rat-sized humans, clothed in dark gray hooded fur coats, nervously halting and scampering about on all fours.

Each cage is designed to study the reactions of one particular creature. Other creatures lurking in the cages are there to test the main one, who is easily identified by the pink bow she wears.

Two groups of ten cages each are arranged together.

The signage over the first ten reads, "Courtship: Densely, Intensely in Love Stage." In those cages, delirious chasing and coupling is taking place among green grass and flowers.

The signage over the other group of ten cages reads: "Marriage: Return to Reality Stage." Shell-shocked, lethargic movement is taking place among warning signs, posted on sticks stuck into an unstable surface of rocks and sand.

Helen is warmly greeted by a research assistant. He takes her hand in his two rat paws; whisker-kisses it, and leads her to the prep room. There is a wire-shelving unit of alphabetized shoe boxes, all labeled "Abnormal Human Wife." Under C is hers: "Abnormal Human Wife, Helen Hemingway Clark." In it are a miniaturizing potion, labeled "Drink Me"; a minute identification wristband; and her case history file. She takes that out and reads it. It is dated 1979:

"Ongoing research is being conducted upon abnormal human wife, specimen Helen Hemingway Clark, age twenty-six, case number 1212121212. The patient is in her second-cage-level of research. She shows a remarkable ability to conform to ever-changing conditions. She has been significantly traumatized, yet continues her attempts to achieve a conclusion. The questions are why does she keep trying and what is she seeking.

"In this experiment, the patient will again be temporarily reduced to the size of a rat and placed in a cage to be scientifically tested on our theory of pleasure/pain reaction. Familiars will again be placed in the four corners of her cage.

The focus of this test is the patient's complex thoughts. She seems to size up the four corners and realize their flip sides."

The technician readies her cage by cloaking the tiny look-alikes of Max Shaw at age twenty-eight, and Steven Clark at age forty-one, in furry-hooded coats. They wriggle as they are lifted into the cage, both chained to their corners. Significant props are glued in place in the other two corners.

She drinks the potion, shrinking to a diminutive her and puts on the ID bracelet, HHC/26/AHW number 1212121212. The technician cloaks her in a hooded fur coat and quickly paw-lifts her from the floor into the middle of her cage.

She takes several steps toward Max who holds out his hands in a welcoming gesture. She halts as she reads the warning signs: "Everlasting Guilt" and "Severe Harm to Others" and "Loss of Personal Integrity." She turns and scampers back to the middle of her cage.

She sees her husband, one hand behind him, steadily watching her from another corner. Three potholes loom before him, labeled: Emotional Rage Misdirected at Wife and "Targeted Degradation toward Wife" and "Beware—Hates Direct Honesty." There's a minefield running down the middle tagged "Loss of Spiritual Health."

She looks in another corner and sees shiny new bottles of wine and liquor on a mirrored shelf behind a gleaming mahogany bar. The warning signs say: "False Escape" and "Painful Headaches" and "Loss of Energy" and "Addiction" and "Loss of Heath."

She looks into the last corner. There's a leather armchair and ottoman, and next to the chair a side table holds an ashtray along with a gold cigarette case and lighter. She reads the warning signs: "Energy Sapper" and "Migraines" and "Addiction" and "Loss of Health."

She turns her attention to Max Shaw. He beckons her. She skitters two steps forward, then hesitates, and skitters three steps back. In this way, she avoids going to Max Shaw's corner and alternately backs into one addiction corner, then the other.

Case number 1212121212 spends hour after relentless hour trying the two escape corners, being laid low again and again by excess drinking and smoking, and crawling back to the middle of the cage after each episode.

Finally, she's splayed facedown in the middle of the cage. She slowly turns over and sees a researcher rat recording, "Inconclusive—Must rerun this set of tests."

At this point, the recurring dream always ends. For twenty-eight years, a rat-scientist has written in the file, and then he has, for twenty-eight years, lifted her out of the cage.

But this time, Helen, who has been analyzing this dream, doesn't let it end. Her instinct kicks in, and she's aware of a missing puzzle piece. A warrior adeptly skirting the minefields, she wills her miniature self to work her way to her husband's corner. He steps to the side, revealing their baby girl holding his hand. It's Camille. Helen holds her baby in one arm and puts the other firmly around her husband's shoulders.

She looks up from the cage to the rat-faced scientists and says, "We've wasted years and years of repetitive testing because we never once discussed the test. How is the intelligence of this experiment defined? In the end, it was my instinct and my common sense that led me to my husband, revealing my little girl behind him as the missing puzzle piece.

"My ability to problem-solve drew me to conclude that the right choice involved tolerating and even embracing the man who limits me, for the good of the group, and the well-being of the child.

"I didn't understand that there is no escaping emotional pain and that the question becomes how to navigate life in the least harmful way. This experiment concludes that intelligent thought evolves through self-control, and shows instinct to be a basic form of intelligence. The selfless act of protecting the innocent is key to true love surviving."

The head scientist says, "What you just watched is an old tape, Mrs. Clark. You solved this experiment several weeks ago, the night you told Max Shaw that he could never reveal himself as Camille's father. And then, last Sunday, he cemented that decision by permanently recusing himself."

Helen popped awake as the laboratory images faded into the forgotten. She hopped out of bed and was brushing her teeth before the current daytime nightmare dawned anew. As this sunk in, the waning battery power of her toothbrush mirrored her own weakening energy.

Fully awake, staring at the bleak reality of this day being the Friday after the Sunday that Max Shaw committed suicide, she drank some coffee and noticed the time was eleven o'clock, which was fine with her. This meant that she only had to stay awake for about nine hours before she could lose her misery in slumber, where every twenty-eight years or so, she might manage to resolve crucial issues.

She began mechanically preparing for her volunteer work. She drank her coffee and showered and dried her hair and had her cereal and yogurt and juice and vitamins and applied some makeup and chose a seasonal dress and put it on along with the matching jacket. She stepped into her sandals, grabbed her matching purse, applied the security of more lipstick and sunglasses, and told herself, out loud, to open the door and leave. She traveled down the elevator, said a chipper "Morning" to this person and that, big proper Helen-smile, and walked out into the sunny day and over the Frank Gehry bridge and through a corner of Millennium Park, and across Monroe Street to the new wing of the

Chicago Art Institute, where she assisted senior citizens in computer graphics.

The walk in the park was anything but. Wallowing in insecurities, she found admiring glances grating because she knew she wasn't admirable. Equally annoying were the passersby who seemed to glare disapprovingly. How dare anyone judge anyone, she thought. In a way, she welcomed the idea of finally looking the way she felt. That should be a requirement; to look the way you feel, to show your suffering.

You don't know what suffering is, she told herself. "Yes, I do," she said out loud, then reduced the volume to a more dignified mumble. "Lose the looks." She'd developed the talk-aloud-to-herself thing in the hospital rehab wing, but outside the joint, people assumed she was speaking into an earphone.

At three o'clock, she decided to call it a day, and to cancel her appointment with Dr. Savage. She got his voice mail and spoke into his machine. "Dr. Savage, it's Helen Clark. I know we have an appointment at four today, and this is the day I'm supposed to tell you about my addiction problems and the rehab experience. Well, frankly, Doctor, and who knows if you're aware of this, I feel insulted every time you dismiss me with your 'time's up.' I, um, don't want to get started on that whole long rehab story unless I can conclude it, and that's not going to happen in forty-five minutes, that's for sure. So I'm canceling our appointment. I understand that I'll be charged anyway, because I'm canceling too late, but that's better than being humiliated halfway through such a difficult memory."

She ended by giving him her cell phone number and asked that he call her to verify his receipt of her message.

She was halfway home when her cell phone rang. It was the doctor. His voice was calm. He explained that the patient did not set the rules. "Fine," she said. "But I don't have to accept them either."

After a brief silence, he capitulated. She was his last patient of the day, so he would, this one time, make an exception and have two back-to-back sessions with her, beginning at four in the afternoon.

"Well, thank you," she said. Damn, she thought. I really don't want to see him. But she turned around and headed to his office. After all, he'd bent the rules. How could she not go? But then again, she thought, the sessions are forty-five minutes long and so two sessions are ninety minutes. What if he said "time's up" when she still wasn't done? What if she needed another ten or twenty minutes?

Enough, she thought. Why do I keep trying to get a grip on this, when it's really not possible? Whatever happens, I'm just gonna go for it. If he insults me, I'll respond in any way I need to.

On her way there, Helen homed in on what she wanted to accomplish in this double session with the doctor. Reviewing the impact that alcohol and drugs had had on her life brought back memories of her first marriage.

*1970 was a life-changing year. It was Vietnam protests and much of America's youth addicted to sex, drugs, and rock 'n' roll. Berkeley College sophomore Helen Hemingway eagerly embraced the times.*

That November, a bunch of Berkeley kids had grabbed their pot and guitars, and caravanned in their psychedelically painted Volkswagen minibuses to pay homage to "the greatest guitar player to ever grace the earth."

They gathered at Greenwood cemetery in Renton, Washington where Jimi's mother, Lucille Hendrix, was also buried.

Amassed at the gravesite of Jimi Hendrix, strumming their guitars and singing the burning, itching lyrics to

"Fire," Helen and Billy locked eyes. "Let me stand next to your fire."

He was a longhaired blond boy of medium height with crazy black eyes, and had the slender build of a pot-smoking youth. He was hunched over his guitar in a flamboyantly sexual pose, singing, "I have only one burning desire."

And Helen? Helen was high, and in this state, Helen was all about desire, from her curly dark hair and big show-me-the-fun eyes, to her recklessly expansive mouth.

Eyes at half-mast, he became fascinated with the way the support-strap of her guitar outlined her curves, resting on her tiny waist, winding around her wide shoulder, and then down, separating her breasts. Even her jewelry seemed to be moving erotically, silver bangles of earrings and wrist bracelets and ankle bracelets and toe rings. "I have only one itching desire."

During the duration of Helen's early teenage "refinement," her authoritarian mother had skillfully worked words of virtue into her everyday conversation with her "wild child." She incorporated the Seven Deadly Sins into Helen's nighttime prayers. Vice and virtue were recited at bedtime. "And, please God, guide me away from the Seven Deadly Sins—lust, gluttony, greed, sloth, wrath, envy, and pride."

Helen would then recite these targeted sins as problem and solution, the flipside of vice being virtue, the flipside of lust being chastity, and so on: "I conquer vice with virtue; lust with chastity; gluttony with temperance; greed with charity; sloth with diligence; wrath with forgiveness; envy with kindness; and pride with humility."

Chastity was as essential as education: The keys to the kingdom were education and marriage.

On one occasion, over bedtime prayers, Helen had worked up the courage to ask her mother what happened to chastity once a woman got married. "That's an entirely different matter," she'd answered. "Your bedroom becomes a place of glorious release…you obviously know something about that. In your case, you experienced something like that in that boy's garage." This crushing response rendered mother and daughter speechless. Then Miriam had burst into tears and apologized. "I'm sorry, darling. That was so tough. The answer is you're supposed to be sexual when you're married. When we're done, when you're educated and married, I'll give you a much kinder answer."

Marriage = Sex. Billy = Sex. Staying in school while married and having sex = finishing one's education the fun way. Not telling anyone completed this folly.

Helen married Billy for sex.

About the third month of her first marriage, she had a miscarriage, which froze their fun for six weeks. Fortunately or unfortunately, this resulted in them getting to know each other.

He didn't understand her tender reaction to the miscarriage—how could he without knowledge of her previous abortion trauma—and he tossed it off as good luck since they had no money and were still in school.

Her hormones were out of control, one minute crying and cuddling with him—he wasn't the cuddling type, nor actually did he like to be touched—the next screaming and swearing that he was devoid of affection. He unemotionally agreed this was probably true.

He dealt with her temper in the same ways his father had with his mother, which was to: (a) get drunk and smack her around, or (b) get drunk and give her the "silent treatment" for a day or two or three—whatever suited his mood, or (c) get drunk and not come home at all.

For the first time in Helen's life, she let her temper loose and exploded into a person she didn't even recognize as she reacted to his physical abuse and emotional withdrawal. She threw items at him, swore, spat, scratched, kicked, slammed doors, and screamed until her voice was gone. Their intense passion had inverted, intoxicating sex turned into bitter rage.

This animalistic display calmed down for a time when their sexual activity resumed, but there was no turning back from what they'd discovered about each other. Once unbridled sex was now cautious and distrustful.

Their marriage had flipped to the other side. They knew that without sex, they were incompatible. A kind of exhaustion set in. The sex was not the same and was chosen less and less often over the escape of drugging and drinking. He said he chose drugs over sex because the high lasted longer. She said doing both was the answer. He laughed at her sexual naiveté. "Show me the dude who can pull that one off."

Apparently Helen had been delusional. She'd thought a highly sexual person stayed that way. Why would they change? Why would they want to?

What she saw coming down the road was this: For the rest of her life, she would be saddled with a mate who was so scarred from his childhood that he heard criticism at every turn of a phrase.

That, plus the brainwashed religious constraints to sexual desire placed on a prepubescent boy. He'd been wired from day one to consider sex a sin. Therefore, once he'd had the orgasmic time of his life with his bride, he felt sated and guilty.

After confessing his "sins," he easily and comfortably returned to his natural habit of smothering his sexuality with liquor. This created an illusion for him—a good boy, having chosen abstinence in the name of religion and all that is holy. Masturbation didn't count.

Helen saw herself with alarming clarity as well. As unsettling as it was, she had discovered the depth of her anger and was appalled by her behavior.

She contemplated her inability to make wise choices for a long, long time. The only reason they'd ended up together—her with her earthy desires and him with his inhibited self-conscious ones, was that, once, in a very teeny tiny space of time, they were overcome by lust for each other.

Their three-month "courtship" had had absolutely nothing to do with their social compatibility, because they'd remained so stoned that they really hadn't heard much of what one said to the other.

They had 'the touch' for each other. Whatever that is, it's not easy to find; once found, a thorough exploration generally follows. That kind of mating instinct travels beyond reason and takes over all that a person understands.

Basically, lust bit the dust.

Helen lent Billy $1,000 to get a place of his own and move out. After all, she had access to money and therefore the freedom to escape being cornered by another idiotic choice on her part. She considered herself better off by herself with a pulsating shower head.

It was at this point that Helen printed out a large copy of the Cher quote and pasted it on her bathroom mirror:

***The trouble with some women***
***is they get all excited about nothing—***
***and then they marry him.***

Being Catholic, Billy requested and eventually obtained an annulment, though it took its dramatic time to accomplish, but during that time, Helen had reestablished her self-control and was back on track by the end of her sophomore year.

Helen arrived for her appointment with Dr. Savage just as the previous patient was leaving. Ooh-Kay, she thought, here we go again. The patient looked like one of her old detox roommates; barely able to keep it together, unmatched clothes slightly askew, nervous return smile after Helen offered a reassuring one and said hi. We're all loons in different corners of the same bin, she wanted to say, but of course didn't.

How many times had she pondered the real difference between them, between another person's state of mind and hers? Perhaps, and Helen truly believed in this possibility, that person was happier, more content than she.

Didn't one's expectations factor into one's happiness? If you expected nothing to work out, there would be no disappointments...unless perhaps if something actually did work out, that might throw you into a panicky state. Maybe you wouldn't know what to do with the success, which would be the polar opposite problem—that of beating yourself up over allowing defeat to keep seeping into your life. My high expectations actually beg for disappointment. Besides which, one or two of my personalities rebel against any good choices I make. I sabotage myself. I shoot myself in the foot.

"Why is that?" she asked herself aloud.

Dr. Savage came out to greet her and let her in the two other doors. She said yes to coffee. They sat, and he began the session.

"So, Mrs. Clark, tell me about your rehab experience."

"Well, as your notes should indicate, I began drinking the summer before my junior year in high school. I was at a party and met some older kids who liked me because they sensed I was one of them. I looked older. I acted older. I was older because of my abortion experience, but no one knew about that.

"Whiskey sours. They taste like a tart kiddy cocktail, and after drinking one I experienced a warm glow of relaxation and silliness that was a wonderful surprise, and such a release."

"So, you were, what, fifteen? And one whiskey sour would get you high? How often did you drink that summer?"

"I snuck out a lot. It was so easy because my dad went, quote, back to his office, unquote, after dinner, and my mom had become an 'evening alcoholic,' so I was on my own. I didn't mind lying, because look what happened when I told the truth. Also, they lied, so why shouldn't I?"

"How fast did your drinking escalate? Did you try other drugs?"

"I really never drank more than two, because they were acidic and any more than that would give me a stomach ache. But I suppose you could argue that the drinking took me in another addictive direction. I began smoking menthol cigarettes. They also gave me a high. Really, whenever I smoked a menthol cigarette, I'd get high, which I loved. I felt confident and fun and funny. That was my reaction to mind alteration."

"And did your habits escalate?"

"Yeah, quite a bit. I drank more in my junior year to contain my sexuality. A lot of guys were after me. I kissed a lot and I loved flirting. This eventually landed me the reputation of being a 'PT.' I couldn't for the life of me figure out what the letters stood for, but my best friend, Cate, said the flirty good girls were called that, because none went 'all the way.' Imagine, I'd had sex and an abortion, yet didn't know what PT meant. Such a combination of innocent and worldly, of hide and seek. Even Cate never knew what I'd been through.

"So those were your addictions until college? Whiskey sours and menthol cigarettes?"

"Well, no. On my sixteenth birthday, my mother threw me a huge graduation-birthday party—"

Savage looked up from his notes, surprised.

She sighed. "Remember, I skipped a couple of grades." Keep up, she thought. Christ.

"And after everyone had left, she introduced me to Mr. Scotch and Mrs. Water. That made me gag, but I managed to gulp it down. The two of us got drunk together. I drove us, don't ask me how, to the local diner for breakfast, and then managed to take an hour getting home. The restaurant was a couple of miles away, so we must have been really fucked up."

Silence.

"What are you thinking, Mrs. Clark?"

"I was realizing that that night was the most fun I'd had with my mother since, um, she made me kill my baby. I guess she got younger and loosened up when she was drunk, and I got funny. We actually laughed a lot that night. She didn't blindside me with another dreary slur about human nature. She just stayed in the moment."

Helen realized she was crying. She stopped, blew her nose and sat up straight.

"So you enter a university known for its wild side, already prepared to keep up with the best of them."

"Not really. I'd never tried any drugs ever. But who doesn't experiment at Berkeley? There was shit being offered everywhere. And it's in my nature to gravitate toward exaggerated people, who live on the edge, who party til they drop. I loved it. My first year at Berkeley? I tried anything you could name. I studied just enough to keep my full scholarship."

"How do you feel about that now that you're mature?"

"Mature? I never claimed I was mature. No, Doctor, just the opposite. It takes all my willpower to act mature. I came from a secretive family, and rebelled against them as soon as I could. So, completing the never-ending misguided circle, I chose abnormality over unrealized potential. Self-destruction runs in families.

"All families," said the doctor.

"Nope, it's just mine. I'm claiming the malady."

"I get the feeling, Mrs. Clark, that you enjoy acting rebellious."

"Well, duh. This kindergarten walk-through is belittling. The point here is to set up the background so that you can understand my addiction and rehab experience, is it not, Doctor? I could tell you story after story about the good times I had at Berkeley, getting fucked up on almost any drug offered me, but that's not why I'm here, is it Doctor?"

"Probably not, Mrs. Clark. But tell me this. Was there any substance that you didn't try? Did you have a line you didn't cross? Was there a limit?"

"Yes. OK. Good question. Let's see. Some asshole served brownies laced with LSD one time, and I had a two-day nightmare. Hideous, just horrible, scary shit. But that doesn't count, because I didn't know. That's a good question, though, Doctor, because it shows some remote character on my part.

"Besides not wanting LSD because I didn't like the trip, my line was cocaine, and heroin, only because I was concerned that I'd like the feelings too much to be able to control myself."

Savage raised his eyebrows appreciatively in response to her drug limits.

She shot him a "don't condescend" look.

He immediately dropped his eyebrows and plowed on. "So...let's talk about your addiction."

"Well, after going way too far I was able to calm myself down by sleeping a lot (no need to mention the whole Billy thing). Toward the end of sophomore year, my best friend, Cate, told me that, as an underclassman, I could get away with not studying, but when I came back for my junior year, I would actually need to buckle down and learn unfamiliar subjects. This was logical to me, and so I quit everything, and by the second day, I was feeling flu-like. The third day, I had the shakes and couldn't eat. The fourth day I threw up, and then had the dry heaves the rest of the day. The fifth day, one of my guy friends came over and we got high together. What a relief.

"I took a different approach. During the summer break, I gradually weaned myself off most of the stuff I was using. I very gradually prepared myself for my junior year and was back to just marijuana and scotch by my deadline.

"So by my junior year, I was back on track, taking twenty semester hours, meeting my future husband, yada yadda. Skip to..."

Savage's phone rang. He looked at the caller ID, and said, "Excuse me," as he held his index finger in Helen's direction, and proceeded to take the call.

Helen flushed with anger. She took several deep breaths and got up to pour herself some more coffee.

The doctor hung up, saying, "Sorry, please continue."

Helen stared at him and said, "Where were we?"

"Refresh me," he said with a deadpan expression.

"See, that's your job, isn't it, Doctor? To track the traumas that I'm wrenching up? To pay attention to the patient in the room and take the call when we're done?"

Savage looked at his watch.

"Oh, brother. Is this going to be a 'time's up' thing?"

"We've got time, Mrs. Clark."

Helen shifted aggressively in her chair and drank some coffee. She looked around the room, trying to locate something pretty to fixate on, another coping skill she'd developed. It seemed to raise her spirits to lose herself in colors and forms. Nothing pretty in Savage's stark office.

"Please continue," he said.

"Fine. I've just described two of my elemental characteristics: one, I've got an addictive personality, and two, I was able to normalize my habit on my own. Is that jotted down there, Doctor?"

No reaction.

"Now we're skipping from 1970 to 2001, because that's my next episodic adventure into the wonderful world of drugs."

"Ah, yes."

"It's September 11, 2001, and I'm walking across the street when a hysterical stranger stops me—in the middle of the Goddamned street—to let me know that New York has just been attacked—America, has just been attacked. Another stunned pedestrian stops to join in the conversation. And then another. So here we all are, everyone in shock, standing in the street on upper Wacker Drive. I'm listening to them describe an unbelievable scene of apparent war, when a car turns the corner, jumps the curb and slowly careens into my right side.

"My hospital stay was two weeks, during which time I underwent two operations. I was on every pain medication I could convince them to give me.

"After months of rehab, I was finally able to move my arm halfway up. We called it 'the Hitler Look.' My endocrinologist decided to put me on a brand-new pain medication because I was still in real pain.

"The drug was amazing and that should have been the tip-off, but no. No, I took those babies every four hours and felt such relief I thought I'd died and gone to heaven. Without the pain, I was able to be more aggressive in my rehab, and I gradually regained most of my agility, though I still can't feel part of the right side of my back. One of the operations involved nerve damage, but shit, no one knows it but my girls and me."

"Your girls?"

"My other selves. I've got my share of personalities. Surely you're not going to argue that we've all got many personalities?"

"No, but we should discuss that another time. I'd be very interested in your account of your 'girls.'"

"Fine," said Helen as she thought to herself, not in this lifetime. I'm done after today. This is bullshit. I haven't learned a thing and now, thanks to you and me, Doctor, I may get hooked on drugs again.

She said, "Skip to a year and a half later. I'm thinking I'm done mending and am as good as I'll ever be, so then I begin wondering how I'd feel without the pain pills."

Dr. Savage looked at his watch and then at Helen. "Well. I'm afraid our time is up." He picked up a pencil and studied his calendar. So, how does Monday at three fifteen work for you?

Silence.

He looked up from his calendar.

They stared at each other.

More silence.

At last Helen found her voice. "Is this a purposeful insult? Are you doing this to see my temper in action?"

"Why would you ask that?"

"Because right now I'm experiencing what is known as 'the slow burn.' You're insulting my intelligence. Or perhaps your basket is full and you can't take any more. Too much whining from too many patients for too many years. One patient blurs into another, yadda yadda, blah..."

She got up as she continued. "You half-listen. Your memory kind of shuts down whenever it wants or needs to. Maybe you're a burnout too, Dr. Savage, like all the other shrinks I've been exposed to."

Grabbing her jacket and purse, Helen walked to the door and turned to finish. "What you just pulled here will be on my list of semitraumas. You haven't helped me. You've made things worse."

She looked Savage in the eyes. "It took me a long, long time to put those memories behind me. And now, at your request, they've all surfaced. You assure me that we'll have a 'unique' double session so that I'll not be interrupted, and then after a single session and, and with me in the middle of my odious recollections, you dismiss me."

Helen was breathing so hard that she had to stop and catch her breath.

Dr. Savage rose from his desk chair. "Mrs. Clark, I apologize. The phone call was to inform me that one of my patients just committed suicide."

"Whh...at? WHAT," screamed Helen. "What are you saying? Are you telling me that I'm now connected to another suicide? What the fuck is this?"

"No. Of course not. I do apologize. Why don't we take a break, say five, ten minutes and I'll make a few phone calls so that I can regain my concentration."

Helen grabbed the grungy, clunky wooden key chain, a filthy piece of surgical tape labeled 'Ladies Room.' She held it away from her body between her thumb and forefinger and went out, leaving each of the three doors open wide.

When Helen returned, she'd freshened her makeup. She removed her jacket, placed her purse on the floor by her right foot, and sat down. She crossed her legs. She recrossed her legs and placed her purse on the floor by her left foot. Next, she picked up her purse, found and lit a cigarette, placed her purse next to her right hip on her chair, and grabbed her empty coffee mug to serve as an ashtray.

She looked defiantly at Dr. Savage, who'd been watching her. "I've been seated in the smoking area," she said. And then she giggled.

He raised his eyebrows, but was silent.

"You, on the other hand, Dick, you're in the nonsmoking section. Please respect the rules." She giggled again.

He smiled. "OK. OK, You've been taking this drug for more than a year and...what? Decide to just stop taking it? You went from using it every four hours to not using it at all?"

Helen took a deep drag. She straightened her back, sighed, and resumed her story.

"I discovered I got the shakes and had those pesky 'flu-like symptoms' by the end of the day. After two days of this, my doctor spoke with me over the phone, at the end of which she told me to come over. I remember that phone call; remember asking if she meant 'now,' and her answering with a definite 'yes.' Knowing that a person has to be in a shitload of trouble for their doctor to make room to see them ASAP, I knew the problem before I got in the cab (puff).

"She told me that she'd looked it up in the latest medical journal. Apparently, one patient in, maybe, a couple of thousand becomes addicted to this painkiller. She looked me straight in the eyes and said, 'You have an addictive personality, so there you go.'

"There you go!" Helen repeated dramatically for the benefit of Dr. Savage.

He pursed his lips indignantly as an act of solidarity.

"I asked why the FDA allowed the painkiller to be put on the market without an addiction warning. She said that it was 'a new discovery,' and that she felt terrible. I remember saying, 'Not your fault' (puff).

"As an aside, Doctor Savage, why, you may be wondering, and rightly so, why would I respond, 'not your fault'? It's because my mother conveniently raised me to be forgiving... not that she held herself to that standard. I was taught to forgive, but saw the example of harboring resentment, so 'there you go' with that whole can of adult worms (puff). Where would we be without our painful childhoods?"

Savage smiled, then Helen laughed and so did he.

"Anyhow...back to me. Blahbety blah blah. We talked about all the amazing painkillers on the market, and how patients and doctors were so eager to have access to the magic of scientific discoveries and their astonishing aid in lessening human misery."

Savage halfheartedly semismiled.

"She wanted me to withdraw by skipping one pill a night for two weeks, down to no pills at the end of two and a half months. She explained that during that time my body would think it had the flu. Gee, sounded like fun to me. The other choice would be to enter a hospital and do the whole detox thing in about a week.

"Of course I chose door number two. I like my pain excruciatingly fast and over.

"My luck continued when days later my doctor had to take an emergency leave to care for her dying mother in Poland. She had no idea when she'd be returning, so she found other doctors for her patients."

Helen stopped talking as the memories flooded in. She took a last graceful drag on her cigarette and placed it carefully in the mug's coffee dredges.

Dr. Savage said, "What about lying on my couch for this part of your recollection. That way you don't have to look at me while you reconstruct this thorny memory."

"Oh!...Well...I'm amazed at your thoughtfu...I'm..."

He got up, rearranged his chair and swept his arm in a gentlemanly gesture of firm encouragement.

As she settled onto the couch, she said, "I've never done this, but I see the value. You want me to deliver a type of...

"Monologue." They both said the word at the same time and then shared a laugh, relieving the tension that had built up between them.

But, on the other hand, Helen didn't like the camaraderie that she and the doctor were developing. He seemed to be treating her more like a colleague, and she wanted to wear the patient costume, so the couch relocation and separation of eye contact was definitely helpful.

Helen cleared her throat, floated back to her detox story, and launched into it.

I called the new doctor chosen for me and spoke with his nurse who assured me that the doctor would handle the matter and that she would take care of the hospitalization details.

When I showed up on the arranged day to enter the detox program, he wasn't there. I sat in the filthy waiting room, alarmed at its condition, and not quite believing what was happening, and certainly second-guessing my decision, which was quickly making its way to my endless poor choice list.

About an hour into my three-hour wait, the admitting counselor unlocked the heavy, grungy glass doors and held one open for my grand entrance. Clutching my suitcase, and holding my cumbersome winter coat, I settled on the couch by the wall and perused what passed for a lounge, central to the patients' rooms. There were seven doors, but, more significantly, two names written on each of them. Apparently everyone had a roommate, not good for someone like me.

All I wanted was to get through the week unnoticed, which is why I packed old comfortable clothes. While I was packing the night before, I'd begun to realize the possibilities of this inmate situation. I pictured what I thought it would be like. Turned out of course that I was pretty far off. OK, I might as well have been sitting in the bleachers at Sox park studying the Cubs' stats. Anyhow, I did have the foresight to pack only comfortable essentials: corduroy jeans, plaid flannel shirt with the double chest pockets so I didn't have to wear a bra, a flannel nightgown, robe and slippers, my toothbrush, toothpaste, shampoo, my hairbrush, tweezers, eyeliner, blush, lipstick, the magnifying mirror, and my kitchen timer that I use as an alarm clock because it doesn't tick. That was the gear for the week, plus the warm-up suit

I had on, and six days' worth of fresh underwear and socks. That's it. Plus the *New Yorker* magazine. Oh, and four books. Plus my pillows of course.

A harried-looking woman carrying a plastic container and wearing credentials that announced she was an aid named Andrea, introduced herself, and told me that she needed to look through my suitcase.

I leaned over and unzipped it, at which point Andrea dumped my carefully packed belongings onto the couch, an act that I found unnecessarily aggressive if not unkind. I remained tight-lipped as I watched her rifle through my items.

Andrea found my tweezers after dumping out my toiletry bag. She confiscated them and delivered my first direct lesson: Tweezers are a weapon.

I asked her why we couldn't have simply unpacked these items in my room. I suggested that I could have put them in my bureau and closet as she inspected them.

She glumly studied me and told me that I didn't have an assigned room because they didn't know I was coming.

I told her that my doctor's nurse assured me that my room arrangements were in order, and asked where the doctor was.

Andrea said the doctor might have a cold. With that, she placed my magnifying mirror in the plastic container.

I remember saying something like, Oh, come on, I can't put on my makeup without that! Can't even see my face.

She yawned at me and told me that glass was considered a danger.

I asked her why she was taking my bathrobe tie and she simply said, suicide, as she threw it into the container. She told me I could put the rest back, and left.

My endless admission to the ward continued as I waited on the lounge couch, covered with a sticky black plastic with rips exposing dirty vanilla foam. I practiced my coping skills, alternating between the I'll-get-through-this-by-amusing-myself thoughts, and the nodding-off-into-a-semidream-of-something-pleasant trick, and the reassuring-myself-that-it-couldn't-possibly-take-much-longer pep talk.

At some point, one of the inmates whose room was several feet away from my couch opened his door. A very tall, muscular, heavily bearded black man locked eyes with me as he approached and towered over me. He grinned widely, clicked his heels and saluted. Bug-eyed, I managed to smile politely, and returned his salute as an act of peace.

He announced loudly that he was a man of the Lord and said you must always be kind to the children. May the celebration of the birth of Christ remind us of the dignity and value in each human life.

This message appealed to me, although the man himself was somewhat intimidating, considering the proximity of his knees to my chin.

Gerald, the boy counselor, appeared in the room, saying, OK, Prophet, let's take a rest, now.

The Prophet said all right and agreeably allowed the aide to lead him back into his room.

Gerald turned his attention to me, said that he'd heard I'd brought books, and asked me if that was right. I answered yes, and he told me that he'd store them for me because they weren't allowed, that I'd be concentrating on myself and focusing on the handouts I'd be getting at the meetings. There's homework, he added.

Taking away my books made me aggressive, and I remember asking how many daily meetings could there be that I wouldn't have any downtime. And homework? How much could there be that I wouldn't have time to lose myself in thoughts other than me for a while? I squared off with him and said something like, are you telling me that you don't encourage relaxing with a good novel before falling asleep?

Gerald squatted to my couch level and patiently told me that I wouldn't be feeling well enough to handle anything besides "what we'll have you doing." He said that the meetings were intense, lasted all day, and I really wouldn't have the energy for anything else.

I got the picture. Or thought I did. They had the days structured as part of the detox. So I fished the books out of my already once repacked suitcase and handed them over. But I kept the *New Yorker*, and he didn't notice.

It's only a week, became my mantra.

So Gerald confiscated my books and told me they were in the process of getting my roommate squared away. I asked him if there were any single rooms, and he replied that there was one. He agreed that that would definitely be best in my case, but it wasn't available for that night. He said that when it opened up, it would probably be assigned to me, if no one else needed it at the time.

Next we went over to a corner table to fill out my paper work. Me lugging my bulky winter coat, my purse and my suitcase. My chair faced the seven doorways, so I had a clear vision of a short, doughy girl being let out of room #204. The girl was beat-up, with purple bruises on her face. Her arms were tied behind her, both wrists wrapped in gauze. A nurse was guiding her toward the hall as she quietly talked to her. The girl shook her head up and down, appearing to agree. As they passed by our table, the nurse told Gerald, that he could get the new patient settled into cot number two.

I numbly followed Gerald into room #204. The room was divided into two spaces, each with its own tiny sink and closet. A nightstand with two drawers stood beside each cot, with reading lights attached to the wall above each one, and a large plastic-covered armchair separated them. A second chair stood in the corner of my roommate's side between her cot and the wall, destroying the symmetry.

Gerald explained that my roommate was on twenty-four-hour suicide watch, so her nurse would be sitting in that chair in the corner by her bed until she fell asleep that night, and then the nurse would be positioned outside the open door until morning. When her shift ended, another nurse would be taking over. He said that the girl wouldn't be bothering me because she never talked after her attempts.

I remember staring at him...having difficulty digesting it. He said something about going to get me some sheets and a blanket.

I remember putting my suitcase on the cot and unzipping it, revealing the untidiness inside. Somehow the mess said it all, and I sort of unraveled. I was overcome by the anxiety of slowly grasped reality. Exhaustion seeped into me and with it that age-old longing for night to come so that I could escape into sleep. How, without a book, I remember wondering. Ah, the *New Yorker.*

My coat had officially taken on its own significance. I guess it's funny now, I mean even at the time it was so utterly symbolic that normally I would have laughed, but instead I did a hot flash number on myself. I opened the tiny closet and hung up my stupid coat. This took up the entire closet. I removed the dumb thing and put it on my bed. I hung up my nightgown and robe, and my flannel shirt and blue corduroy jeans. I placed my slippers on the closet floor. Next I placed my underwear and socks in the bottom drawer of the nightstand. I took my pen and pad of paper out of my purse and put them in the top drawer, placing my kitchen timer on the top. I took out my two down-filled bed pillows and placed them neatly on top of the plastic-covered mattress, troubled over the issue of cleanliness.

I remember wondering why I hadn't packed Lysol. Of course the answer was that if I'd known I'd be wishing for Lysol, I wouldn't have gone there in the first place. I put my toiletry container on the sink counter, unzipped it, and removed the silver cup holder for my toothbrush and paste, and a bottle of water, which I put next to the water faucet. There was still the matter of the coat.

As it happened, I wouldn't even need that heavy a coat by the time I finally left. The weather would have turned warmer when I next experienced it beyond the grimy windows. I put the quilted, tufted, hooded monster-coat in my suitcase, which I placed on the top shelf of the closet, and I closed the door.

Helen stopped talking.

"What are you thinking, Mrs. Clark?"

"Well, why am I telling this story in such a detailed way? 'I closed the door'? What the hell bearing does that have on my ultimate experience?"

"Actually," said the doctor, "it's significant. What you've been able to do here is be in the moment and describe your experience thoroughly. This helps me to pick out key moments that you may not identify as such. So, please, continue."

"Hmmm. OK."

I remember sinking onto the edge of the plastic mattress and grabbing my long hair, holding it up, away from my flushed face and neck, and taking a deep breath. I thought, c'mon, humor, I know you're in there.

And then I thought of Eddie Murphy in *Bow Finger.* If he was stressed, he'd say, "You gotta keep it together, man; you got to remember the words: Keep it together." And then he'd chant, "Kit kit kit kit, keep it together, keep it together. Kit kit kit kit."

I let my hair fall back down around my face and shoulders and sprang off the bed, thinking, Kit kit kit kit, keep it together, keep it together. I can do this, I thought. A week was nothing. How bad could it get? Keep it together: kit kit kit kit. Things weren't as grim as they appeared. Or what if they were? A week was nothing. Nothing at all.

Gerald returned with sheets and a blanket, and when I asked him if I could have a couple of extra blankets because I get very cold at night, he said to follow him, he'd show me where the supplies were kept, and that way, I could help myself to whatever I needed whenever I needed it. I remember one night, a couple of weeks later, when I was shivering so badly that I padded down that linoleum hall three times for three additional blankets.

They shot me full of methadone to get me off the wonder drug.

At this, Dr. Savage blurted, "Say again?"

Helen turned to see his stunned expression. "That was their fucking treatment plan. They discovered that the wonder drug had an opiate effect comparable in strength to that of a heroin addict."

Savage aggressively cleared his throat. "That's a new one. Please go on."

Helen closed her eyes and continued.

I was high on methadone for a few days. Those were a couple of great days. Every aspect of the place was extraordinarily fascinating.

But then, by day three, no high. But no pain either, because of the methadone. A week goes by and I'm feeling good. I'm ready to leave. But they tell me that I've only just begun, that they didn't know the extent, and that it will take weeks.

In short, no one knew how to get me off the wonder drug. But withdrawing from methadone was common knowledge. So? They hooked me on methadone to cover up the painful withdrawal. Without any attempted explanation at all, they had created a situation where I would be bunking in this place for another three or more weeks. There was no real accountability because of the no-assigned-doctor thing. The doctor's on leave, the doctor's on vacation, the doctor on call is out for the day. He'll/she'll be in tomorrow sometime, they'd say.

Finally a doctor showed up, and answered some of my more pressing questions. I was told that the reason I'd ended up there was that I wanted to remain close to home and that the locked down detox unit was the only game in town. Unfortunately, due to government support cutbacks, the detox unit also had been forced to downsize. This meant that the sane and insane cohabited—went to the same discussion groups, the same addiction classes. They ate together and slept two in a room.

After a fairly brief rundown of personal history, the doctor agreed with the drug decisions already in place. As if a choice remained at that point. So it was settled, well, resettled. Since I'd been dependent upon an opiate for over three years, it would take the power of methadone to get me off.

In lieu of an explanation, and because he was short on time—what with his handling his cases and some of my doctor's as well—he told me it was a difficult withdrawal and asked me if I was strong enough to go through it.

Number one. What if I wasn't, and, number two. That's a perfect dare for a feisty gal. I gave him the A+ answer that he knew I would—of course I was up to whatever it took. He said good and left with a see you in a day or two. He left without giving me any description of what I'd be up against. And of course I'd been too scattered to ask.

My body began seriously craving the drugs it was being denied, and the drill turned tough and really God-awful—every morning with the wake-up at six a.m. and each morning feeling even worse. Shower, dress, pills, breakfast, exercise, pep talks, AA meeting, lunch, group discussion, craft class. I loved the intensity of the craft class, hung out in there as often as possible, made trivets with tiny colored tiles, and taught others about design. Group therapy, pills, dinner, ending with a final group discussion, identifying what we'd accomplished, which was basically getting through the day.

I napped as often as I could get away with, but some counselor or another usually came and dragged me to class. I'd ask if I had to and they'd answer, No, you don't have to, but if you want to get out of here...

A week later, I was beside myself with shakes, chills, and itchy skin, slept in my clothes under my covers whenever possible, and began calming myself by chanting while I struggled with the now difficult chore of putting on my shoes for meals.

Mealtime had taken on true significance. Before eating, it was line up for pill time. And then onto the mess hall, knowing the pills would be kicking in soon. Through trial and error, I found the combination of cherry Jell-O and vanilla ice cream to be the least offensive meal. Actually it was delicious. It remains a staple item in my civilian life.

So there I was in boot camp: Sleep, up, pills, eat, show up for mandatory class, and listen to something I could have taught in my—Sleep, up, pills, eat, show up, sleep, up, pills, eat, show up, and sleep.

When my kitchen timer beeped me awake for mandatory class, I'd swing my feet off the bed and onto the floor, bend over and verrry slowwwly wrestle on my shoes, chanting: One two, tie my shoe—three four, open the door—five, six, get my fix—seven eight, don't be late—nine, ten, eat again. One two, tie my shoe—three four, open the door—five, six, get my fix—seven eight, don't be late—nine, ten, eat again. One two, tie my stupid shoes—three four, open the stupid door—five, six, get my stupid fix—seven eight, don't be fucking late.

Meals for me were wretched. I knew I had to fuel my body, to eat three meals a day, and drink water and more water to keep myself hydrated.

Thank God for the Jell-O and ice cream. The rest of the food wasn't nearly what I'm used to, and it's a challenge to eat with the kind of company who chew with their mouths open, who aggressively and consistently belch, who strike up conversations with each other on the absurd assumption that anyone understands anyone else, and who then wig out.

And yet, they tried, which touched my heart. The people who weren't in the first throes of the shakes would make the effort to communicate with one another.

Meanwhile I tried to stay in a zone of hanging tough, and talked as little as possible, because I had observed that it was hard to not be misunderstood. For example, what could begin as one inmate striking up a conversation could swiftly spin out of control as the person speaking uncovered a troublesome memory. A tirade of nasty words could ensue. One or the other would sometimes move to another table for relief, a movement of endearing logic.

My way of coping with these edgy exchanges was to listen, show concern, and when it became my turn to speak—when the person would stop and look expectant—I'd say, you're right, or, absolutely, or, yep, or in some cases, that's right, and good luck, as I made my exit. Of course this isn't just a skill meant for psychiatric wards—it's one we all use in ordinary life. See, there really is the thinnest line between them and us. It's maybe a pill away.

One day there was a woman who plunked her tray down across from me and just sat there, shaking as badly as myself, staring right at me. I ate slowly, holding my bowl right below my chin as I tried to spoon the Jell-O and ice cream into my mouth. I knew she wanted me to recognize her presence, but the challenge was to say something noncommittal, so I didn't mistakenly set her off. I pictured myself running for public office, and it came to me. I pursed my lips, offered a slight grin, and said earnestly, Never pluck your eyebrows when you've got time on your hands. She let that sink in. Yep, she nodded. You got that right. She removed her food-warming lid, and grabbed her utensil, as she put her face way down near the plate in the hopes of getting most of the food into her mouth.

One gal, six feet tall with flaring nostrils and an attitude, was a three-peat and proud to tell the score to anyone who would listen. "Let me tell you how it is here," she would say. "In other parts of the world, people celebrate Friday, because it's the end of the workweek and time to party. They call it TGIF, thank-God-it's-Friday. But here we like Monday. We call it TGIM, thank-God-it's-Monday, because we're relieved we just got through another tempting weekend without surrendering to drugs, that we survived another lonely weekend without blowing our brains out. That's how it is here." I remember thinking what a fascinating way to put it. Around about the eighth time of hearing the exact same speech, I moved to another table.

There was a peppy young repeat who really cracked me up, because he just blurted out whatever occurred to him without editing his thoughts. He was a crazy salad toss, a sort of forthright yet unintentionally offensive comic. But I figured out that he wasn't going for rudeness at all. He just thought it was funny to get any kind of rise out of someone. At our group therapy sessions, all he'd have to do, practically, is open his mouth and I would burst out laughing; he loved that he made me laugh, which encouraged him to spiral into ever-crazier blurt-outs. I nicknamed him Bozo, which he liked, and it caught on. Humor strained the counselors' patience, so Bozo was given many time-outs.

I remember once in the mess hall, when he sat at the head of the table. As usual, he chose a way too appropriate topic. He looked at the new guy sitting next to me, grinned and said, "You're a loon." I actually felt the guy's foot stop shaking, not a good sign. I leapt into the fray. "There's an abundance of loons," I agreed. It worked.

He turned his attention to me. "Your elevator doesn't go all the way up to the top." He grinned wider. "You're short a full deck of cards." I grinned back. The new guy's foot was back to shaking; we were safe. Bozo was delighted with our game. "You're two bananas short of a bunch." He giggled. "You're one quart short of a gallon." I laughed.

"You're…you're two tacos short of a fajita." This was apparently his favorite, because he broke into such riotous laughter that he began choking, so a counselor rushed over and held his arms over his head, and then took him away for some alone time.

The Prophet lived on an alternate level. When he ate, he would forget to swallow, just kept stuffing food into his mouth until it began squishing out the sides of his mouth onto his cheeks or falling onto his chin. The aides would remind him to swallow. After he ate, he would ask for another tray of food. And after eating that, he would go into the kitchen and get several sandwiches, all the while looking around to make sure no one could take his food from him. Whenever the kitchen was open, there was the Prophet, hurriedly taking whatever he could hold.

Fifteen days into my supposed seven-day treatment plan, I began my own plan—to get out. It was simple. I would act energetic and create a healthy appearance with the aid of makeup. I would thus be signing myself out before dinner.

Heads turned when I showed up in the six thirty a.m. pill line, all sparkly in my makeup.

I met my first resistance and had my first clue when an aide at breakfast gave me the following day's menu to fill out. "Ya know what?" I said with great gusto.

"What?" she said, mocking my cheerfulness—the fat fuck.

"I shouldn't fill this out, because I'm going home today."

"Reeeally," she said, and then left as I was saying, "Yep." She returned swiftly, saying she'd hate to see me have to eat any old thing tomorrow in case I needed to stay on past the next meal or two. She again presented me with the menu.

"That would be pretty bad," I agreed, and immediately began writing in my usual a la-carte items, my cherry Jell-O, my vanilla ice cream, my vitamin D milk. I was elated to discover macaroni and cheese as a choice for the next night.

I'm heavily detoxing, I'm shaking from head to toe, unless I force myself to be still, which is mighty tough and takes practically all my pathetically limited energy. Apparently whenever I doze off, someone has been inserting shaved ice into my middle-aged veins. I'm having difficulty breathing with the drug toxins now coursing out of me. My skin itches so badly that I'm taking three showers a day.

My temporary relief right then was the act of paying attention to my a la carte menu. In that moment of my fucked-up life, going without that temporary pleasure, and the future temporary pleasure that I was ordering, and could look forward to counting on, mattered to me more than the intangibility of freedom. Because, when I stopped and thought about this freedom thing what would that be? The freedom to have all those horrible feelings alone at home for empty hours and hours until my beautiful, anxious husband came through our door at the end of the workday not having any clue at all about my condition?

No, these were my people. We understood each other's condition. In other parts of the world, they celebrated

Fridays, but here we liked Mondays. Here our existence had a simple formulated reliability. This, I needed.

Totally spent from my public charade of feeling absolutely well enough to return to my natural habitat, I trudged back to our room and crawled onto my cot. I was teeth-chatteringly freezing cold, but could not even muster the energy to pull a blanket over me.

It was too much.

Helen sat up on the couch and asked Dr. Savage for a glass of water. As he got it, she deftly located the vial of Valium in her purse and slipped two into the side of her cheek, then politely thanked him and drank them down. Soon she was again prone, this time so relaxed she seemed to be back in the hospital's harrowing detox ward, simply reliving it...

My nap was abruptly halted when an aide scared the shit out of me by looming her mammoth body over my cot. "There's a doctor waiting to see you in the conference room. Walk this way." I couldn't have walked her way if I'd wanted, because, unlike lard-ass, my thighs were independent of each other.

He was doing paper work when I entered. I scratched my arms and sat across from him. Another doctor I'd never seen nor would I see again, and he said to me:

"I hear you want to go home, Helen. Is that right?"

"Yes."

'You're depressed?'

"Depressed is a relative word, Doctor. Right now, it's just before pill time and lunch, and some fat cow jolted me awake from shake sleeping." I offered him a good look at my shaking hands.

"That will subside over time. It's part of the drill."

I stared.

"So, are you depressed?"

"I'm crabby. I was sleeping, so I didn't know how awful I felt, but now I'm awake and I feel horrible."

"Are you depressed?"

"...Could you stop insulting my intelligence, please, and get on to something concrete."

"Depression is concrete."

"OK. The subject is depression. You. You are depressing me. 'Depressed,' Doctor? No. I'm feeling lighthearted, detoxing in a mental ward. Have you ever tried what you're expecting of me? Have you ever tried sharing your white upper-middle-class frustrations with people who live in boxes in the out-of-the-way corners of lower Wacker Drive, humans who don't even know how messed up they are—do not have a clue how impossible their situations are—could spend the next twenty years trying to climb out of a hole that's so deep they'll never ever see the light of day? Ever? And yet they try. So, if you tag me clinically depressed, Doctor, because I'm overcome with sadness for these people, then I tag you a lazy fucking burnout."

He stared, not a nice stare, a how-dare-you stare. The pompous prick then got mean. "You cannot get out of your depressed state by yourself, Helen. I can offer you choices: Prozac, Zanax, Elavil, Serzone, Paxil, Depakote, Haldol. You need something to go home with when you leave, which won't be now."

"Oh, my God," I said. "What are you people doing to me?"

I cried. He watched.

"We...this has turned into a drug debate." I sobbed. "Doesn't anyone get the fact that I don't do well on drugs? That all I want is my drug-free life back? That these depression drugs can have side effects so crippling that they create an even larger problem? Doesn't anyone believe in character overcoming depression? Has anyone bothered to review my personal history—have any of you bothered to ask me about my accomplishments—achievements I could not possibly have pulled off in a clinically depressed condition? Anyone?"

On day seventeen, I was taken off methadone completely. Now I was withdrawing from the original opiate and another opiate as well, with nothing for pain other than Motrin for aches, and Bentyl for stomach cramps. Nothing for the shakes. Nothing to relieve the feeling of ice in my veins. Nothing to alleviate the skin itch of released toxins. Nothing to do about the exhaustion that rendered me barely able to support my body in a sitting position.

I remember a group therapy class from that day. The inmates were encouraged to talk about their troubles—how they were feeling about their stay and why they had landed themselves there.

A newcomer, must be all of nineteen, is looking angry. He seems to be wrestling with his emotions. One of the social workers, an excellent leader, targets him to speak.

"You're looking like you have something to say," she says to him. He's surprised by her attention.

"Not really," he says as his color deepens.

"Are you finding the subject difficult?" she asks gently.

"What's the subject?" he asks belligerently.

"Why are you here? How are you doing?"

"I'm not supposed to be here…with these people," he mutters aggressively. "Pot was all I was on. This is bullshit," he says, as he turns his face away.

As I sit in the conversation pit with these people, my arms clutched tightly to my chest and my legs sprawled out in front of me, I find myself quietly humming a song through the clenched teeth of a recovering addict: "Getting to know you, getting to know all about you…" I shift my position to ramrod straight, sitting on the edge of my seat, then to elbows leaning on knees. I shift again, surrendering to the temporary pleasure of scratching my itchy skin, knowing I'm just provoking it. The itchiness increases immediately.

The coleader for this particular session is an overweight, heavily made up, irritating woman, named Janine, who seems on the verge of having control, but not quite in charge of whatever that might be. "OK, people," says Janine, "let's begin with a question: Why are you here?"

"Deja vu all over again," I mutter.

Janine pivots her neck to face me. "Helen, why are you here?"

"For my personal growth," I reply tersely through clenched teeth.

There is nervous laughter from several patients.

Janine keeps her poker face and asks again. "Why are you here, Helen?"

I open my eyes wide, emulating a small child. "To serve the medical profession as a human guinea pig?...One small step for mankind."

There are giddy laughs from the group.

Janine raises one eyebrow and takes a deep breath, "Helen, why are you here?"

I sigh heavily and speak in a monotone. "I'm here to overcome an addiction practically hand delivered to me by the awesome American duo: our self-serving ill-informed medical profession, and our greedy pharmaceutical conglomerates with their subservient glad-handers in Washington, who have conspired to lead us down pill lane. Pills will pull us through, slash, pills will make us rich."

Funniest thing, but that very night, yet another actual doctor, never saw him before or since, showed up to speak to me.

I posed the question of the day to my substitute for the substitute doctor. I said that I was convinced that I could have had this bad a time on my own. "So, Doctor, why am I here?"

"We monitor you every three hours to make sure your vital signs don't jump below the level of safety" was his answer. "You're depressed," he continued. "You're a depressed person, and we think you need meds for this depression. And we really can't sign you out without a med plan."

I said, "Let me ask you something, Doctor. Why would I consider yet another drug on which to become dependent when I'm not even free of the drug I came in to rid my system of yet, nor the drug you gave me to rid me of the original drug? Why would you suggest such a thing, when I have stated several times that all I want to accomplish here is to be drug-FREE?"

"Because you're depressed."

One in our group, David, was a welcome "ordinary" for me, a thirty-something alcoholic who came onto the ward the day after a serious drunk, having spent the night in the emergency room downstairs. He was educated and had come to the ward of his own free will, just as I had done. I watched him detox and normalize. He was focused on cooperating, learning, getting better, and getting the hell home.

When he began the detox phase two, getting off the meds given to him to get him off the booze, I decided to bond with him. "Listen, I just wanted to tell you that this is the most difficult phase of detox. Just ask me, the old expert," I told him earnestly.

The grateful look he returned melted my heart. We began sharing thoughts—discussing what just happened in the such and such group, and playing cards.

One night, I was playing gin rummy with David. The table was angled in such a way that we were both faced in the direction of my room, affording us an all-too-clear view of a drama that would play out.

God was about to humble me further.

My final roommate, Pam, all but unraveled the toughness I'd worked so hard to gain and maintain through my five weeks of ward life. David and I watched the young girl arrive and spend her first hour in the common area by my bedroom door, holding hands with her distraught mother, who offered words of comfort to her sad daughter.

As I watched this scene, I vowed to not say a word more than necessary to her. After stewing awhile, I snapped my chewing gum loudly and ranted to David. "Just Goddamn perfect. That's all I fucking need. Shit! All I need right now is to get tenderly engaged in comforting someone. Fuckin' A."

David whispered, "Maybe that would be a good thing—surely good for her."

I continued passionately snapping my gum, and said, "For her, yes. But for me?" I pointed to my shaking legs as an example of my jumpy physical state. "Imagine what my brain is doing to keep calm," I said. 'I've been told and told to focus on myself. The whole time I've gone to these classes day after day, the counselors have consistently advised me to self-focus, to help myself; that I can reach my core problems and deal with them if I apply the same passion to myself that I've always applied to my daughter, my mother, my friends, even my neighbors. And my husband," I concluded with another loud series of snaps.

David said, "That makes such sense. You have every right to concentrate on yourself, Helen, and I'm glad you are. But where would I be if you weren't here? You helped me tremendously, just advising me and being my pal."

"Don't tell me that," I said.

I was so intent on hanging tough that I told David I couldn't watch the mother-daughter thing going on in front of us, and I suggested we go to the television room where the night owls gathered to eat candy and watch vapid talk shows.

He said no, he'd rather read the old contraband *New Yorker* magazine I'd lent him.

Interestingly, the news wasn't allowed, but talk shows were big. That night, Bozo was in the TV room, so that helped. We got goofy, One side of your toaster doesn't pop up, and so forth. And everyone thought the formulaic television comedian was a real hoot. Goofy laughter is truly an answer. In retrospect, I see that I developed a broader understanding and deeper appreciation of the term, goofy, during my incarceration with so-called mental patients. Being off-center has little meaning when the center keeps shifting.

The beloved temporary comfort of sugar-high snack time occurred at two in the morning, wherein the door to the tiny "snack kitchen" was unlocked, and everyone eagerly took whatever they wanted, and ate and drank it. When lights out was enforced I crept into my darkened room, quickly yanked off my shoes and jeans, and climbed into my cot without even brushing my cookie-coated, milk-furred teeth.

I lay there facing the wall, curled into a fetal position, hugging myself to still my shaking, itchy body, trying to think, feeling deeply conflicted and unworthy. I was so strong compared to these people, how could I possibly be selfish enough to consider myself more in need than any of the others. But especially that child in the next cot.

I awakened at sunrise. I shifted in my bed and turned over to meet the tragic eyes of my young roommate.

"Are you OK?" came the child's thin little voice.

"Surviving," I said, and closed my eyes, trying to be dismissive.

Deathly quiet followed my callousness.

I couldn't go through with it. The child was too in need, so I opened my eyes.

"How are you?" I asked, cautiously. I was praying, please say fine and let me shake myself back to sleep.

"Oh…I'm OK. I'm just so tired."

"Me too," I agreed. "That's the thing. Just no stamina at all."

I racked my ravaged brain for something to say. I dug into my pathetically sparse repertoire of interesting conversation, and pulled up the fascinating story of why I was in the hospital, figuring the girl was probably curious. What I didn't see coming—what I was so completely unprepared for was the three-word story the child eventually told me.

I said, "Four years ago, I came through surgery with my right arm somewhat immobile. The pain was too intense to bear physical therapy. So my endocrinologist suggested I take a new drug for the pain. Virtually no side effects had been reported. The plan worked well. After months of therapy, I could rotate my arm. It still hurt, as well as my back, so the doctor suggested that I stay on the drug. Three years later, I began to wonder if I still had any real pain, so I discontinued the pills. For one day. At first I thought I'd caught the flu,"… blah blah blah…and then it was the girl's turn.

"What about you?" I asked politely, still hoping to not be moved by this sweet young girl.

"I have AIDS," she replied.

…I have AIDS was her reply.

I remember the ringing in my ears, and my heart seemed to stop for a moment. I could not think of anything to say. I couldn't breathe. There we were curled up on our twin cots, facing each other. We could have been telling cute little secrets at a Girl-Scout overnight. We lay like this, staring at each other as she waited for me to react. This little girl's fate was simply beyond words.

She wanted me to ask. She needed me to ask.

I wanted to kill the staffer who put this sweet girl in my room. You can bet it was well thought through. They knew I'd be better than the others with her. But was that the best thing for me? To force me to help someone else, when I was suffering such a crippling withdrawal?

I said, "I'm Helen."

"I'm Pam," she said with an almost palpable relief. She had a friend.

"Do you want to tell me about it?" I asked.

"I was with my boyfriend, once," she said, "on prom night."

"Once," I repeated.

She sighed. "Mmmhmm. After that, I wasn't feeling well, and I just became more and more tired. And then, finally, I had all kinds of tests done. And then they said, AIDS."

"I can't believe this," I said. "This is too horrible. It's just horrific. I'm so sorry."

The effort of hearing the news and then reacting to it so exhausted me that I actually fell asleep. She did as well. We awoke to the breakfast gong, in the same exact face-to-face positions.

I smiled.

"Hi, Pam," I said softly. "Breakfast was just delivered to the cafeteria if you're hungry. You can go in your night-clothes if you want. Need to use the bathroom before I do?"

"No thanks," she said sweetly, sadly getting up, looking in the mirror, smoothing her hair and opening our door to shyly peek out.

We walked to breakfast down the hall, past the phones where what's her name was holding court through the airwaves, telling some poor slob that "here we celebrate Mondays," and I remember wondering bitterly how many Mondays were left in Pam's life. I showed her the ropes and found a quiet corner for us to eat. Everyone was eyeing the new kid. "Don't make eye contact," I advised. "You'll meet them in class. They'll get to know you."

And of course she said exactly what I didn't want to hear: "But you'll be there with me, right?"

My stomach was in knots all morning. We went to group therapy as I schmoozed the group. (Pam's fine. Pam's with me.) The delight on David's face clearly indicated he'd thought I'd bravely risen to the occasion, which frankly made me want to puke.

Later that morning, she was preparing to shower before the temporary relief of pills and lunch, and I nonchalantly told her I'd mosey on out to the common area to give her some privacy. "Just open our door when you're done."

She thanked me in a tone of almost devout appreciation. My throat closed up and my eyes teared, and I needed to go home. My maternal feelings were raw with the bitter injustice of it all. There was nothing I could fix for Pam or for anyone. I could live here and watch all this misery, or I could go home and maybe fix me. Twice, I snuck into our bathroom to quietly cry. I needed to go home.

Things got simple. Pam was told she'd be moved to another floor for three days of testing, so she and her mother prepared to relocate.

Another roommate, Trixie, was checking in, designated to bunk with me. There was talk among the staff. It was decided that Trixie would get room #204 to herself for now, and that I would get a-room-of-my-own—the one single room in the whole place was mine! I was pathetically overjoyed. Everything is relative.

My very own room was located down the hall past the phones and just off the common area. We gathered there for our morning exercise choreographed by a staff member. It consisted of getting off the couch and stretching one way, then the other, and then holding our arms straight out from our sides for a full half minute. A certain spatial ability was required, because everyone had to shuffle to the left, no right, no left, so we wouldn't bump into each other. This screamed stamina for the strung-out lot of us as we attempted personal dignity by concentrating on not plowing into each other.

We also had our formal morning pep talk for the day in there. We'd mumble self-conscious encouragements to each other. One day at a time, man. Incoherent excuses about the unrealized plans from the day before would be followed by the grand new plans for this brand-new day. Our television was in that room too, only allowed on at night. And the nighttime snack kitchen, locked during the day, was but a slipper-and-robe-donning moment away from my very own private room.

Complications set in as I packed up to move. My makeup, which I hadn't used since that day I tried to paint myself normal and leave, was nowhere to be found. I looked in the four places it could possibly be, and then reported it missing. An incredibly short time later, it was returned in a small plastic basket. One of the patients had mistaken it for her own. We dialogued, with me wondering how that could be when it was in the drawer below my sink, and the counselor's detailed explanation, "Well, here it is, anyhow."

I quickly settled into my suite. By then it was dinnertime, so I collected Pam and her mother to have a last supper together, and found a safe table in the back by a window, where no one would bother us. Wrong. We were immediately joined by a skinny, mousy-looking woman I'd seen flitting around for the last couple of days, probably my age, but with fewer teeth. She hadn't yet attended any classes, but just sat around observing...mostly me, come to think about it.

We ate. No one talked. Fine, I thought. I'm good with silence. Not really. My internal Miss Manners was furiously telling me to speak up and be entertaining. But my crabby detoxing self was telling the interloper to fuck off.

"Looks like the last snow of the year out there," I managed.

Pam and her mother nodded sadly.

Mouse just looked at me with her raccoon eyes. I sized her up; talk about too much eyeliner...and what's with the missing left eyebrow...?

Mouse got up to leave, turned back to me, and said, "I'm sorry."

"OK," I said, the way I always did when some noodle was singing in a different time zone.

The next morning, as I was shuffling through the ritual of waking up to eat when I wasn't hungry, I went to brush my hair and couldn't find my hairbrush. It wasn't in #204, but Trixie was, and boy did she have a mouth on her. She did not like me. "You are really something," I said, brightly. "Wow, what an outfit." She liked me better then.

My hairbrush was discovered in Mouse's room.

Later, when I came back from a lecture on manic-depressive disorder, I passed Mouse who had on a mound of my color lipstick and my color blush.

"Sorry," said Mouse.

They didn't know how she'd managed to slip past everyone and sneak into my room. They were mystified as to how she managed to get my tweezers out of the locked storage closet. And then the decision that finally set me off was made.

I was taken aside by a counselor and told that they'd had a special meeting about my stalker. I needed to understand that she wasn't being malicious. On the contrary, she simply wanted to be me. They'd decided that since I was the stronger person, she should be given my private room, and I was to bunk with the new loud girl back in #204. "Let me get this straight," I began...My voice escalated off the charts as I raged about the injustice of their decision.

After I was done, the counselor congratulated me on letting it all out. "This is the first time you've really opened up, Helen," he beamed.

"What are you saying," I asked, hoarsely, "that this is good for me?"

"Yes, Helen. You're showing how you really feel."

"About this particular decision," I yelled, "about a moronic decision to give a stalker my room because she wants to be me. And I get to bunk with a hooker who won't shut up. What about my seniority?"

"You're depressed, Helen. You need to get on a med program and get out of here."

I walked out of the conference room and practically tripped over my stalker. She looked at me with total sincerity and apologized again.

"I'm sorry," she mumbled.

"Too heavy on the blush," I said.

And time for the final doctor chat. I'd asked to see a doctor on Thursday, on Friday, and on Saturday. On Sunday night, one finally showed up.

I cut to the chase. "Why won't you sign my release papers?"

"Because you can't be released without meds."

"Why?"

"You're clinically depressed."

"I was supposed to be here a week."

"You're clinically depressed."

"You're right. I've become very depressed with this ill-managed clinic, run by overweight burnouts…That's not a show of temper on your face is it, Doctor?"

"Tell me about your outburst over your room arrangement."

I did a short laugh. "That's simply a reaction to the typically illogical decisions made around here; scattered logic, and no accountability. Have you even read my notes? And yet here I am in your care—your care—with another ill-informed and therefore superficial diagnosis, another aggressive attempt to slot me into a condition, medicate me, and send me on my way, out into the bigger world and into the uncaring hands of some other arrogant shrink who can trial-and-error me through another haphazard round of..."

His response was to tell me to lower my voice, please.

Mine was to say I would not in the least, to thank him for finally showing up, and wonder if he could help me out about the thinking that was behind my needing to see a doctor last Thursday and no one showing up until dinnertime on Sunday, at which time he yanks me out of the cafeteria just as I'm about to eat the only good thing on the menu, the hamburger deluxe, special order.

Dr. Feel Good led me to a private side room and shut the door, and the interrogation was on. "How depressed are you?"

"I need to go home, that's how depressed I am. You live here," I suggested. "I'll go home. Then I'll come pull you into a little side office in a week or five and we'll talk about your mood."

So there I was in a tiny muffled room where I was again being coaxed into taking antidepressants. He said, "It must have been hard for you when your best friend died of cancer." He glanced up from the notes in my file, hoping for a five-star performance of unabated grief.

"What was her nickname...Other?"

He might as well have ripped out my heart. My feet began shaking as I gripped at self-control.

I swallowed vomit.

"Helen?"

"Hard...on me? Naw. At the time, but...now is now."

"And your accident with the resulting operations and therapy. Three years! My God, that must have been difficult to handle."

My lips were quivering and my voice was shaking. I wasn't up to shielding myself. And what the fuck was he doing? Breaking me down so that I'd beg for an antidepressant?

I set my jaw and hung tough. "That's old news. All over. Now is now."

"There is an antidepressant that could help you not feel so intensely about these past traumas," he began. "It's a new drug and hardly has any side effects. You could begin to feel some relief before you even leave the hospital, so that, in two to four weeks, these problems could shrink into the past and stay there."

I decided to not respect his professional title of doctor as the slimy bastard set out to shove me into the convenient slot that I had consistently rejected as wrong for me. I asked for his business card and studied it.

"And then what, Ed?"

He blanched at the Ed thing and then plastered a smile on and concluded with, "And then you live out a normal life!"

"That was already happening before I became addicted," I said.

"Well, you can say that if you need to, but the fact is you talk a good deal about your past traumas." He smiled condescendingly.

I remained composed, unwilling to break under his bullying. I sighed dramatically and said, "Ed, that's only because everyone here keeps fucking asking me about them."

The doctor's tone of voice got an edge. "Noooooo, actually, we ask what troubles each patient. You keep going into your past."

Now I began speaking very slowly and succinctly. "That's because,—and you people should know this from my personal file,—I have to go into my past to find something troubling to talk about. I'm content with my current life. Other than the addictive drug. Oh, wait; now it would be other than that and the methadone withdrawals, I like my life a lot of the time. My past issues are not of the recurring type.

My back operations happened long ago. And my childhood happened even longer ago.

"So," I continued, "in these discussion groups I've been attending, there's me—a pretty happy and accomplished midlife person—and then there's the rest of the group composed of people the same age as my adult child, only with bipolar and self-infliction problems, or older people more nearly my age, one difference being that I live in a high-rise overlooking the whole city and their last address was a box on the street. Where is the commonality here, Ed?

"Why am I still here, Ed?"

We said it together, me playing the conductor with my hands—"Because you're depressed, Helen."

I rose out of my chair to finish my thoughts. "And you know what, Ed? The difference between our lots in life is conflicting for me all on its own. I don't share your superiority over the chasm between me and the other inmates. I feel really badly for them and keep fighting my urges to help them all. So not only am I coming off two potent drugs, but I'm up close and personal day after day after day with these horrible victims of life's cruelties. And that's Goddamn fucking depressing,...Ed."

In the end, and after spending six times longer than the originally agreed upon time, I made a decision to spring the joint, and resorted to play-acting to achieve this end. I was still feeling the agony of my now double withdrawal symptoms, but could no longer see any benefit to hanging around while a new bunch of sad characters began to fill the vacated beds of those having been sent to various homes.

Later that day, when Helen was safely back in her bedroom, she would remember relating the story of her detox to Dr. Savage, laying on his couch and telling him, but what she didn't recall at all was ending the session with him.

After the Valium wore off, she thought she remembered being rather abrupt. It really couldn't have ended another way, she reasoned, because an abrupt beginning brought on by a need to digest an abrupt death probably required an abrupt ending.

She remembered that she'd stood up and said, "I need to leave here too, Dr. Savage. The more I talk about this, the more I talk about this. It's not going anywhere for me. I know everything I'm telling you, and I know what it means. I don't dislike you, Dr. Savage. I'm simply beyond this type of therapy. I know what I've got to do. Relating my experience of living through detox has simply reinforced what I already knew, which is that I can't rely on doctors and drugs to fix me, because you…not to be rude, you don't know enough.

"Thanks for this week though. You were helpful. That's, I think, where 'modern' medicine is right now—pills provide a temporary solution. The real work comes from within and there's no getting around it. Sooner or later, everyone sits down to a banquet of consequences. Guess it's my turn to be the host and the chef and the guest. My mother always said, and now I clearly see—there really are no easy solutions, and there really is no substitute for hard work."

She remembered his reaction. Dr. Savage had risen from his desk, assured her she could call anytime, and they'd shaken hands.

He was on the phone before Helen was out the second door.

Simon & Garfunkel's "The Sound of Silence" thrummed in her head. (Hello, darkness, my old friend, I've come to talk with you again…)

*God gave women intuition and femininity.*
*Used properly, the combination easily jumbles the brain of any man I've ever met.*
~ Farrah Fawcett ~

*Above all, be the heroine of your life, not the victim.*
~ Nora Ephron ~

# SATURDAY

By Saturday, Helen was so sleep-deprived that every move she made seemed clumsy. When she got out of bed, she stepped on her reading glasses, cracking the frame. When she was making her bed, she rammed her big toe into a suitcase stored underneath, painfully cracking a toenail. As she yelped and grabbed her toe, her bathrobe got caught on the bedpost, ripping the side pocket all but off.

In the kitchen, she banged the side of her head into an open cabinet, and broke a nail emptying the dishwasher. She burnt her tongue on hot coffee and lit the wrong end of a filter cigarette.

But the dramatic mishap occurred around lunchtime.

A mean-spirited crippled lady lived in the building. She aggressively maneuvered herself around in a customized electric wheelchair. Her bitter temperament led Helen to refer to her as "Sunny" behind her back, and it stuck.

Several months previously, she'd got hold of a black puppy she named Lucifer. The cute little Doberman puppy was frisky and playful and was seldom put on a leash. But now,

Lucifer had grown to the height of a petite woman, still frisky and unleashed. Sunny's spirits seemed buoyed by watching her frightened neighbors scurry out of the way.

Some folks sought out their two-inch-thick book of condo rules and found it clearly stated no unleashed dogs were allowed in the common areas and, furthermore, the leashed dogs were relegated to the service elevator only.

The case of the unleashed Doberman had been discussed in gossipy whispers for the past several weeks, with the consensus being: (a) The lady should be reminded of the rules and required to follow them just the same as everyone else. And (b) If she still did not obey the laws set forth, she should be fined as a punishment—how much was still a debate.

Clearly the leadership should have managed this problem, but didn't, under the heading of not wanting to reprimand a cripple.

People suspected management was waiting until "something happened" rather than addressing a "potential problem." They were.

That Saturday, Helen went to get the mail. While waiting for the elevator, she began studying her bruises, wondering how much fun a person could possibly have in one morning.

Having lost her focus, she entered the elevator and automatically pressed the button to go all the way up to the pool instead of down to the lobby. It took a while for the elevator to go up and come back down. Under the heading of bad luck, had that time delay in her journey to the mailroom not occurred, the next event wouldn't have either.

Annoyed with the stupidity of her morning, when the elevator stopped at the lobby level Helen aggressively shot out the opening door. Doberman was poised on the other side. Utterly confused, he regarded the situation as an attack and reacted by furiously growling as he leaped onto a thunderstruck Helen, pouncing on her left hip and thigh and throwing her to the back wall of the elevator, where her head bumped.

Although Helen had never been a screamer, she did, in fact, scream. She shrieked as she too went into attack mode. After an episode in college involving being beaten up by her first husband, she'd taken boxing lessons, during which she'd learned protection strategies, such as how to disable someone by punching them in the Adam's apple. This she managed to do to Lucifer.

"What have you done?" yelled the bug-eyed Sunny.

"He fucking attacked me, you idiot," roared Helen.

"No," snarled Sunny. "What did you do to provoke him? Call an ambulance," she screamed down the corridor.

"No, don't," yelled Helen. "We don't need one. Calm down everyone," she said to the gathering group. "Just go get James to come help."

As Lucifer whimpered, and his mistress raged on, Helen crawled over to the elevator buttons to push "Doorman." Sunny had somehow gotten a wheel stuck while struggling to swat Helen, but she still managed to grab Helen's hand. Helen pulled loose, banging Sunny's hand onto the front tray of her utility vehicle.

James the doorman was at the elevator within seconds. His initial facial expression was one of concentration, a man in action, but it changed to total fear as he saw the loose and yelping Lucifer. "Back up. Back up," he commanded Sunny. "Where's the damn leash?"

Helen saw it in Sunny's basket, and knowing how soon the dog could regain his strength, she grabbed it and attached it to the immobile dog's collar, securing the handle tightly to the brass elevator railing.

Meanwhile James grabbed the walkie-talkie from his belt and called maintenance to assist immediately. Two showed up, both looking petrified as they saw Sunny's Doberman, who'd somewhat recovered his senses and was now baring his teeth and growling. It was a nasty low and vicious kind of growl that no one ever wants to hear, unless they're someone like Sunny who has the dog's meal ticket loyalty.

All this time Sunny had been trying to get one of her tires freed from being stuck in the entrance crack of the elevator. She was beet red and screaming, "Stop it."

Helen tried to help her but was spat on and pushed away. The maintenance men untangled Sunny's vehicle, while Helen multitasked retching and escaping the crime scene, while uttering a thick, "Thanks, guys, we'll sort this out later." Gagging a combo of reprised coffee and orange juice, she got into the next elevator going up to the safety of her unit, which her shaking hands managed to unlock.

Wiping Sunny's spit off her face with the sleeve of her sweater, she hobbled down the hall to her bathroom, and made it to the toilet before throwing up. Brushing her teeth rose to the number one spot on her priority list. That checked, peeling off her clothes, and showering took over as number one. After she washed off the dog odor and human spittle, she stood under the soothingly hot running water and allowed no thoughts, just pleasant visuals—the bright white of the bathtub, the shiny silver of the shower hardware, and the clear purity of the water.

Finally calm, Helen relived the bizarre chain of the day's events. She began that kind of hysterical giggle she'd always had when life shifted into the roughest kind of slapstick. So far today, I've injured myself doing housework, gotten slammed by a Doberman, temporarily paralyzed him, and physically fought with a cripple. Oh, and was spat at.

When was the first time she'd had that giggle reaction, she wondered absently.

She remembered.

It was the day of her forced abortion when her mother was driving her home and broke the silence of Helen's excruciating sadness by saying, "Thank God everything is back to normal."

It was the day her first husband physically attacked her for pouring a full bottle of Jim Beam down the kitchen drain.

It was the day she'd discovered and confronted her husband, Steven's emotional infidelity.

It was the day she'd rudely rebuffed Helen Nevada's offer of friendship.

It was the day her father lay dying in the hospital, and she helped her mother through the odyssey of dealing with his mistress.

She hadn't giggled over the suicide though. Perhaps it was still too painful.

Helen took a nap.

The two hours she slept revived her spirits and helped soothe her wounds.

She went into the kitchen for coffee and turned the phone back on. There was a message from Steven, saying he was at the loop office, and she should walk over and meet him. They could see several movies and have dinner. Helen called to remind him that they had a dinner date with a condo couple they hardly knew. Steven had made a date with them at the barbecue, and they'd already canceled twice.

"We've got reservations for the four of us at LaScarola, Steven," said Helen, testily.

Steven said, "Helen, why are you so crabby with me? Did I do something?"

"No," she answered. "Not a thing. Nothing. Nothing at all."

"I see," he said. "What did I fail to do?"

"Anything, Steven. You're not home. You haven't even asked me about my therapy sessions. Basically, you're just waiting for me to get over this and be my old self again. Well I'm not my old self. I'll never be my old self again. And I need some support, Steven."

He coughed to clear his throat and keep his voice even. "That's what I thought you were getting from this Dr. Average." This was meant as levity, and actually Helen grinned, but let it pass.

"Savage," corrected Helen, primly. "Let me remind you, Mr. Clark, that you once needed constant special attention. It may have been a long time ago, but I came through with aces."

Silence.

"Helen you can't possibly mean that these two tragedies are comparable. You're comparing your husband's tragic accident to the suicide of a neighbor you knew socially. I mean, my God, Helen, I liked Max too, and actually I'm still upset about what happened. By the way, you never asked me how I was feeling."

Helen thought this over and realized Steven was correct in his analysis as far as he knew. She was stunned by her lack of comprehension, and immediately tried to behave within the perimeters that would apply if, in fact, she'd only known Max a little while as an amusing neighbor instead of the love of her life.

She said, "Oh for the love of God, I don't know what's come over me, honey. You're right and I'm really sorry. I didn't ask you. 'Course you didn't offer either, but still. How do you feel about witnessing a suicide?"

Steven's voice was sad. "Beyond the fact that suicide is horrible, beyond that, I liked Max. A lot. He made every party more fun. If I was bored, all I had to do was locate Max. Actually, I think the feeling was mutual, because he sought me out a lot too. And…I really thought that if you got to know him and Janet better, we two couples could end up hanging out together. I really looked forward to that."

As she listened to this innocent view, Helen had been holding her nose to stop her tears and processing how thoughtless she'd behaved in Steven's eyes. She also suddenly realized what a chump Max had played Steven for, which created newly formed feelings of protection toward her husband. "I'm sorry, Steven. I really am very sorry for selfishly throwing my anxieties at you."

Steven sighed the sigh of a man who thinks his wife is back to normal and obviously loves him. "Thank you, Helen. Let's try to put this behind us as much as possible."

He's being so gracious, thought Helen. He has no idea that a part of my life has flipped. Forever. She would have to sort this out later, but for now, she went into her automatic mode, taught by her authoritarian mother, of behaving appropriately no matter what.

"Well, OK," she said. "I'll be fun for everyone tonight. And I guess you'll just have to punish me in bed later on."

He didn't react to the double entendre the way Max would have. No one would ever react to her the way he had. Ever again. Helen felt flat, and exhausted from the charade of it all.

"That's my Helen," said her husband of thirty-two years. How about, you choose a movie and I'll meet you there."

"No, you decide. I can't.

"OK, I'll swing by and get you, and we'll walk over together." He was trying his best to help her along.

Self-disgust said hello as the old "kill-me-now" entered her thoughts.

"After the movie," Steven continued, "we'll change and enjoy an evening of good food and interesting company. Well, actually, I have no idea if they're interesting. But I'll enjoy your presence, anyhow."

"Me too," she managed.

Helen kept a framed picture of her and Max taken at the beach that fateful summer when she was twelve and he was fourteen. She took it from its hiding place on the highest shelf in the farthest corner of her closet inside a flowered hatbox. She placed their photo on her vanity and as always, melted at their innocent smiling faces.

Forgetting she'd already showered until too late, she was drying off as she faced herself in the vanity mirror. She stood there for some time staring at each part of her beautiful body and then into her eyes. This is the girl that Max loved, she thought sadly. She remembered the "takeoff" on the Mother Goose nursery rhyme that fourteen-year-old Max had paraphrased and recited to her again and again as he touched her.

Helen began reciting the rhyme as she looked at various parts of her anatomy.

This is the girl that Max loved.
This is the face
That belongs to the girl that Max loves.

These are the eyes
That are on the face
That belong to the girl that Max loves.

This is the smile
That comes from the mouth
That is on the face
That has the eyes
That belong to the girl that Max loves.

This is the mouth
That is also for kissing
That is on the face

That has the eyes
That belong to the girl that Max loves.

These are the breasts
That are caressed
That are on the girl
That has the eyes
That are on the face
That has the mouth
That smiles and kisses
That belong to the girl that Max loves.

This is the entrance
That is for sex
That causes delight
That follows the kisses
That are on the face
That has the eyes
That are on the girl
That has the breasts
That are caressed
That belong to the girl that Max loves.

This is the heart
That is tender and true
That belongs to the girl
That has the breasts
That are caressed
That are on the girl
That has the eyes
That are on the face
That has the mouth
That smiles and kisses
That follows with sex

That causes delight
That belongs to the girl that Max loves.

Today, Helen added,
This is the body
That has the womb
That had the babies
That caused the tears
That led to the death
That broke the heart
That belongs to the girl that Max loved.

Tears filled her eyes. The saddest girl in the world looked back at her. She heard Steven unlocking the front door. She saw on her French clock that it was 3:15 already.

"Hello," Steven called out pleasantly.

Helen yelled, "Hi, honey. I'll be out in a few minutes."

"Take your time," he answered. "The movie doesn't start 'til four."

"OK." She put the photo away, took several deep breaths and got on with the day. She gave herself a silent pep talk as she dried her hair and applied her makeup. Today is the only day like this you'll ever have. Make the most of it. Stay in the now. Forget the past. Create the future.

After throwing on slacks and a sweater, she found her husband in the kitchen, snacking on cashews. She kissed him hello, said, "All set," and off to the expected pleasure of the movie they went.

At 7:30 that night, Helen emerged from her bedroom looking stunning in her black knit suit, with a soft pale blue camisole underneath. She wore pale blue and black striped high heels and carried a matching purse. You could see her diamond earrings sparkling through her shiny black hair.

Her good-looking husband was checking his watch, waiting right outside her door. He knew she was always five minutes late, so it never failed to irk her that he purposely intimidated her by waiting there like that. He looked at Helen, smiled and said his usual perfunctory "You look gorgeous."

Yeah, I do, she thought. So what? Max would have gone nuts over her appearance, but not Steven. No desire there.

Steven wore a dark gray suit with a crisp white shirt and a navy-and-blue striped tie. She simply said he looked great too, although she wanted to unbutton his suit coat and give him an amorous chest hug. It would only have embarrassed both of them, because he wasn't into that anymore.

The handsome Clarks met their new friends, Buck and Thelma Peterson, in the lobby. Helen had no idea who they were, but Steven recognized Buck because they'd made the original date.

"I'll get the car," announced Buck. "And you stay with the Clarks, Thelma."

Neither Helen nor Steven could tolerate small talk very well, but the situation called for it. They small-talked through the car ride, into the restaurant until they all gave their drink orders. Helen avoided her urge to be sarcastic. No need to offend normal people.

As they sat there facing each other, Helen had the oddest sensation that they were smirking at her.

Finally Buck said, "So?"

"Yeah," said Thelma.

Both were looking at Helen with what seemed to be anticipation.

Helen smirked back. "What's the deal?"

Buck barked.

"Exactly," said Thelma.

"Details, please," said Buck.

"What don't I know?" asked Steven.

Apparently the Doberman incident had scurried through the grapevine, and their new best friends wanted a blow by blow. Helen preferred the role of backup rather than lead, especially now that being social had landed in the task category. Yet here she was on stage faced with an obligatory performance.

Steven stared, dumbfounded. "This is your idea of 'nothing much' when I asked what you did today?"

She'd actually forgotten it happened and grinned as a cover-up.

He flashed her his eager tell-me-something-funny smile.

She felt she owed him. "You could say I had a crash course in elevated animal behavior," she began.

It was easy enough to get drinkers laughing with a goofy rendition of an already over-the-top true story. They all went through another round of drinks before she managed to move the subject away from herself.

"So," said Helen. "How did you two meet?" Watching couples describe how they met was always good for a while, and at least it would be new.

It turned out that Thelma was Buck's "trophy wife," though they hardly put it that way. When Thelma was thirty-two, she was hired by Buck, then forty-six, to work the front desk of his insurance business. Apparently, her qualifications were her good looks and her smoker's voice. Obviously, Buck took an immediate interest in Thelma. It took Thelma a while longer though. After all, Buck was a married man with two teenage girls—"enough to make me move out right there, if you see what I mean," said Buck.

"Yeah," said Helen, "that's sure a reason to leave. Those teenagers. They are murder."

Buck looked momentarily confused. Steven taped Helen's foot.

The story continued. So, even though they were hugely attracted to one another, he for the looks and youth, she for the looks and money, Helen supposed, Thelma had refused to even have lunch with him for a good three weeks. About a year later, Buck was divorced and married to her. The hurry was that Thelma really wanted to have children and she was thirty-two, for God's sake. So right off the bat, they had a girl and then another one. Buck admitted that the whole thing sort of bit him in the ass when those two girl babies became teenagers, "which they are as we speak."

Totally taken by surprise at his candor and the fact that he was willing to make fun of himself, Helen almost spewed her mouthful of wine, as she snort laughed.

This encouraged Buck to continue making her laugh, so he said, "Not to mention the four weddings."

Helen placed her hand on her chest as she convulsed over this.

"The first two at the Drake Hotel, for Christ's sake."

"Well isn't it time to hire another thirty-two-year-old to work your front desk?" Helen asked with a smirk.

Thelma was not at all amused, but clearly this notion had crossed her mind, under that annoying life lesson of what goes around comes around. "Yeah, Bucky, maybe I should just come back and work the front desk for you—just to be on the safe side."

Steven saved them from escalating their awkward banter by saying, "Looks to me like Buck's got enough woman to handle already."

Thelma blushed and smiled at Steven in a flirty way.

Buck realized he'd been thrown a life preserver and grabbed on, with both hands. "Man, you can say that again. She's one energetic tiger, that's for sure."

Helen played along with this save-the-couple intervention by offering a quirky summation. "So," she said, "Some things are funny and some are…just not…like garlic gum is not funny, for example."

"Eww." said Thelma.

Buck puffed out his manly cheeks in fake disgust.

Steven laughed, which always pleased Helen, plus he was entering into his routine of stepping up to the plate for her when she went too far. For some reason, Helen got a real kick out of putting Steven in that position. It was a tease of sorts.

Their entrées were served and another bottle of wine was ordered.

Thelma threw up her hands and said, "All right, all right, enough about us. Your turn to tell us how you met."

"We have different renditions," said Helen. "Want his first, or mine?"

"I'll start," said Steven. "Honey, you chime in anytime I get a fact wrong."

"Sure," snickered Helen. "Remember though," she warned, "you've asked a teacher to tell you a story. This could be a while."

"Well! Thanks for that," said Steven, as she and the Petersons shared a chuckle.

"It's 1972 and Helen is a second-semester junior at Berkeley and signed up for my beginning computer class, which is taught at eight a.m. to establish who's serious.

"Berkeley's tough. You've got to have brains and stamina to get there and get through it. We establish rules of order from the get-go so no one's wasting their time."

"You do," said Helen. "That's what you like to do. Not all teachers are so stern, but as an upper classman, I knew what the score was anyhow."

Steven and Helen smiled playfully as they recalled the beginning of them as a couple.

"OK," said Steven. "First day, the twenty students show up early. The sign on the blackboard says Welcome to Computer

101. My name is Professor Clark. Please check off your name on the blackboard list and take a seat at one of the computers.

"Now, keep in mind the significance," Steven said to Thelma, "This is 1972. The future of technology lies in computer literacy and we are among the privileged pioneers. It's an amazing honor, a huge deal to be in that class."

Thelma thanked his inclusion of her with a wide smile.

Steven said, "I describe the course, ask the students to turn on their machines, and begin explaining the various parts to them. I can see they're all listening except for one, and she is clicking away on hers."

Helen took over. "He walks up behind me and sees that I'm composing a paper for advanced English literature. I'm so into my thoughts that I practically jump out of my seat, as he says, what's your name and what are you doing.

"I stand up, so he doesn't have such a spatial advantage and begin. My name, Professor Clark, is Helen Hemingway, no relation.

"He says, would you mind demonstrating what you know about this machine, Miss Hemingway, no relation?"

"I take this as demeaning," Helen told the Petersons, "so I answer sarcastically.

"I could, or I could just tell you that we share a common goal, Professor. Yours is to educate this class, and mine is to ace this course because, as a second-semester junior, I've got a big load, and I need one to slide on.

"The class snickers.

"Steven just stares at me. No offense intended, I add.

"None taken, he says. 'But nevertheless, see me after class, Hemingway.'"

Steven said, "I teach the rest of the two-hour class and notice that after the break, Helen doesn't return. But then, as the last student files out, there she is walking toward me. She faces me and says something like, Professor Clark, I'm going to be straight with you. I've read your syllabus and, frankly, I could teach the course. If you'll just tell me your objections, we can see where this will lead."

Helen took over and said, "He grins. I can see he's trying not to, but he does anyway. So then I say that I've looked at his morning schedule and since he doesn't have another class for an hour, I've taken the liberty of bringing coffee and doughnuts, so should we go outside where it's a beautiful day?"

Thelma sipped her wine and said, "Boy, you were one mature cookie."

"That's for sure," said Buck. "Steven, did you like her right away?"

He grinned at the memory. "I really did. What an original. She was also gorgeous. She was wearing jeans with a T-shirt and blazer, and sandals with painted toenails. She had an amazing body. She had rich, dark hair down to her waist, and the sexiest smile. You'll notice she's got one front tooth that sticks out just slightly."

Helen blushed and said, "It's not sexy, just crooked. She posed her teeth for the Petersons."

"No, that's sexy," said Buck.

"So what happened over coffee and doughnuts?" asked Thelma. "Were you attracted to the professor too?"

"Oh, yeah," said Helen. "He was so nonchalantly in charge. He got a kick out of me teasing him, but I saw that he clearly knew how to keep control of his students. Plus there's nothing sexier than a man dressed in a suit and tie who's concentrating."

"True," agreed Thelma.

"Well," said Steven, "I actually had no idea how to control this beautiful, intense radical. I guess that was part of the attraction. Helen was a rebel, but a polite one. As I got to know her, I saw that she knew how to state her strong opinions in such a way that others saw the point without getting teed off. Now that's a talent."

The waiter came over for coffee and dessert orders. This took a while, but in the end, they decided to order the flourless chocolate cake. Thelma wanted to know how in the hell you could bake a cake without flour, so they ordered one to show her.

"Well? Go ahead, Steve," said Buck. "What happened over coffee and doughnuts in the beautiful outdoors?"

"I actually still remember what Helen suggested, even the way she put it. She tells me that she is normally crawling into bed at seven thirty a.m., so of course this early thing wouldn't be working out. But she had figured that she'd make the effort for the first class, and then hand in whatever was required at the end of the semester. Or, she says, she could take the final right now, and pass and would that take care of the problem? Would that satisfy me?"

Buck said, "What a pistol."

"Yes, well I was always completely confident in an academic environment. In high school, it was where I could escape from my parents and more importantly where I shined. I've always loved studying, learning, teasing my future husband." Helen smiled across the table at Steven. In the candlelight, he could have been the thirty-three-year-old Professor Clark again.

"And your answer to the beautiful twenty-one-year-old, Professor Clark?" Thelma asked.

"I tell her that I can see where she's coming from, and I might consider her proposals, if she took my advanced computer technology class in her senior year. She asked what time it was offered. I said I hadn't decided that yet. How about eight to ten p.m., she asked. Sure, I said, What the hell difference did it make? She made me feel that way, like loosening up and being comfortable with myself. I've had other students ask for similar breaks, but only Helen ever managed to move me. It was her confidence, her gentility. She was thoughtfully rebellious, and this intrigued me. I knew I had to keep seeing her. And eight to ten p.m.? Perfect for getting together afterward."

"Did you feel that way too, Helen?" asked Thelma.

"Steven was everything I imagined a mature man should be," said Helen. "I had been resisting male advances since... high school, and he didn't come on to me. I loved that. Also, he was quite the handsome professor. Later, I learned that half the girls on campus had crushes on him. He was that powerful manly combination of tall, dark, and handsome, with the low confident voice. He smiled easily and joked with his students and got a kick out of them, but never did he lose control of his role as their teacher. And he never flirted, like so many of the other teachers and professors. In fact, I, me, the prude of the West Coast ended up seducing him."

Buck tried to get Helen to tell them about the seduction, and when that didn't work, he suggested they all have a nightcap at their place.

Steven got out of it gracefully by looking at his watch, saying time flies when you're having fun, and then telling them he had a lot of writing to do the next day—notes to his students to be handed to them along with their grades.

Thelma said, "You must be one of those teachers that students wait in all-night lines to sign up for their class, Steven." Helen wearily noted that Thelma had already developed a crush on the professor.

Home and exhausted, they talked about the evening as they prepared for sleep. They both had fun. The Petersons were nice and openly friendly and funny. Funny was important. Although the evening had been intellectually ordinary, it had been emotionally stirring.

They went to sleep feeling better about their relationship. It never hurt to retell your first passionate moments of falling in love.

They both fell asleep recalling how they had finally connected sexually, the morning after her Berkley graduation, and how their wedding was discussed with her parents on the evening of that same day.

*Professor Steven Clark waited until Helen Hemingway was graduated to begin their sexual courtship. Helen invited Professor Clark to join her and her parents for a dinner celebration after the graduation ceremony. Helen's parents loved him on the spot. So accomplished. So handsome. Such a gentleman.*

Steven got a kick out of Helen calling her father "Captain Businessman" and her mother "Mrs. Housewife." Although there was no clue during drinks and dinner, Steven could sense Helen's reserve.

That night, Helen's parents went back to their hotel around 11:00 p.m. and Helen wanted to stay up until morning. There were many parties to check out, but Helen was beyond that scene. They stopped for a bottle of champagne and cashews and walked to Helen's studio apartment. Steven had never seen it and reacted by saying that he was stunned at the artistic atmosphere Helen had created. He said that she'd never told him she was an artist, to which Helen quickly responded by saying emphatically that she was not.

Helen had had the place since her freshman year at Berkeley, so there was a "scrapbook wall" composed of mementos from her crazy drug days, the posters, the protests, the wild psychedelic designs. Interspersed with her freshman and sophomore years of complete craziness were serious black-and-white photos she'd taken for the school newspaper in her junior and senior years, when her behavior was less crazy but nevertheless still radical, showing rebellion against injustice, but also showing happy students, studious students.

There were two closets, one for clothes and one a fold-away bed. She'd painted on the wall and over the doors a mural of phrases and words she especially liked. They were organized into gradations from "hell," which was red and black and brown, on up to "heaven," which was pale blue and silver and gold. All the weather conditions appeared in the middle: sun, rain, snow, sleet, tornado, monsoon, overcast, and fog.

Helen's mural was a very telling picture of her personality, and Steven studied it thoroughly.

Hell was solidly involved in the sins. Pride, Envy, Anger, Avarice, Sloth, Gluttony, and Lust were entwined and connected in a ribbon effect, with an overlay spelling out "Captain Businessman," and "Mrs. Housewife" in Graffiti shadow-lettering.

"Heaven" had a kitten, and two cats. It had a map of the Berkeley Campus. Her friends' names created a circle. Steven felt his stomach flip as he saw a heart with "The Professor" on it.

Groups of books were stacked on either side of the bay window, with a view of the quad. There was a couch at the window, above which hung a lush fern plant in an elaborate macramé holder that Helen had crafted. Stacks of books supported a large top of edged glass creating a coffee table.

Helen was preparing their champagne party in the strip of a kitchen in front of the fourth wall. With each of her trips to Tijuana, Helen had brought back a few more Mexican tiles, and added them to her kitchen counter and wall. High on the wall was a yellow neon sign that said, "BIRD."

Steven sat at one of the two counter stools as Helen was pouring the champagne into fluted crystal Champagne glasses. "Pretty fancy glasses for a college kid," he remarked.

Helen explained that her parents had insisted on accompanying her to school and wouldn't leave until she was safely installed in this hugely expensive but tiny apartment. There were no furnishings, so as soon as her mother returned home, she sent the couch, the bar stools, three lamps, new linens, and a whole kitchen filled with "extras" she had laying around the house. "So these fifty-dollar glasses? They're extras from my mom's kitchen," said Helen.

"How sweet and generous of her," said Steven.

"She has her moments," said Helen.

Steven asked what the bird sign was all about. Helen smiled a self-confident smile that melted him on the spot, and she told him about her gang of girlfriends who all nicknamed each other. At first they called her Hummingbird, instead of Hemingway, and then Hummingbird just became "Bird."

"But you can't call me that," announced Helen. "It's a pal thing."

"Does this mean we're not pals?" asked Steven.

"No but I mean that in a good way," she said.

"Well, come over here, then," said Steven, "and we'll make a toast." They stood inches from each other. He touched his glass to hers but he also left his hand touching hers as he toasted, and she loved his gentle connection. "Here's to Helen Hemingway and all her many unique accomplishments." They smiled and sipped some Champagne. The longer he made no move to hold her or kiss her, the more Helen began to wonder if he might be gay.

Later in their life together, Steven would admit that he was terrified that she wouldn't like the way he kissed or that she wouldn't want his kiss. A thirty-three-year-old professor, Helen would laugh. That's so hard to believe. But he would defend his position by telling her how very much he wanted her to marry him.

Without even seeing if we were sexually compatible, Helen would ask. And he would answer that he knew they would be. He just knew.

Neither knew the other's sexual past, because they'd decided it was beside the point.

They talked until dawn, and at 5:00 in the morning, she made them breakfast. Steven suggested they take a walk to his place, so that he could shower and change, so Helen showered and threw on a summer skirt and a t-shirt and sandals. Out into the gorgeous day they went.

His place was on the other side of the campus. Helen liked it. It was a small one-level white stucco bungalow with a red tile roof and arched windows and doorways throughout. There was Spanish tile in the entranceway, leading to a small front room where there was a plush round sectional couch facing a tiled fireplace, flanked by floor-to-ceiling bookshelves filled to their limit. In the middle of the black-and-white striped sectional couch was a round glass and iron table holding oversized books.

His stereo system stood on a long library table under two arched windows. Another wall had framed artwork depicting open space, ranches, and horses. There were some handsome family portraits as well.

"Well, feel free to look around," he said. "I'm going to shower so we can get to the early showing of that underground movie you were talking about."

Helen stood there. Totally amazed that he still hadn't touched her. She said, "Professor Clark, how do you shave?" Taken off guard by the question, he said that he, uh, shaved with a straight-edged razor.

"Really," said Helen. "Did you know that I had a barber friend who taught me how to do that? Would you like me to show you when you're out of the shower?"

"Uh, sure," he answered.

Helen strolled around Steven's house and became convinced that he'd inherited all this splendor from a family member, or perhaps several. Not only was the house in perfect condition and order, it was spotlessly clean. Every room had built-in bookshelves, all filled.

She looked out the huge arched kitchen window onto a stone patio. Rows of flowers ran along the stone path leading to a vegetable garden. Well, she thought, I'm twenty-two and he's thirty-three. Maybe in eleven years, I'll have this adult look in my place wherever that ends up being.

Steven came out in a terrycloth robe, and found Helen in the kitchen still looking out the window. His wet hair was slicked back, which made it look even darker. "Say," he said. "I heard you were the new barber in town. Do you have time to give me a shave?"

"Why, yes I do," she answered. "This is my shop. We'll need three washcloths and a pan of hot water and your shaver and soap. You'll sit on this chair and I'll put my tools on the table."

"Right," he said.

Helen found a pan and filled it with steaming water. She took the three washcloths from him and put them in the pan of hot water.

"OK," she said. She threw a white kitchen towel over her shoulder and tucked another around Steven's neck.

"Would you prefer this standing up or sitting down?" she asked.

"Uh, sitting down," he answered.

First she took the washcloths out, one at a time, ringing each one and placing them around his nose, covering his face including his eyes.

"Oh, man, that feels great," he said through a washcloth.

She let the steamy washcloths open his pores as she ran her fingers through his wet hair, massaging his scalp. He moaned. Next she refilled the pan with hot water and put the cloths back into the pan. She lathered his facial hair and then began the gentle, but firm scraping of the blade on his face. When she was done, she put the steaming cloths back on his face, leaving only his nose uncovered.

Helen faced him in his chair and climbed onto his lap, her legs on either side of him and the chair. He was so aroused that she lifted herself up slightly so that she wouldn't hurt him.

Steven removed his washcloths and said, "I think, uh, sir, that you could achieve better leverage if you, say, removed your underpants."

Helen stood up, reached under her skirt and pulled them down and off.

"Like this," she said.

"Yes, exactly. Then if I open my robe and you lift your skirt, and get back on top of me, I can adjust myself into you...like that."

Helen let out a moan and then just kept moaning. Steven was breathing hard and moaning too, as she moved in and partially out of him. He was holding her head and kissing her with such desire, and then he put his hands under her T-shirt and gently massaged her breasts. She put her bare feet on the floor for leverage, moving with more force and faster. She experienced an intense climax. He stopped to let her fully enjoy it. Then she began moving again for him and after another few minutes this caused her to come again. This time he couldn't stop himself and he came with her.

It took them a long time to calm down. And then all they wanted to do was to climb between his sheets and do it again, because during the three semesters that they had known each other, they were already good friends and respected each other's minds. Both Steven and Helen were relieved and excited that they made love so easily together—in a way the final test of a soul mate.

At four in the afternoon, Steven's grandfather clock struck the time, and Helen suddenly realized they were supposed to be meeting her parents in an hour at the classy restaurant north of the campus.

Steven took over. "Call your parents and say the reservation is for six and that we'll pick them up at five thirty. I'll shower quickly and throw on a suit and tie, then drive you back to your place."

"Good," said Helen. "I love the way you take over." He threw off the sheet and looked at her and said, "We could save a lot of time if you want to shower now…with me."

Helen laughed. How sexy is that, she thought. "Yes, Professor, you're always correct."

They didn't save time, but they had fun and then raced like hell, and pulled up in front of the Hemingways' hotel right on time.

After their drink order, Helen excused herself to use the ladies' room. Steven said he'd walk with her to use the men's room. The restrooms were located off a beautifully appointed hallway, with a glowing atmosphere created by the golden tones of the wall sconces. There was a huge vase of fresh flowers sitting on a table between the two restroom doors. No one was around, so Steven took the opportunity to put his hands on Helen's waist and draw her near to him.

"Helen," he said, "I love you."

"I love you too, Steven," she said, with a wonderfully serene smile she didn't even recognize.

"I know your parents are leaving early in the morning for their drive back, and I know that you hardly ever see them, so how do you feel about me asking your father tonight for his permission to marry you?"

Steven would ponder her initial reaction every so often for years to come. So would Helen.

She said, "I, well I, I'm only twenty-two. I…could be too… young for you. How do you know how I'll turn out?"

His initial reaction was amusement. It was such an honest and innocent response. He grinned, and said, "You've already turned out beautifully. And you seem to have grown up a long, long time ago."

Helen put her arms around Steven and pulled him close. She whispered that she would be honored and delighted to marry him.

They were in love. They were in lust. They were in heaven.

After the drinks, and the meal itself, Steven, seeing how much Helen's parents enjoyed a drink, suggested they go into the smoking lounge for an after-dinner liqueur. "Perhaps a cigar," he said to Mr. Hemingway.

"Do you smoke, Mrs. Hemingway?" asked Steven.

"I do on occasion," she answered. "Is this an occasion?"

Everyone thought that was worth a laugh, even Helen's mother.

As they smoked and drank, Steven turned his attention to Helen's parents. He said, "I've loved your daughter since the first day we met, and I'd like your permission to marry her."

Helen's father was taken aback, but her mother just beamed. "Well," she said, "you're eleven years older, so you'd probably be up to the task of keeping her grounded."

"Mother!" exclaimed Helen.

Mr. Hemingway chomped down on his cigar at the remark. He spoke up. "I see clearly that your union could be propitious. I think Helen's mother means to imply that our daughter is only twenty-two, and might not be prepared yet for marriage and its routine."

"I'll speak for myself," said Helen's mother. "We all know that Helen has a wild side."

She turned to Helen and asked her what kind of a wedding she'd like to have. Helen gave her the only answer her mother would have accepted. "I trust you implicitly, Mother. Whatever result you're looking for is what you deserve to have." She said this somewhat snidely, but no one caught it. Her mother radiated.

Helen continued, "I'll be here until June, wrapping up my extracurricular activities, so anything you want to arrange is..."

"Well, but this summer, right," said Steven.

"Perhaps this fall, this fall would probably be the earliest I could arrange everything," said Mrs. Hemingway. "Harold and I had no say in our wedding, so this will be my first and only chance to plan a big, beautiful wedding."

"How, how big are we talking here," asked Helen.

"Well, our side alone goes well over one hundred fifty, probably two hundred, counting the friends you've made here," her mother answered. "And that's another thing. Protocol dictates that all out-of-town guests should be completely taken care of. This means airfare, hotel accommodations, and meals. Then there's Steven's family and friends."

Helen sat there with a blank expression on her face, waiting for this to be over. She put herself into another zone, removed herself from any emotion her parents might evoke. They talked on, ordered more drinks, all got slightly inebriated.

And then it was time to ask Steven all about his family. This, Helen found interesting. Steven came from a complicated family, and she was high enough to find his being put on the spot amusing. She grinned at him. He gave her the you're-being-infantile look. She giggled. He cleared his throat, and launched into his family, so to speak.

"Well, the short version of my people would be this: I was raised in Wisconsin. My parents divorced when I was eight.

My mother's mother had died the year before, so she asked her father to come and live with us. She said she could handle my little sister, May, who was seven, but she needed a man to help her boy. This turned out to be the best thing that ever happened to me, because my grandfather was my hero. He encouraged my athletic endeavors, sat at the table every night while I did my homework, and raised me to be a gentle man. My mother was able to stay at home to raise us, thanks to my grandfather's generous financial support.

"Good job," mumbled Helen. "Tell only the good parts." Steven mugged the show-a-little-mercy look.

Steven continued. "So, let's see, as far as wedding guests from my side of the family: There's my mother, Louise, my grandfather, Henry, my little sister, May, her husband and four children, my mom's sister, Ida, my dad and his wife, Bunny, their three adult children. (Larry, Curly, and Moe, he muttered to Helen. This she loved.) And, uh, then, as far as my friends go, it's up to you. I've got a lot of friends, though. There are my childhood friends, some of my fraternity brothers from the University of Wisconsin, My peer group at Berkeley. I don't know how big you want this to get."

Mrs. Hemingway's eyes were twinkling as she said, "Well, we'll just see."

Helen knew that her mother's enjoyment was twofold. The wedding planning would be of great enjoyment to her. Finally an unencumbered wedding. The other part of her fun, though, was sticking it to her husband. This wedding would be hugely expensive. As much as Helen disliked her mother at that point in her life, on some sisterhood level, she felt a slight giddiness that Miriam finally had the chance to be unmercifully vengeful to the part of her husband who had been adulterous.

When it was finally time to go, Helen put on a good show during the car ride back to her parents' hotel, and wished them a safe trip, all the while giving herself an inner pep talk. This is nearly the last time you'll have to devote yourself to them. We just have to get through the wedding and that will be that. Everything will be fine after that. No surprises, just a nice life with her man, Steven. Right?

Wrong. She no longer had illusions about adult life. She now knew what she'd suspected all along. There's a flip side to everything, and you never know what corner it's around.

Helen thought about the advice Steven's seventy-four-year-old grandfather had offered the almost four hundred guests at their unforgettable wedding. Every once in a while, Henry Clark just popped into her mind. That night, he had come up to the stage microphone and spoken of Steven so lovingly, and ended his speech with how happy he was that Steven had found his soul mate, Helen. What a soul mate, he said playfully. And then he said he had a piece of advice for this young married couple, just beginning their life together.

He said, "Life can be very, very long if you're not doing what you love. Cut your own path and go for it. Remember the necessary words—unconditional love, and stamina. These will take you through your whole life together."

Now that she'd lived half her life, (or more, who knew?), she couldn't agree with the advice. No. It just wasn't that fucking simple. If all there was to it was unconditional love and stamina, then where did Max Shaw fit into the picture? Where did pure sex fit into life? What about complications, such as Camille's conception, for example? Think of all the years of happiness Max had given Steven by way of Camille.

Helen desperately needed to think this through. Perhaps she should have told her psychiatrist what her real current problems were. In a weird way, though, Helen felt she would be betraying Steven to tell anyone about Camille's conception. No one knew. No one in the whole wide world.

Now.

Her mind played "My Sweet Lord" over and over again.

*In the long run, we shape our lives, and we shape ourselves.*
*The process never ends until we die.*
*And the choices we make are ultimately our own responsibility.*
~ Eleanor Roosevelt ~

*Follow your passion. Stay true to yourself. Never follow*
*someone else's path*
*unless you're in the woods and you're lost and you see a path.*
*By all means, you should follow that.*
~ Ellen DeGeneres ~

# THE SECOND SUNDAY

After awakening at her usual nocturnal cookie hour and read-lulling herself back to slumber, Helen sprang awake again at 4:30 a.m., then cover-tangled fitfully for another hour, tossing to a Steven thought, flipping to Camille, turning to a Max thought, flipping to Camille.

She semidreamt, aware that she was in an out-of-body nightmare. She was looking down at a flat glass plate. On it, she saw her image reflected in a teaspoon of liquid, along with her mother and Steven and Max and Camille. She heard murmurings, but couldn't make sense of them. She watched as the liquid began to move and their faces became commingled in the swirling liquid. She backed away, her eyes refocusing to allow a bigger view. She saw that she'd been looking through a microscope and, with sudden clarity, realized they were cultures in a Petri dish.

She awoke, soaked and shivering; threw off her covers, got up, put on socks and flannel pajamas and a robe; lit a

Fantasia, snuffed it out; lit another and sat in her red leather arm chair, smoking and figuring out what in the hell her life had been all about, and what, for God's sake, was that nightmare telling her. Jesus!

Helen never had kidded herself about her affair with Max flipping to the dark side. But without Camille around, she simply hadn't cared. Personal pleasure was such a rare, uneasy choice for Helen. But, she was so in love with Max. Just this one time, she'd thought. Just that once, she chose living in the now of herself…just that once. Caution thrown to the wind had briefly been an ecstatically warm breeze before plunging to a tsunami. And here she was, reeling from the momentary pleasure that brought lasting disaster.

Perhaps that kind of exquisite pleasure cannot be sustained. Of course it couldn't be. How could it be? It couldn't. It wasn't.

*The disaster had come only a couple of weeks ago. Steven was at work, Helen was teaching senior computer training down at the Cultural Center as a volunteer, Max was working from his home office, and decided to walk out into the sunshine to Starbucks for some coffee. He was revolving out the main condo entrance, when who should be hopping out of a cab, but Camille Clark, home on holiday from Cambridge, earlier than expected, as a fun surprise.*

*In a heartbeat, Max recognized the possibilities of this chance meeting and began working it to his benefit on the automatic pilot he'd used his whole life long, that of charismatically doing exactly what he wanted to do, or thought he wanted to do.*

*To Max, this chance meeting was righteous destiny. Now was the moment for careful action. Time spent charmingly could coax wishful thinking ever closer to chosen reality.*

Mr. Charisma helped Miss Key-to-the-Kingdom out of her taxi, reminding her that they'd met briefly at some condo thing before her mother had whisked her away. She didn't remember, because it hadn't happened, but she'd heard about him through her dad's descriptions of condo life, Max Shaw being a highlight.

They began chatting. He said her parents were gone for the day. She was disappointed. He sympathized, "What a bummer," and explained where Steven and Helen were, as an assurance to Camille of how utterly close their friendship was. She took it. He seized this opportunity to nonchalantly suggest they have lunch at the outdoor cafe across the street in Millennium Park. She thought that was a fun idea and really was famished because, of course, she wouldn't touch the airplane food. A beaming Max put Camille's luggage in a holding area near the doorman's desk, and off they went.

They were both wearing sunglasses, but ever the think-ahead guy, Max knew if they sat at a corner table, the trees would shade them and eventually they'd both remove their eye camouflage. This was his opportunity for Camille to discover her first essential clue. It was his plan that she discover who he was, the truth of their relationship slowly sinking in. Once that happened—and he fully intended to methodically pursue this to its eventual conclusion—then it would be possible for him to take Helen and their daughter away from Steven. They belonged to him, not Steven.

"So, how fun are all those 'clicky' condo dinner parties for you, Mr. Shaw? My dad tells me that you can turn any party into a riotously good time. He says they'd be nothing without you. He gets a real kick out of you. Man, the park looks amazing. And the lake and all the boats. It's always fun to come home. I just love Chicago."

Max was delighted to hear that Steven liked him so much that he praised him to his family. One more inroad toward Helen's desire for a life with him.

He said, "Yes. The park is gorgeous. Never get tired of it...so what does your mom say about those goofy parties?"

"Um...hmm...I don't think she's mentioned them. She writes more about what she and Daddy do for city fun—the plays they see, the restaurants they try, their old friends who come to visit...That's always fun for them. They love to entertain their guests by showing them their favorite places."

(Chest pangs of jealousy.)

Now they were seated exactly where Max had envisioned them sitting. "I think we just got lucky," he said to Camille. "We beat the lunch-hour crowd because it's only eleven thirty."

"What a nice shady area," he said, and removed his sunglasses.

"Yeah," agreed Camille as she put hers on top of her head.

Their waitress asked what they wanted to drink, and Max held out his hand toward Camille, saying, "Ladies first."

Camille pondered whether to have a drink. She liked to drink pinot grigio, but not at 11:30 in the morning with a neighbor she only sort of knew through her parents. "I'll have a Pepsi," she said, "with a lemon, please."

"I'll have a Pepsi too," said Max, "with a bourbon, please." He winked at Camille.

Camille smiled, but she felt slightly uncomfortable. His eyes were amazing,...but...something else, she thought.

Max looked back into her eyes, and thought, finally, she's noticing. Put it together, Camille. They're your eyes, for Christ's sake. He asked her how the flight had been, a purposefully mundane question so she'd easily be able to automatically respond while focusing on the eye thing.

"The flight was, you know, long and tedious. But I read a great book, *The Secret Life of Bees*, by Sue Monk Kidd, which I highly recommend, maybe not so much for you, but perhaps your wife and, well, do you have a daughter, Mr. Shaw?"

He drank some water. "Janet and I were unable to have children after her first experience of miscarrying." Max phrased his answer perfectly. He hadn't lied. He and Janet could not have children. But he did, most assuredly, have a daughter.

"I'm sorry," said Camille.

"It's all right," said Max. "We've done just about everything else. And my sister has two boys. They spend summers with us. They're about your age, actually, if you'd like to meet them when they return from their boat trip next week." (Wanna meet your cousins?)

Camille smiled politely. This was always happening to her lately—parents matchmaking for their sons, nephews, best friend's kids, and on and on. "I'll be back in London, but thanks for the thought."

"If I did have a daughter," began Max, "she'd probably have eyes exactly like yours."

Bingo!

Camille stared into Max's eyes. Then she stared at Max's eyes. So familiar. He wasn't flirting, was he? No. Wait! That was it. His eyes were the same shape as hers, the same unusual turquoise-blue color, and they were outlined by black eyelashes. How very unusual.

She narrowed hers. "And why would that be, Mr. Shaw?"

This threw him off. He couldn't be direct, or Helen would never forgive him. "Well because we've got the same incredible eyes, that's why. We could be related, for Pete's sake."

(Too bold? Maybe not.)

"That's it," she exclaimed. "That's what's disconcerting about you. We have got similar eyes…and they're quite unusual. I mean, have you found that anyone else has this color, this kind of turquoise-blue color?"

(Be careful here, buddy-boy.)

“Uh, just in the movies…and I’m fairly sure they wear colored contacts.”

“Do you?”

“What?”

“Wear…”

“Wear colored contacts? Hell no.” He laughed at the idea. He was, to be sure, happy with his looks, but he’d never thought of enhancing them. Why would he?

“Ah. Thank you,” he said to the waitress who placed his glass of essential alcohol in front of him. “Shall we order?”

They both ordered salads, another drink for Max, and began eating the warm French bread set in a basket on their table.

“I’d be happy just eating this. Mmmm, this sweet, whipped butter is delicious,” she said.

Just like her mother, thought Max. What a thoroughly delightful young lady his daughter had turned out to be.

Camille’s cell phone rang, to the tune of “Reveille,” which always made her laugh. Max laughed too. My God, he thought, she’s got Helen’s exact laugh. Her beautiful mouth spread wide, allowing the infectious giggle to escape.

Camille excused herself for taking the call, “but my friends are trying to get a plan going, so…”

Max said, “Sure, of course.”

She didn’t stay on long, but when she clicked off, she looked at him, again staring at the eyes. Something…somehow a level of discomfort was rising, sort of creeping her out. “I, um, I’ll bet I took you away from your work, and my friends are coming over soon, so…is that cool, if we leave after we finish our salads?”

“Sure,” he said. “Cool. We can get ice-cream cones at the park pagoda for the walk home if you’d like.”

“I’d love that,” his enchanting daughter said with a smile.

Helen arrived home about 4:00 p.m., opening the door to the sound of a bunch of raucous girls. Her heart leapt with joy as she grabbed her daughter and held her close. All seven of Camille's friends earnestly hugged her mother. The Clark home had been the party-place forever, so Helen knew them all well. She believed her duty as a stay-at-home mom was not only to provide a safe place for gathering, but also to know the influences in Camille's life.

Helen was about to discover an alarming new influence who'd managed to slip onto the Clark family stage through a side door.

Steven was having his weekly faculty meeting, which always lasted through dinner, so the girls began begging Helen to at least join them for a while at their favorite restaurant in Chinatown. Helen was considering this and about to say yes, when Camille asked if they could wait awhile to eat. She said she wasn't really hungry yet, "because she'd had a pretty big lunch with Max."

"Max?" asked Helen. "Max who?"

"Max Shaw, Mom. You know, one of your condo friends."

Helen's smile froze on her face. "Who?"

Camille described their spontaneous lunch. "What a fun guy he is," she said.

The loose cannon who lived ten floors above had found a target.

"He sure is," replied Helen. "Excuse me a minute, ladies, I need to check my phone and e-mail messages, and I'll join you for a glass of wine when I return. Maybe not for dinner though, because sometimes Steven gets home early and then we eat together. Or," she said as off-handedly as she could manage, "perhaps we could meet up with you for dessert."

Helen lit a cigarette the minute she got to her desk in the library, breathless as the full weight of what this luncheon meant sunk in. She listened and looked at her various messages.

She learned that Steven was, in fact, going to be late. She e-mailed him back to call her when he was on his way home in case she needed anything from the local grocery store. She did not tell him that Camille was home because she needed time to straighten something out.

Next, she called Max, said she "really couldn't talk but that she was free until around eight tonight, if he wanted to come over in a couple of hours."

He said, "Great."

She said, "I'll call to let you know when it's safe—probably sixish."

"Perfect," he said.

You won't think so once you get here, thought Helen furiously. Her heart felt as if it was pumping out of control.

Helen took several deep breaths, lit another Fantasia, and joined the girls for a glass of wine, before they went on their happy way. She cupped Camille's beautiful cupid face and told her how delighted Daddy was going to be to see her later on that night.

*At 6:13 p.m., Helen called Max to announce that the coast was clear. He was in her front room within minutes. By this time, he'd had three bourbons, and she'd had almost a bottle of wine.*

She grabbed Max's face in both her hands, kissed him hard on the mouth, and backed up.

She stiff-armed his advances, putting him on high alert.

Body ramrod straight, face of stone, she spoke with deliberate control.

"Max, do you remember the scene in *The Godfather: Part Two* movie that's set in Cuba? The one where Michael Corleone is courting a bunch of mobsters in a crowded nightclub when he realizes that his brother Fredo has set him up?...and Michael cups Fredo's face in his hands and kisses him hard on the mouth?"

"Yes, yes, I do," answered Max as he recalled the scene. "It's...sort of...it's a Mafia kiss of death."

(Uh oh.)

"Exactly," said Helen. "That's what you just got, Max. As of this moment, you are dead to me." She raised her hand, palm out, to stop him from talking. "You crossed the line, Max. There are so many lines that we've crossed. But this line. This line? This is off the edge. You finally went too far for even me.

"I told you that Camille was off limits. That you could never call her your daughter. I'm just wondering, Max. Did you really think I'd still embrace you? I told you that you could never ever have Camille, that I would never shatter her world, or Steven's, by exposing her complicated identity.

"Why would I ever put my own happiness ahead of hers? I wouldn't. I couldn't and I wouldn't. And her happy pink satin childhood is hopelessly, helplessly, wonderfully, happily connected with Steven Clark—with the man who nurtured her, the man they both know is her father. Period.

"There is no one without the other. To deliver the shock of such a truth to Camille would be to tell Steven, and to tell Steven would be a death knell. It's the eye of the storm. It's... it's ruination for everything I've so carefully orchestrated for Camille."

Huge intake of air. Vacant icy stare.

"I'm blocking the threat of your avalanche. We're done."

During this diatribe, Max had been inching closer to embrace her. If he could just get her into his arms, he would have the chance to convince her that it was all so innocent, that he would never purposely sabotage Helen's rules.

"Helen, baby..."

"Don't 'baby' me," she screamed. "All you've ever, ever done is mess with people, especially me." She yelled as she hit herself in the chest and walked down the gallery hall into the kitchen. "You don't have any respect, Max. You have no parameters." Her hands shook as she attempted lighting a cigarette. She slapped his hand away as he tried to light it for her. "Don't touch me," she screeched as she scurried into the party room.

A highly flushed Max got himself a drink at her bar and poured Helen a glass of wine. He put the wine on the cocktail table next to the couch he now carefully sat upon. "Helen, let's just look at this logically," he began.

She clenched her teeth. "There is no logic to this, to us, Max. I love my husband and I love you. But I respect my husband and I don't respect you. Camille may be our baby, but Steven was the man who raised her. Camille would never have turned out as well if you'd played the father. Notice the key word in that sentence, Max. Played. You play at things, Max. You're a boy. You've never grown up. You're an alcoholic. I remember telling you one time that one of these days these character flaws were going to bite you in the ass. This is that day, Max."

Max was sitting very still, which had a calming effect on Helen. He looked so sad.

"There's no one who kisses better than you," she continued, but in a kind voice, "...who caresses better than you, who makes love better than you. No one can make me laugh as hard as you. No one understands my body and certainly my past as well as you. No one. But Max, there's more to my life than just me."

She took a moment to catch her breath.

Max said, "I..."

"...No wait, I need to finish. I would love to turn back the years, but...and, you know, in many ways, that's just what we've been up to. We so desperately wanted all those years we should have had together that we, I don't know, tried to regain some of them. Our relationship was formed—if you can even use that term for such a short period—was formed when we were still children…so, actually, it makes sense that we would go about our affair in a childish way…Oh, God, Max…that just took all the wind right out of me," she said, and began to cry.

"You know what you mean to me, Helen. I love you so much it hurts. I think about you all the time. I…"

Helen interrupted him. "Max, don't you see? That's an adolescent attitude. You never grew up. I had to keep my shit together because of Camille. Max, you and I are too sexual for our own good. We're too wild. We're too everything when we're together. It's not lifelike. It's got to end before you do something that cannot be reversed. You'll never learn when to quit. I can see that now. You don't get it."

"I can get it, Helen. Just tell me," pleaded Max.

"But I did, Max. I told you straight out that Camille was strictly out of bounds and that I would never be yours, and I would never leave Camille's father."

"That's it, isn't it?" asked Max. "It's not that you won't leave Steven, but that you won't leave Camille's father. You won't walk out on Steven and into my arms, because it would mean shattering Camille's life of security. Isn't that it, Helen? Does it really boil down to one or the other of you being happy?"

Helen's anger was back. "Get out your calculator, Mr. Smug. There are three people who think they're happy, and keep in mind that people who think they're happy probably are."

Helen raised her hands to tick off the numbers. "So: Steven, Camille, and Janet believe they're happy. Two others, Max and Helen, think they're OK, but would rather ratchet theirs up to more, much more happiness...Let's see...Kill three happiness/gain two. Sounds like a Chinese proverb. Confucius say, NoGo."

Max smiled. He loved her so completely. She was irresistible even as she argued. She needed to talk this through to finally grasp the inevitability of them together.

Now Helen was getting so irritated, was so frustrated that Max wasn't understanding how he'd screwed things up, that she poured herself even more wine while continuing to chain smoke. She brought the bottle of bourbon over to the coffee table and plunked it down. She knew he'd want more.

"See, this, Max, this is why we could never end up together. We would end up like, what was that movie with Faye Dunaway and Mickey Rourke? They were smart, chain-smoking alcoholics, amusing each other every day at their favorite bar. They were losers."

"That isn't a good comparison at all, Helen," said Max, pouring himself another drink. "Reminds me of a good story though. An ocean liner pleasure boat sinks and the three people who manage to save themselves by quickly jumping into the only available boat and paddling away from those who are drowning are a priest, a rabbi, and an atheist..."

Again Helen interrupted him, "What the hell are you doing, Max? You're, you're still playing...incredible."

"The joke I'm telling has a point to it that directly relates to what's going on right now," said Max flatly. "You know, Helen, I may be a party boy and maybe that's not so appealing to you because you're trying so hard to be uh...good, and, and uh, proper. But, baby, you are drawn to people who live on the edge; you love the excitement of testing life to its limits. And let me remind you that many people with that type of personality are alcoholics. And why? Because life is too cruel to take it seriously and too brutal to ignore any enjoyment when it comes your way."

This quieted Helen down. His points were compelling. "Even if I agreed with you, Max, it's still my duty to protect my family against any physical or mental harm. Especially if I can see it spinning into a wind funnel and heading their way."

"But at the expense of your own happiness?" asked Max.

Helen drank half her glass of wine and said with forced patience, "Let's try it another way: Happiness is fleeting, Max. And I will not take it at other people's expense."

He said nothing.

"...And you know what else? I am happy a lot of the time. By living carefully, thoughtfully, gracefully, one can avoid most pain. Steven and I have a routine to our lives that's... comforting. No evil lurking just around the corner."

Max looked dark and almost menacing. "I take it the lurking evil is me."

Silence.

Max said, "No one can give you sexual pleasure like I can, Helen. You know that, don't you?"

Helen blushed. She hadn't told Max of Steven's impotence. She lit a Fantasia. "Steven was...is, is a good lover. He always satisfied...satisfies me."

"Yeah," said Max, "but not enough, and not in a variety of unexpected ways. And...you know something...I have a feeling that his accident left him unable to satisfy you, because really, Helen, if he's as good as all that, why would you risk everything to be with me?"

Helen felt a strong surge of desire run through her body as Max spoke of their sexuality, a physical yearning so intense that she was reduced to sitting on the edge of her sofa and clenching her teeth, willing herself to keep control. But Max sensed it and seized the moment to rise and scoop her up. He put his hand high up inside her skirt and kissed her ears, sending shivers all over her body.

Max's phone rang. He didn't answer it. Helen's home phone rang, and they could hear the message being recorded on the machine. It was Steven's voice and he was saying that he'd be home late. "Don't wait up. Sorry, honey, I'd much rather be with you."

Meanwhile, Max removed his hands from Helen and grabbed his cell phone from the coffee table to check on who'd called. It was Janet. He listened to her message. "Max, it's Janet. Where are you? I'm going to see that new movie with Patty, so I'll be home in about two hours."

Max and Helen stood there staring at each other, she, feeling horribly adulterous, and he, feeling wildly jealous of Steven and glad that Janet was occupied.

"Was that Janet?" asked Helen.

"Yeah. Yes it was. She's gone to a movie, so we're safe for at least two hours on both ends."

Helen clenched her teeth. "Have you heard nothing I've said, Max Shaw? There is no 'we.' I'm sorry. I'm sorry for the four of us. Our spouses think they're happily married. And you and I are, or were, content with them until we ended up living in the same building. Sex and laughter aren't everything, you know, Max." Even as she said this, she began grinning.

"Actually, Helen," said the smiling Max, "I know you don't really mean that. Maybe they're not everything, but they're first and second on my list. We've both been bitten in the ass when we practiced loyalty, and, I don't know...wealth isn't all that great. You can't buy love, or good sex or a genuine laugh. Health. Health is important. But why be healthy if you're not going to parlay that health into fun?"

"You know what, Max? I can't completely disagree with you. But I can say this: You now scare me. You've cornered me into the extremely delicate position of needing to protect the innocent. That would be Camille and, peripherally Janet and Steven.

"Did you really think that if you stalked Camille…"

Max's eyes dilated. "Stalk her! That's not…"

"You might as well have. And don't interrupt me. Don't you get that you'd be separating Camille from the one man in her life who has always provided for her, protected her, loved her, liked her? Why would you want to devastate anyone like that, but especially your own…"

"Flesh and blood," Max finished for her.

Silence.

"You're used to seducing people into playing along, with no regard to the personal repercussions, or…or even that they've been made a fool."

"I don't purposely make fools of anyone," said Max hotly.

"Realllly. You became pals with Steven. It was easy for you, in fact. See, that bothers me. How could you be great pals with a guy while you're secretly fucking his wife? That really bothers me. I was able to justify cheating on Steven because of the convenient 'he's got it coming' rationalization. But you didn't know that. I never told you that Steven went through years of taking out his anger on me after a car crash he was in…well you were there…there in the hospital…you knew about the accident…"

"Yeah, I was. I was there all right. And so was Camille, if you want to examine that more thoroughly…"

"I don't," said Helen. "That wasn't my point."

"But it is a point, right?"

"No. Well, yes. What was I even saying…OK. I was making a case for me committing adultery by pointing out that after Steven's accident, he pulled some really damaging shit on me, really awful…but, but you didn't know that, so for all you knew, you were ravaging a good marriage…which, actually, it is in many ways. I'm getting drunk. This is horrible."

"But, so aren't we really in agreement? Aren't you saying, you deserve…"

"So, yeah," said Helen. "Yes. I'm saying I deserve to have fun. We. We deserve to be together,...but again, not at the expense of others."

"What he doesn't know won't hurt him."

"BONG." She yelled it so suddenly and loudly that Max upended his drink.

Giggling, she said, "You're a denialist."

"Whoa, no, not that."

"It's not funny."

"Yes, it is. See, now who's the denialist? It's fuckin' funny."

They both broke into peals of laughter over this absurdity.

Helen excused herself to pee. She gathered her selves and returned in a somber state, knowing this desperately needed resolve.

Max was mulling over his possibilities.

Helen spoke. "It's Camille that we're talking about here, Max...Camille and Steven. No one can be allowed to come between them. Why would you want to break such a sweet bond?"

Max poured another bourbon. He reached across the cocktail table and filled Helen's glass with wine.

As Helen watched him, she had a light-bulb moment, and said, "It suddenly occurred to me that we both have lines bearing unseen signs of Do Not Cross. We now know that my line is you befriending Camille. I'll bet yours is taking away your party, your Jim Beam, and of course your Nat Sherman Black & Gold cigarettes. So...Camille is mine, booze/tobacco yours."

Max held his cigarette between his thumb and middle finger, and took a deep drag. He drank half the bourbon in his glass. He looked Helen straight in the eyes and said quietly, "Is that what it would take?"

Helen defiantly folded her arms across her chest. She laughed sarcastically. "Yeah, Max. That's what it would take.

For you to graduate out of your adolescent phase, sober up, and figure out who the hell you are besides a seductive party boy."

"If that's what it would take, Helen, to have you, I can do that."

"...OK," said Helen. "Um. Let's see how you're doing by the end of next week. And...during that time, you and I will agree that you will have no contact with my family or myself."

"Fine," said Max. He stood up. "Is that the deal, then? I give up booze and cigarettes and you give up Steven?"

"That's it," said Helen.

What Helen thought she knew was that she had just bought the week Camille would be home. What she further believed was that Max would not be able to face himself without his self-medication, his bourbon, his cigarettes. She dared not even hope that he could and would have the character to follow through, and that she might end up with him after all, with Max, where she'd always belonged.

What Max thought he knew was that he could and would do anything to live out the rest of his life with Helen, where he'd always belonged.

"You need to know, Helen, that what I did today was meant to show you how Camille and I bonded. Our time together was so easy, so natural. Camille likes me. I can tell..."

"Stop," screamed Helen. "I see very clearly what you've done. You've made your first move. Let's just leave it at that."

"Right," said Max. "Want me to go now? He moved to kiss her."

She again put her arms straight out, stopping him.

"You're killing me, baby," he said.

"You're killing me too, Max. Isn't that what we've always done?"

"You're my Goddamn world, Helen," he said softly as he picked up his cigarettes, and cell phone.

"I am not, Max. You want what you can't have. That's all."

The phone rang and rang. Then Camille was recording a message.

"Mom, I'm gonna stay over at Beth's tonight. We're partying, and I don't want to drive like this. I'll see you and Daddy tomorrow. I love you."

Click.

Helen put her head down, staring at the floor, willing herself not to let Max hold her.

"We've got a whole hour to ourselves," whispered Max, beseechingly.

"We have no more time to ourselves," said Helen. She was crying, but he couldn't see her face, and she somehow managed to keep her voice even. "Ever," she said.

Max watched a tear run down her face and two others trickle down her neck onto her sweater. That was it. He grabbed her and held her to him so tightly that she couldn't move. "Now, listen to me, sweetheart, I'm going to do exactly what you've asked of me. I won't try to see our dau… Camille. And I won't drink or smoke for the whole next week. A week at a time…right? I…don't need to be the party boy you think I am anymore, Helen. I'm…tired of amusing everyone, and…really, I'm tired of not feeling so great. You energize me though. Only you, baby, I just want to be with you."

He backed slightly away from her. "So I'll see you in a week. OK?"

He managed a heartbreakingly bright smile just for her.

She couldn't speak.

"OK?" he repeated.

Helen managed to whisper, "OK," and kiss his cheek. He let her go and saw the anguish in her eyes. He promised to keep his word, placing his pack of cigarettes in her left hand, then cupping and kissing the palm of her right one, the pleasure of it making her weak-kneed. Max closed the front door quietly. And he was gone.

Forever.

Now, sitting quietly in her armchair, watching the sunrise over the beautiful Chicago skyline, Helen realized that the question had become, what to do with all these memories. She'd cried so much during the last week that she felt strangely calm right now, maybe sated for the moment. Yet she knew there were many more tears to shed. She'd grieved over Max before, cried over him for years, but never because he'd left the planet. This was the darkest void.

Helen was a person who alternated between hearty self-confidence and excruciating self-doubt. Good decisions came in waves. Same with bad ones.

She attempted to rein in her various personalities so that as team players, there could be some clear thinking. She—they attacked her decision from different angles. Could she somehow manage to secretly grieve? Since Steven and Camille knew nothing of her haunting memories, should she just keep the whole Max-and-Helen story to herself? Why involve them now? Why harm the relationships among the three of them?

The most compelling desire centered on Camille, of protecting the innocent. Steven too, but most especially, Camille. So, for example, if Helen told Steven and he reacted badly, he could end up harming Camille emotionally, maybe not even meaning to, but a life story directly involving him that he wasn't even aware of, could flip him to his dark side, where in the heat of the moment, who knows who would be safe, including Camille.

Now that Max was dead, Camille's smooth life would never be upended with the knowledge that Max was her natural father. Helen couldn't think of a single reason to tell her.

So it really wasn't a question of should she tell Steven and Camille the truth, but how she could seem functional in their eyes as she mourned. How could she camouflage her desperation as she came to terms with the knowledge that she caused the suicide of her soul mate? Could she keep that to herself for the rest of her life?

Sifting through the facts, she puzzled over her life choices. Many had been made with hopeful honesty. Conceiving Camille had been one of her good choices, hadn't it? And recently, breaking it off with Max was meant to be a good and wise and selfless choice. The thought occurred to her that, as atrocious as it was, his death put an end to the loose cannon in her family's life. Too many lines had been crossed to ever regain control if Max had continued living in the same condominium.

And Max would never have let go of the possibility of getting the true story out. That was his nature, both seductive and ridiculous, depending upon the subject. He was open in a world of chaotic compromise and surrender. His charisma had been his ace in the hole for most of his life. Until last week.

But, still, it didn't have to end in death. Or did it? Had his death been inevitable? Did fate intercede and hide his letter that begged Helen to see him? If she had gotten the letter, could the circumstances have ended differently? Many scenarios came to mind.

Helen realized that if there was ever a time to be pragmatic, this was it.

Around about 11:00 a.m., Steven peeked into Helen's room where he found her curled up and sleeping in her armchair. He was showered and dressed for the day.

She opened her eyes as he was quietly closing the door to let her sleep.

"I'm awake," she said sleepily.

"Why are you sleeping like that?" he asked.

Helen smiled sadly. She was tired and conflicted and caught off guard. "I couldn't sleep more than a few hours, so I got up to…to read."

Steven walked over and bent down to kiss her. She warily kissed him back, expecting him to let her be, to go make the coffee or something.

But Steven stood over her. He had something to say.

Helen looked up. "Yes? Do you want something, Steven?"

"Yeah, Helen. I do. There…Is there…something you want to tell me, something I should know? Because just go ahead. Let's just get whatever is going on over with."

Helen squared off with her husband, her friend, her love, the father who so thoroughly loved her precious Camille.

Although Steven's years of adulterous flirtations had cost Helen dearly, he had remained strong in Camille's eyes.

Steven is still among the walking wounded, partly because he has to live with the guilt of hurting me, thought Helen. But he learned to put away his personal despair and appreciate what's left of his life.

He did that with my help. In his darkest moment, I gave him a brand-new love object. Max and I gave him that. He's been able to remain strong in Camille's eyes, to keep that love intact, and that gives him his biggest sense of pride. He wouldn't have that without me, without Max. But I wouldn't have her without Max either. I wouldn't have a love object to hang on to myself!

She began stumbling through some words while she made one of those life-altering decisions.

She said, "All things considered…It's just that…It's really as simple as…Well." And she thought to herself, Let's get it together, girls, this is what self-control and selflessness is all about. Here it is. Grow up. Now would be the time. Now would be good.

She was looking into Steven's anxious, searching eyes.

She pulled from a memory of long, long ago when her mother had told her so much more than she ever wanted or needed to know. She'd learned through that experience that some things are better left unsaid.

"No," Helen answered. "I'm sorry I seem to be overreacting to the suicide. You know me—I'm the drama queen who showed up in your computer technology class trying to reinvent the rules. That's me."

She looked earnestly, tenderly into her husband's troubled eyes.

She watched the relief flood his face and thought her heart would break with compassion. She rose from her chair and put her arms around his waist. Helen hugged her husband gently, firmly, for a long time, feeling the tension slowly leave his body. He wanted to believe her. So he did.

"I could tell you something that would…uh, let's see… that would…that could help me get through…," began Helen.

The phone rang. Why now? Why right then when so much hung in the balance? They let it go to the answering machine.

"That would what, Helen?" asked Steven.

"Um…clarify…well…why I always stuff my feelings…"

It rang again, the family signal that a member is calling and you should pick up the phone. They each went to a phone, knowing it was Camille. She said she was just checking in, wanted to make sure the last week hadn't been too awful for them.

Steven held a remote phone and quietly walked to just beyond view of Helen on the den phone. Helen was holding her jaw tightly between her thumb and index finger. He took over the conversation by replying that the week had been horrendous but they'd gotten through it just like they always got through everything, with determination and love.

Camille anticipated the familiar answer, but said she wanted to hear Mom's view of the situation. Helen covered the mouthpiece and took what she felt to be the deepest breath she'd ever taken. She placed her hand over her heart and spoke in a calm, clear voice as she assured her beloved Camille in a positive yet truthful way that things were settling into place, that Dad had been helpful, that she had begun a to-do list, which was well known as her coping skill for moving on.

Steven interceded with the good-byes, said could they call her later in the day and asked what time would be good. "I've got my watch on, Mom," said Camille. "And I'm lookin' at six p.m. your time, midnight here."

Helen laughed too hard and managed a "Good job, kiddo," and a "Love you, darling," before she hung up the phone and walked quickly to the safety of her bathroom. She shower-cried and emerged in her robe to find Steven searching the movie section of the paper.

He looked at Helen and smiled. "You know, this is our brunch-and-movie day, Helen." He glanced at his watch and feigned surprise. "There's that documentary playing at the Music Box. We'd better go now if we're going to make it."

Utterly worn out, she stared at him a beat too long.

His face took on an anxious expression.

Minimize the casualties, she thought.

"We'll make it," she replied, and disappeared into her closet to throw on some clothes.

She didn't see his look of relief.

What had passed between them before Camille called was the high-wire act without the net. Then TheNet had called, halting an alarmingly delicate situation. Was that phone call intuitive?

Steven said he'd get the car and meet her in front. She didn't hear his voice catch.

Helen muffle-yelled from her closet that she'd close the windows in case of rain. He didn't see her barely capable of dressing herself—confusing the neck of her T-shirt with an armhole.

Back on track.

As Helen closed the kitchen window, she thought to grab the week-old grocery list.

Back on track.

Mrs. Steven Clark was deliberately baby stepping, back on track.

Applying the confidence of lipstick, she set out to brave the humans.

She didn't pay attention to the movie, but sat in the safety of darkness, trying to get a handle on her rambling thoughts.

The Chicago song "If You Leave Me Now" played in her mind as she thought about the lovely couple of years she'd had with Steven before his accident.

What...have...I...done?

Helen thought: Thirty-five years ago, in a computer class at Berkeley, Helen Hemingway and Steven Clark had been drawn to each other in a magnetic way. They had "fallen in love" and had the time of their lives for two years. And if fate had not mercilessly stomped its reconstruction boot down on them...

No. Clear thinking negates using the if word. Logic takes a walk when the if word comes to town.

In 1976, fate did intercede, twice. First Steven's accident and right on its heels, Max with his gift.

There really was no getting around the fact that Max had given them Camille...or the beginning of Camille. Without Camille, there would probably be no Steven and Helen right now, in 2007. They would have ceased to exist as a couple way back in the day.

But wait. That's actually an if thought…if Camille hadn't been conceived.

So no, wrong path again.

What am I trying to figure out? thought Helen.

And here it was. Helen's life as Helen ended the day she gave birth to a live baby girl. From then on, she was first and foremost Camille's Mother. Camille's needs had trumped Helen's at every turn of the road since her birth in 1976. It was as simple and as complicated as that. Helen had struggled a long, long time with her resentment over her husband's apathy. She had grown used to it and put it in a place. She'd trained herself to keep her needs to a minimum.

And then Max had shown up. Max: her best daydream and her worst nightmare. Her delirious pleasure over his desire faced off with her fierce protection of her daughter, and the showdown wasn't even close. Game over. Camille gets the happy card.

*When I make cookies…*
*I think of you*
*Daisies are your favorite flower…*
*When I see daisies…*
*I think of you*
*Grandma's hands are your hands…*
*Are mine*
*When I look at my hands…*
*I think of you*
*You are in my thoughts, in my heart…*
*I think of you.*

~ Jessica Judge Schott ~

# BIOGRAPHY

In May of 2014, Kimbeth Wehrli Judge published a well-received collection of short stories, *Mothers and Others.*

Encouraged by public applause, she has now published her first novel, *The FlipSide.*

Kimbeth is the mother of three grown children and grandmother of five. She lives with her husband in the heart of Chicago.

To learn more, click onto her website, kimbeth.com

# ACKNOWLEDGEMENTS

Thank you to my heartfelt *Mothers and Others* fans who strongly encouraged me to publish this novel.

Pam Ahearn, Mary Hayes, Mary Ellen Brinker, Tom Burke, Jerry Crimmins, Isabella Goldberg, Joan Goldberg, Jane Hasil, Jennifer and Lance Jansen, B.J. Judge, Rick Kogan, Mike Miller, Herb Nadlehoffer, Mary J Peterson, John Schott, Jen Schottke, Nancy Stewart, Marcy Twardak, Don Wehrli, Mary Lou Wehrli.

I'm grateful for the wonderful memories of the extraordinary Father Robert Botthof, a man among men who enthusiastically supported all my writing.

Thank you to my loyal early readers who patiently read drafts of *The FlipSide*:

Sharyn Behnke, Beryl Byman, Ronda Channing, Kelly Judge Goldberg, Joan Jones, Gina Judge, Nancy Lee Turpin, Cathan McGovern Sowden, Mary Supina.

Thank you to Ben Sugar for his technological skills.

A special thank you to my daughter, Jessica Judge Schott, for her lovely poem.